THE NINTH PAN BOOK OF
HORROR STORIES

THE NINTH PAN BOOK OF
HORROR STORIES

Selected by
HERBERT VAN THAL

*No one of these stories
has been previously published*

PAN BOOKS LTD : LONDON

This Collection first published 1968 by
PAN BOOKS LIMITED
33 Tothill Street, London, S.W.1

330 02144 3

Printed in Great Britain by
Cox & Wyman Ltd., London, Reading and Fakenham

CONTENTS

ACKNOWLEDGEMENTS

The Editor wishes to acknowledge the following permissions to quote from copyright material:

Mr Raymond Williams and his agent, London International of Park House, Park Street, London W1, for 'Man-Hunt' and 'Smile Please'.

Miss Dulcie Gray and her agent, London International, for 'The Fly' and 'The Happy Return'.

Miss Lindsay Stewart and her agent, London International, for 'Strictly for the Birds' and 'Jolly Uncle'.

Mr Martin Waddell and his agent, London International, for 'Bloodthirsty' and 'Old Feet'.

Mr Adobe James and his agent, London International, for 'An Apparition at Noon'.

Mrs Rene Morris and her agent, London International, for 'The Baby Machine'.

Mr Walter Winward and his agent, London International, for 'Stick With Me, Kid, And You'll Wear Diamonds'.

Mr Raymond Harvey and his agent, London International, for 'Father Forgive Me'.

Mr John Burke and his agent, David Higham Associates Limited of 76 Dean Street, Soho, London W1, for 'A Comedy of Terrors'.

Mr Alex Hamilton and his agent, Jonathan Clowes Limited of 20F New Cavendish Street, London W1, for 'Not Enough Poison'. Copyright © Alex Hamilton, 1966.

Mr Peter Richey and his agent, London International, for 'Don't Avoid The Rush Hour'.

Mr James McArdwell and his agent, London International, for 'The Green Umbilical Cord'.

Miss Tanith Lee and her agent, London International, for 'Eustace'.

The Ninth Pan Book of
HORROR STORIES

MAN-HUNT

Raymond Williams

THE DARK crouching figure ran clumsily across the ploughed field to the shelter of a solitary tree. He fell on his knees out of sheer exhaustion and clung to the rough bark with his wet hands. Perspiration trickled in little rivers down his burning face. His hair hung like black seaweed over his forehead. The moon crept out from behind a black cloud, shed some light sparingly on his trembling body and slid back behind another black veil. 'God, don't you start showing your silly yellow face,' he gasped, straining his eyes upwards to the night sky.

He staggered to his feet, leaning heavily on the stout trunk. His prison clothes were ripped and filthy. He knew he could not afford to take too long a rest, he must keep going, they couldn't be too far behind him. A few faint yelps in the distance tightened his nerves. The dogs – they had the dogs on him now. He had seen them patrolling the prison grounds; great black beasts with dirty yellow eyes which always watched you wherever you went, long white teeth just waiting to sink themselves into your skin and rip you apart.

He stumbled away from the tree in the opposite direction to the yelps. Dogs were so fast you just couldn't outrun them. They always outran foxes and stags and got them in the end; he was no match for a fox, well not in speed maybe, but in cunning – that was a different story. Yes, when it came to cunning why he could teach the fox a thing or two. What about the cunning way he had lured June Kent back to his room just over two years ago? What about the way he had out-manoeuvred her, raped her and finally killed her? Didn't it call for cunning the way he had cut up her body and disposed of it piece by piece all over London? The old fox had a long way to go to catch up with him, a very long way to go.

And then he couldn't help laughing as he remembered his final stroke of genius when the police finally caught him. He could still see the faces of the jury as he performed his 'madness' act in court pretending to talk to little men on his own shoulder. His face split open with a delighted grin – and that bit when he told the judge that he had to obey the moon when it winked at him.

The silence of the night was suddenly ripped open by his hysterical high-pitched fit of laughter. He was laughing too much to go on. He sank to the ground and rolled on to his back laughing and panting, 'John Blandon, we find you guilty but insane,' he spouted in a deep voice. What a simple lot they were in that courtroom – guilty but insane. Little did they know how sane and cunning he really was.

The smile vanished and the giggle died in his throat at the shrill bark in the distance. He had forgotten the dogs, he must pull himself together, it was dangerous to rest and dwell on his clever exploits. First things first, his main problem now was getting away from these savage brutes. 'Come on, Foxy, run,' he said to himself to spur his mind back to his plight. He thrashed his way through the wet grass and sharp bushes torturing his brain to find an escape. Suddenly he saw the weapon to beat the pursuing dogs. Water, black running water. Once in the stream he could travel down with the current and find his way out on to the other bank; then let the dogs try and find him. 'Clever old Foxy, you've done it again,' he muttered. He lowered himself over the lip of the bank into the gurgling stream. A sharp pain stabbed through his groin as he splashed in. 'Hell, this water's cold,' he gasped. Then he was pulling strongly with the current along the twisting black valley. I wonder if foxes can swim, he thought. If they can why don't they when the hounds are after them? Before he could answer himself he saw a bright yellow light in the distance. Police torches he thought immediately but they couldn't have got this far already. Then by straining his eyes in the direction of the light he realized it was too large a mass of light for a torch. Could it be a window, the lighted window of a small cottage perhaps. There was only one way to find out. He swam to the side and clawed his way from the swirling water up the slimy mud bank.

Inside the small kitchen in the flickering light from the oil lamp a middle-aged, white-haired woman was laying the table. She hummed to herself while her daughter scooped white steaming mounds of potato on to the two plates. 'I think we're just about ready mother,' she said tossing her shoulder-length blonde hair back with an automatic flick of the head. 'I'll just cut some bread then dear. How many for you?'

'Just one thanks,' she replied setting the two steaming plates on the table. The cheerful face had stopped humming with the concentration of slicing with the long gleaming blade of a carving knife. 'We must get a bread knife next time we're in town, Pat,' she said. 'I'm always frightened when I use this thing.'

She left the knife and loaf on the side table and took the white slices across to the other table. They both sat down and were just about to start when the door burst open and a grey blur flew to the side table, picked something up and turned to face them. Mother and daughter, both shrieking, were already up and cowering against the wall before the man spoke.

'Shut up and listen or I'll slit your noisy little throats.'

He stood there in a wet grey uniform with drips of water falling from his black hair. 'I'm on the run, see, and you're going to look after me until I'm ready to leave, and if you get any other ideas then you'll be arguing with this.' He thrust the carving knife with a sharp jab through the air in their direction.

He soon discovered that the cottage had a well-concealed cellar below the main room, a perfect hiding place when the guards came, which he knew was just a matter of time before they did. He had just finished bolting down some of their evening meal and changed his wet uniform for some old clothes found in a trunk when he spotted the round pools of flashing light approaching the cottage. He acted a quick mime of what would happen to Pat if her mother talked and disappeared down the wooden rungs to the cellar. With trembling hands and thumping heart the mother closed the trap door lid, replaced the carpet and rocking chair on top and waited for the knock at the door.

Below in the pitch blackness of the cellar John Blandon had Pat pinned between his body and the damp stone wall. His left hand was clasped over her mouth while his right held the cold steel against her throat. The voices floated down to them from above. 'No, sir, I haven't seen anyone.' 'I should keep all doors locked tonight, madam,' it was a deep stern voice, 'you see this man's a mental case, very dangerous.' 'Oh my goodness, what did he do?' the voice was high pitched with just a slight tremor. 'Well, maam, he, um,' there was a nervous cough 'he raped a young girl and killed her about two years ago.' He felt Pat's body stiffen and press harder against the wall. 'Oh, my God, no!' came the woman's voice from above. 'Nice girl she was from all accounts,' the deep voice was continuing 'something Kent her name was, bits of her turned up all over London. So you see you keep this door locked lady and don't look so worried we'll get 'im before morning never fear.' After a few calls of 'Good night' the footsteps faded and the door closed. John Blandon was still free. He grinned in the darkness and pressed his body hard against the girl. 'You heard what the man said little girl,' he purred, 'so you'd better be very nice to me tonight, hadn't you?' He felt the girl's head nod in reply.

When he was out of the cellar again, the carving knife still waving, he ordered the women to take some old sacks and cushions to the cellar as their beds while he would lie on the couch above. When they had gone below he searched around the cottage. He found £11, a gold watch, a dark blue overcoat, a pair of sunglasses and a pair of pyjama trousers. After pocketing the money he undressed, put on the pyjama trousers and settled down on the couch with a few blankets over him and the knife close at hand.

He lay back gazing at the dark shadows flickering on the roof above, thinking how cleverly he had got away when he heard a creak from the direction of the trap door. He shot up grasping the knife tightly but what he saw made his grip

relax by degrees. Emerging from the cellar and coming towards him was Pat in a black négligée. Her face looked
radiant in a lamp light with the golden tresses of her hair
draped over her shoulders. Her firm round breasts protruded
sharply through the thin négligée each neatly tipped with a
darker shape. He gasped and stared in disbelief. It had been
over two years now since he had seen a woman and now this.
Was he dreaming? Was he really here with this wonderful
female beauty? 'Well you did say I had to be nice to you,'
she said cocking her head to one side as she spoke. He was
still unable to speak when she reached his side; the moving
body held him in a spell. He dropped the knife to the floor
and with two huge hungry hands reached out to sample the
tempting goddess. So intent were his eyes on drinking in the
beauty, while his hands ravaged across the smooth soft flesh,
that he did not notice the goddess raise her right arm with a
dark green bottle in it or bring it down swiftly towards
his head, but he felt the blow on his left temple and had a
vague recollection of tinkling glass as the warm breasts
slipped from his hands and he fell into a deep pool of darkness.

His head ached, his eyes hurt when he opened them. He
groaned and tried to move but couldn't. As feeling began to
seep back into his numb body he realized he was tied down
hard to the top of the kitchen table. He was unable to move
an arm or a leg. Above him he saw the two faces of mother
and daughter just watching him and saying nothing. 'Oh what
did you . . .?' he began as his head cleared.

'So you're awake are you, Mr John murdering Blandon.'
It was the white-haired mother who spoke, her green eyes
glinting at him. 'So you thought you'd got away with rape and
murder.'

'Now just a minute,' he started, 'I'll do a deal with you.'

'We don't do deals with you, do we, Pat?'

'No mother, not with him.'

He looked at the other face. It also looked hard and full of
hate.

'Are you ready, Pat?' 'Ready when you are mother.'

'Right, now he's awake we'll start.'

He felt a sharp thrill shock his body as Pat's smooth fingers undid his clothes. Then the room shook with his screams as he saw the mother holding the long carving knife in her hand. The knife vanished from his view and his scream reached a higher pitch as he felt a violent gnawing pain. His scream was continuous as the carving knife sawed back and forth in the strong determined hands. Then with the pain scorching through his body until he was on the verge of collapse he saw the red-bladed knife again.

'Why, why. Oh why?' he croaked appealingly.

'Why? I'll tell you why,' spat back the older woman, 'because it was my daughter June you debauched with your filthy body, my precious lamb you hacked apart and packed into bloody parcels. Well you won't rape any more girls now as long as you live.'

THE FLY

Dulcie Gray

ARTHUR PONTNEY grunted and shifted in his armchair. His wife Maria looked at him contemptuously. What a revolting sight he was! His mouth hung open and flaccid. His mottled purple face sagged. His pig-small brown eyes were closed; shuttered by the blue-veined wrinkled lids. His heavy body lay sideways, and his large red hands hung loosely over the sides of the chair. He was snoring soundly.

Maria sitting opposite him, had been reading by the light of the table lamp beside her. The book was a romance; the story of a middle-aged woman who could still in certain lights look like a girl, and who was being ardently pursued by a handsome, slim, and distinguished-looking man. If only she were free of Arthur she too could re-live her life. She, too, looked (she fondly believed), like a girl in certain lights, and Major Maltravers, tall, slim and distinguished, had given her what she was sure could be interpreted as an encouraging look, the night before last at the Bottomley-Smythes. But whether the Major had or had not been giving her the eye, one thing was indisputable, she must be free of Arthur.

Arthur had ruined her life. He had proposed to her when she was too young to realize what she was doing, and having married her, had deflowered her with an impetuosity which she had found disgusting. Her mother's vague references to the pleasures of the bridal bed had in no way prepared her for passion, and Maria, though she had fought strongly, had been vanquished by a delighted Arthur who had found her resistance stimulating. Maria had complained bitterly by telephone to her mother, who had murmured that all men were beasts who had to be endured because of their money. They had to be given in to from time to time, she said, but a clever woman could always get her own back in other ways.

'But I don't want to get my own back,' Maria had said surprised. 'I married because I thought I loved Arthur. I'm not a prostitute.'

At this her mother had laughed until the fish she was eating at the time (the telephone call having disturbed her lunch) nearly choked her, and even after a paroxysm of coughing so violent that she had to retire to bed for the afternoon, she had still shaken with laughter all through the rest of the day.

Uncomforted and resentful Maria had finished her honeymoon at Bournemouth, and returned to the marital bungalow at Wraysbury.

The years passed, and Maria bore her lot stoically, but she never forgave Arthur for the fact that he demanded sex from her, or her mother for failing to prepare her. She kept the house spotlessly and cheerlessly clean and tidy. She cooked grimly unappetizing meals, and took to dressing in despairing tweeds and masculine hats. She kept a series of small intolerably noisy dogs to replace the children that never came, and talked loudly and commandingly, laughed loudly and without humour, and smoked incessantly, having managed to find a way of sticking the cigarettes to her bottom lip like glue, so that she need never be without one, almost whatever she was doing.

Arthur snored one last time, with a noise like tearing paper, sat up in the chair, and looked round him in apparent bewilderment. Then his eyes came to rest on his spouse. He belched noncommittally, and she with an angry sniff returned to her book.

What a boring bitch she was! How had he ever been taken in by her? And how was it possible for any human creature to have changed so completely? He had met and married a frail, dark-haired elf. He had achieved a statuesque Amazon, with a voice like a buzz saw, and the looks of a shire horse. All the money he had made, and he had made plenty, failed to alleviate the tedium of his domesticity. Maria's very generous dress allowance failed to provide her with one garment of which he approved. The very generous housekeeping allowance gave him no culinary treats, and Maria's taste in furnishing was deplorable. However attractive the house he bought for her, she managed to reduce the interior to the level of the first bungalow in Wraysbury. He sighed.

Maria raised her eyes from the book. 'It's ten o'clock,' she said, 'I think I'll go to bed.'

'Very well dear,' said Arthur.

'Coming?' asked Maria, gathering her knitting together, preparatory to her departure.

'In a moment,' replied Arthur, with his eye on the whisky bottle standing on the sideboard.

Maria followed his glance, and her lips tightened. 'Don't be too long,' she said.

That was another thing. Arthur drank, and at night his breath always smelled of whisky. He had long since ceased to importune her, but even now she could remember with horror his love-making after he had been drinking. His heavy body and laboured breathing. The fumbling. The smell of the whisky, the elephantine heavings, and the final grunts of satisfaction. Revolting beyond belief. But now, and this was even worse, he had found someone else. A chit of a girl. A blonde. His secretary. So-called. Maria would lay a bet her secretarial work didn't depend on her typing or her shorthand. She snapped her spectacle case shut, and with the book, and a box of chocolates under her arm, she made for the door. 'Good night dear,' she said.

Arthur nodded. 'Good night.'

Maria went out of the room, and Arthur went to the sideboard, gave himself a generous whisky, and returned to his armchair. My God how he wished little Mabel was here! There was a good kid for you! Kind, friendly, good at her job, and good in bed. He didn't know what an old buffer like him had done to deserve her. But the kid liked him. Actually liked him. Had chased him in fact. Not the other way round. Even though he'd been damnably attracted he hadn't wanted to seduce her because she was such a sporting little thing, and he didn't want to harm her. She had long blonde hair. Eyes as blue as the sky, a little nose which turned up at the end, a lovely smile, not to mention the figure of an angel. He loved her. Old enough to be her father. Humble enough to be full of gratitude, he loved her, and he could never marry her, because he was married to Maria. Besides the kid must find someone of her own age.

Upstairs, slowly getting ready for bed, Maria was dreaming for the thousandth time of a life without Arthur. But how to get rid of him? Their doctor liked Arthur, and was no fool, so poison was out. Maria didn't know how to use a gun, so all that splendid armament in the gunroom downstairs must go to waste. No phoney shooting accident was therefore possible, and suddenly to learn to shoot must inevitably arouse suspicion. She had already tried to tamper with his car. Twice. But both times Arthur had foiled her. Apparently in all innocence. And he now had an extremely competent chauffeur. So what? What could she do?

It was a lovely summer evening; still quite light. Maria went over to the bedroom window, and looked out into the garden. There was a paved courtyard which ran all round the side of the house, and the drop from the bedroom was quite a long one. The tall house had its drawing-room on the first floor and its bedrooms on the second. If only she could persuade him to fall out of the window! With his weight, he'd be certain to be killed. But how? How?

A fly buzzed angrily in the corner of the farthest pane, by the sash cord. It began crawling up the window, reached the centre glazing bar, fell back on to the sill, and started again.

Arthur hated flies. Had a real horror of them. He said he had some sort of idiotic premonition connected with them. He hated all insects, bees, wasps, ants, and above all flies. They sent him nearly mad. Couldn't she make something of it? Surely. Surely. But what? She'd made a thousand plans. Rejected a thousand plans. The twice she had tampered with his car had nearly killed her herself, from sheer excitement. The plotting. The preparation. The mounting tension as Arthur going about his ordinary business had finally reached the car. The fantastic disappointment when her plan had miscalculated.

She'd been to a demonstration of hypnotism the other day. The hypnotist had sent several of the audience in the perfectly ordinary drawing-room at the Bates' house first of all into a trance, and then had suggested that they should do all sorts of things; absurd things like wearing wastepaper baskets on their heads, or kissing absolute strangers, or reciting childish poetry in a child's voice. And important business men, and their self-important wives had done everything he had told them to do. All he had done was to talk to them, and make these absurd suggestions. Couldn't she learn? Then indeed she could fabricate a fool-proof accident! Especially with a window like this one in his bedroom. It was immensely tall, and the sill started only a foot from the floor. 'Arthur,' she would say. 'Arthur I'm going to send you to sleep. Sleep. Sleep. Sleep. That's right, Arthur. Now Arthur, why not take a walk? Don't be frightened, Arthur. That's only a fly buzzing. It won't harm you. Just a little fly buzzing, trying to get out of the window into the lovely summer air. Up it crawls. Up up up it crawls. Buzz buzz. It's fallen again. Why not help it out, Arthur? Why not open the window and let it out? Dear little fly. Nothing to be ashamed of. Walk to the window, Arthur, open it from the bottom. Gently now. Carefully now. Open. Up. Up. Up. That's it. That's the way. The fly has gone. Out of the window. D'you hear me, Arthur? Out of the window. Why not follow it, Arthur dear? It's perfectly possible. Climb on to the sill. Steady yourself against the sides. Poise yourself, and then dive! Dive Arthur. Dive damn you. Dive!' She raised her voice in spite of herself, almost to a scream. She opened the window herself, and peered out on to the courtyard below.

The fly, with monstrous stupidity, had removed itself to the top half of the window, and was now crawling up the panes there, ceaselessly trying to get out – but endlessly failing.

Maria could almost see Arthur's dead body in the courtyard below as she looked over the edge of the sill. She gloated on it in her imagination with great satisfaction for several seconds, then, playing a game to herself with such intensity that she almost believed it to be true, she hurried over to the telephone shouting 'Help. Help. Help.' She pretended to lift the receiver, dialled the doctor's number, babbling with grief and horror told the doctor of the accident, and then still in her imagination with Arthur's dead body now on the bed beside her, she telephoned all her family and friends, all of whom came one by one into the bedroom to comfort and commiserate with her. It was very satisfactory. And completely absorbing.

The door was suddenly flung open and Arthur came rather unsteadily into the room. Maria gasped. 'Good heavens you gave me a fright!' she exclaimed.

Arthur looked at her disinterestedly. 'Why aren't you in bed?' he asked. 'You came up hours ago.'

'Exactly half an hour to be precise,' answered Maria coldly.

'What have you been doing?' asked Arthur.

'Thinking about hypnotism,' said Maria truthfully. She closed the window, trapping the fly in the room.

'Hypnotism? Why? What about it?' asked Arthur.

'I told you I went to the hypnotist at the Bates' the other night, and I was just thinking how clever the man was.'

'A lot of nonsense!' exclaimed Arthur.

'It isn't!' said Maria. 'It's extraordinary. He did marvellous things, and it couldn't have been a put up job.'

'Don't believe in it,' said Arthur. 'Stands to reason it's rubbish.' He headed for his dressing-room next door, and Maria began creaming her face. She was unaccountably angry at what he'd said, and she scrubbed her face viciously with her face tissues to remove the cream. She heard Arthur plunging about the dressing-room. He seemed to be banging into the furniture, and her lips curled in contempt. Couldn't even hold his drink. Disgusting. She sat staring into her dressing table mirror, and saw with emotion the deep lines running across her forehead, and down from her nostrils to the sides of her mouth.

Arthur returned in his pyjamas. 'Hypnotism!' he snorted scornfully. 'Bird brain!'

'One day I'll show you,' said Maria. 'I'll learn how to do it, and I'll practise on you. Then you won't call it rubbish!'

Arthur made for his bed, and sat on the edge, making the springs creak.

This infuriated Maria even more. How often she had lain in her own bed and heard Arthur snoring and shifting in his, while she herself had stayed awake for hours wishing away her whole life, because he was alive.

'It only takes intelligence and belief,' she said. 'I'll learn, I promise you.'

Arthur looked exaggeratedly serious. 'Maria. Maria. You're going into a trance,' he mocked. 'A trance. A trance, Maria darling.' His voice went absurdly high and he laughed at her maddeningly. 'Oh, Maria, you're going into a trance,' he repeated. 'Clever Maria. Idiot Maria.'

Maria lost her temper. 'Shut up you bloody fool,' she said, 'and get into bed. You're drunk.'

'Hypnotize me, darling,' taunted Arthur. 'Hypnotize me into bed. It only takes intelligence and belief. Hypnotize me.'

Maria went and stood in front of him. 'All right,' she said. 'I'll try. Look at that light, Arthur.' She pointed at the light in the centre of the ceiling. Arthur looked at it obediently. 'Good. Now you feel as if you are swaying, swaying, swaying. You feel as if you are swaying, swaying, swaying.'

To her amazement Arthur, glassy-eyed, began swaying. 'You want to go to sleep. To sleep, to sleep,' she crooned, and again to her astonishment, Arthur's head began to nod on his chest, though his eyes still remained glassily open. 'You want to shut your eyes,' she urged with enormous excitement. 'Shut your eyes. Shut your eyes!' Arthur shut his eyes. 'Now you can't open them. You try, but you can't.' Arthur flickered his eyelids but his eyes remained shut.

Almost unbelievingly Maria went on. 'Now you want to go for a little walk dear. A walk round your bedroom. You're going to be very careful not to trip into the furniture, and you'll walk right round the room, then you'll sit at my dressing table, pick up my hairbrush, and brush what remains of your hair on your balding head.'

Arthur rose slowly from the bed, walked carefully round the large depressing bedroom, painstakingly avoiding the beds, the chairs, and the tables. He wandered about for a little while, then made his way with equal care to the dressing-table, where he sat down, picked up Maria's brush, and began brushing his hair. For a horrible second Maria thought he had opened his eyes but with great relief she realized it was just a trick of light. He calmly went on brushing his hair.

Maria's mouth was dry, and her heart was pumping. She had never been so excited in her life. She tried to control her voice, but had to put her hand to her chest, where she seemed to have a violent pain from a constriction of her breathing.

'Now,' she said quietly and intently. 'Now you want to go to the window, Arthur. Carefully now. Very carefully.' Arthur went to the window as he was told.

Almost in a trance herself, Maria heard a fly still buzzing at the pane, and for a moment, Arthur in his trance seemed to hear it too, and he faltered.

Breathlessly she said, 'You're going to open the window, Arthur dear, to let the fly out. You don't like flies, do you? But the fly is your good angel, if you did but know it. And mine. He's going to lead you out into the summer night, right up to heaven. Open the window, Arthur. That's it. You help that little fly, and he'll help you. You're going to love flies from now on. You're going to love this, Arthur. Pretty flies. Good flies. That little fly will teach you to fly, Arthur.' She paused a moment to smother a smile at her own joke.

Arthur like a zombie opened the window. He pushed it up from the bottom as high as it would go, then with his hands one on each side of the frame he stood rigid.

'Now, Arthur dear, you're going to dive. You're going to dive out into the night. Like a bird. A swallow dive. See, your little friend the fly has already gone. Out into the night. Dive, Arthur dear. Dive.'

Slowly Arthur took his right hand away from the frame. Fascinated Maria watched him. But he stood still.

'Dive, Arthur dear. Dive,' encouraged Maria.

He remained where he was, his left hand holding the frame; his right hand hanging by his side. A huge ponderous irresolute figure.

Maria became impatient. 'Go on, you drunken fool. Dive, damn you,' she whispered.

Was it only her imagination that he braced himself for a moment. She watched him minutely, her heart still thumping in her almost uncontrollable excitement, but still he stood there right in the centre of the window.

Maria crept stealthily towards him. 'Dive, Arthur. Dive,' she urged. 'Dive, Arthur. Dive.'

Silently she lifted her arm to give him a push. Just one vicious fatal push, to send him crashing on to the paving stones below. It was high above her head when suddenly with the speed of light Arthur wheeled round, collected her round the waist with his right arm, put his left hand over her mouth to prevent her screaming, and sent her hurtling through the window to her death.

She made no sound as she plummeted to the ground, arms flailing, nightdress billowing, until with a sickening crash her face smacked into the iron door stop outside the front door. Then with an extraordinary cry, she gave one convulsive heave and lay still, her face turned sideways and streaming with blood.

Arthur peering out of a window, watched her motionlessly for some moments, then he walked over to the telephone and dialled the doctor's number.

'It's my wife!' he babbled, imitating the voice he had heard Maria using before he came into the room. 'It's horrible. She's thrown herself out of the window. She's been practising self-hypnotism or something. Oh God, I can't explain now, but come over old man. Dead? I don't know. I haven't dared look. I called you at once. Yes, yes, of course I'll go but she fell out when I was nearly asleep, and I've only just seen her lying down there, absolutely still. You'll come, won't you? Yes, OK. I'll go straight down. Yes, yes of course. Poor Maria. Yes. Yes.'

He put down the receiver, put on his dressing-gown and slippers, went downstairs into the drawing-room and gave himself a stiff whisky, then made his way out of the house, to see if Maria was actually dead.

She was. Her face was gashed open. The summer flies were buzzing round her, and one eye lay on the flagstones beside her. On it a fly was crawling, while another explored the empty eye socket.

Arthur laughed. 'Good flies. Pretty flies. I'm going to love flies from now on,' he said. 'You're my good angels. My passports to heaven.'

He turned away and was violently sick but the flies went on buzzing happily, enjoying hugely the blood that streamed from Maria's face.

THOU SHALT NOT SUFFER A WITCH. . .

Dorothy K. Haynes

THE CHILD sat alone in her bedroom, weaving the fringe of the counterpane in and out of her fingers. It was a horrible room, the most neglected one of the house. The grate was narrow and rusty, cluttered up with dust and hair combings, and the floorboards creaked at every step. When the wind blew, the door rattled and banged, but the window was sealed tight, webbed, fly-spotted, a haven for everything black and creeping.

In and out went her fingers, the fringe pulled tight between nail and knuckle. Outside, the larches tossed and flurried, brilliant green under a blue sky. Sometimes the sun would go in, and rain would hit the window like a handful of nails thrown at the glass; then the world would lighten suddenly, the clouds would drift past in silver and white, and the larches would once more toss in sunshine.

'Jinnot! Jinnot!' called a voice from the yard. 'Where've you got to, Jinnot?'

She did not answer. The voice went farther away, still calling. Jinnot sat on the bed, hearing nothing but the voice which had tormented her all week.

'You'll do it, Jinnot, eh? Eh, Jinnot? An' I'll give you a sixpence to spend. We've always got on well, Jinnot. You like me better than her. She never gave you ribbons for your hair, did she? She never bought you sweeties in the village? It's not much to ask of you, Jinnot, just to say she looked at you, an' it happened. It's not as if it was telling lies. It has happened before; it has, eh, Jinnot?'

She dragged herself over to the mirror, the cracked sheet of glass with the fawn fly-spots. The door on her left hand, the window on her right, neither a way of escape. Her face looked back at her, yellow in the reflected sunlight. Her hair was the colour of hay, her heavy eyes had no shine in them. Large teeth, wide mouth, the whole face was square and dull. She went back to the bed, and her fingers picked again at the fringe.

Had it happened before? Why could she not remember properly? Perhaps it was because they were all so kind to her after it happened, trying to wipe it out of her memory. 'You just came over faint, lassie. Just a wee sickness, like. Och, you don't need to cry, you'll be fine in a minute. Here's Minty to see to you. . . .'

But Minty would not see to her this time.

The voice went on and on in her head, wheedling, in one ear and out of the other.

'Me and Jack will get married, see, Jinnot? And when we're married, you can come to our house whenever you like. You can come in, and I'll bake scones for you, Jinnot, and sometimes we'll let you sleep in our wee upstairs room. You'll do it, Jinnot, will you not? For Jack as well as for me. You like Jack. Mind he mended your Dolly for you? And you'd like to see us married thegither, would you not?

'He'd never be happy married to her, Jinnot. You're a big girl now, you'll soon see that for yourself. She's good enough in her way, see, but she's not the right kind for him. She sits and sews and works all day, but she's never a bit of fun with him, never a word to say. But he's never been used to anyone better, see, Jinnot, and he'll not look at anybody else while she's there. It's for his own good, Jinnot, and for her sake as well. They'd never be happy married.

'And, Jinnot, you're not going to do her any harm. Someday you'll get married yourself, Jinnot, and you'll know. So it's just kindness . . . and she *is* like that, like what I said. Mebbe she's been the cause of the trouble you had before, you never know. So you'll do it, Jinnot, eh? You'll do it?'

She did not want to. The door rattled in the wind, and the sun shone through the dirt and the raindrops on the window. Why did she want to stay here, with the narrow bed, the choked grate, the mirror reflecting the flaked plaster of the opposite wall? The dust blew along the floor, and the chimney and the keyhole howled together. 'Jinnot! Jinnot!' went the voice again. She paid no attention. Pulling back the blankets, she climbed fully dressed into the bed, her square, suety face like a mask laid on the pillows. 'Jinnot! Jinnot!' went the voice, calling, coaxing through the height of the wind. She whimpered, and curled herself under the bedclothes, hiding from the daylight and the question that dinned at her even in the dark. 'You'll do it, Jinnot, eh? Will you? Eh, Jinnot?'

Next day, the weather had settled. A quiet, spent sun shone on the farm, the tumbledown dykes and the shabby thatch. Everything was still as a painting, the smoke suspended blue in the air, the ducks so quiet on the pond that the larches doubled themselves in the water. Jinnot stood at the door of the byre, watching Jack Hyslop at work. His brush went swish swish, swirling the muck along to the door. He was a handsome lad. No matter how dirty his work, he always looked clean. His boots were bright every morning, and his black hair glistened as he turned his head. He whistled as his broom spattered dung and dirty water, and Jinnot turned her face away. The strong, hot smell from the byre made something grip her stomach with a strong, relentless fist.

Now Minty came out of the kitchen, across the yard with a basin of pig-swill. With her arm raised, pouring out the slops, she looked at the byre door for a long minute. To the child, the world seemed to stop in space. The byreman's broom was poised in motion, his arms flexed for a forward push; his whistle went on on the same note, high and shrill; and Minty was a statue of mute condemnation, with the dish spilling its contents in a halted stream.

A moment later, Jinnot found that Jack Hyslop was holding her head on his knee. Minty had run up, her apron clutched in both hands. Beatrice, the dairymaid, was watching too, bending over her. There was a smell of the dairy on her clothes, a slight smell of sourness, of milk just on the turn, and her hair waved dark under her cap. 'There now,' she said. 'All right, dearie, all right! What made you go off like that, now?'

The child's face sweated all over, her lips shivered as the

air blew cold on her skin. All she wanted now was to run away, but she could not get up to her feet. 'What was it, Jinnot?' said the voice, going on and on, cruel, kind, which was it? 'Tell me, Jinnot. Tell me.'

She could not answer. Her tongue seemed to swell and press back on her throat, so that she vomited. Afterwards, lying in bed, she remembered it all, the sense of relief when she had thrown up all she had eaten, and the empty languor of the sleep which followed. Beatrice had put her to bed, and petted her and told her she was a good girl. 'It was easy done, eh, Jinnot? You'd have thought it was real.' She gave a high, uneasy laugh. 'Aye, you're a good wee thing, Jinnot. All the same, you fair frichted me at the beginning!'

She was glad to be left alone. After her sleep, strangely cold, she huddled her knees to her shoulders and tried to understand. Sometime, in a few months or a few years, it did not seem to matter, Minty and Jack Hyslop were to be married. Minty was kind. Since Jinnot's mother had died, she had been nurse and foster mother, attending to clothes and food and evening prayers. She had no time to do more. Her scoldings were frequent, but never unjust. Jinnot had loved her till Beatrice came to the dairy, handsome, gay and always ready with bribes.

'You're a nice wee girl, Jinnot. Look – will you do something for Jack and me – just a wee thing? You've done it before; I know you have. Some time, when Minty's there . . .'

And so she had done it, for the sake of sixpence, and the desire to be rid of the persistent pleading; but where she had meant to pretend to fall in a fit at Minty's glance, just to pretend, she had really lost her senses, merely thinking about it. She was afraid now of what she had done . . . was it true then, about Minty, that the way she looked at you was enough to bring down a curse?

It could not be true. Minty was kind, and would make a good wife. Beatrice was the bad one, with her frightening whispers – and yet, it wasn't really badness; it was wisdom. She knew all the terrible things that children would not understand.

Jinnot got up and put on her clothes. Down in the kitchen, there was firelight, and the steam of the evening meal. Her father was eating heartily, his broad shoulders stooped over his plate. 'All right again, lassie?' he asked, snuggling her to him with one arm. She nodded, her face still a little peaked with weakness. At the other side of the room, Minty was busy at the fireside, but she did not turn her head. Jinnot clung closer to her father.

All the air seemed to be filled with whispers.

From nowhere at all, the news spread that Jinnot was bewitched. She knew it herself. She was fascinated by the romance of her own affliction, but she was frightened as well. Sometimes she would have days with large blanks which memory could not fill. Where had she been? What had she done? And the times when the world seemed to shrivel to the size of a pin-head, with people moving like grains of sand, tiny, but much, much clearer, the farther away they seemed – who was behind it all? When had it started?

In time, however, the trouble seemed to right itself. But now, Jack Hyslop courted Beatrice instead of Minty. Once, following them, Jinnot saw them kiss behind a hayrick. They embraced passionately, arms clutching, bodies pressed together. It had never been like that with Minty, no laughter, no sighs. Their kisses had been mere respectful tokens, the concession to their betrothal.

Minty said nothing, but her sleek hair straggled, her once serene eyes glared under their straight brows. She began to be abrupt with the child. 'Out the road!' she would snap. 'How is it a bairn's aye at your elbow?' Jinnot longed for the friendliness of the young dairymaid. But Beatrice wanted no third party to share her leisure, and Jinnot was more lonely than ever before.

Why had she no friends? She had never had young company, never played games with someone of her own age. Her pastimes were lonely imaginings, the dark pretence of a brain burdened with a dull body. She made a desperate bid to recover her audience. Eyes shut, her breathing hoarse and ragged, she let herself fall to the ground, and lay there until footsteps came running, and kind hands worked to revive her.

So now she was reinstated, her father once more mindful of her, and the household aware of her importance, a sick person in the house. The voices went on whispering around her, 'Sshh! It's wee Jinnot again. Fell away in a dead faint. Poor lassie, she'll need to be seen to ... Jinnot – Jinnot ... wee Jinnot ...'

But this time, there was a difference. They waited till she waked, and then questioned her. Her father was there, blocking out the light from the window, and the doctor sat by the bedside, obviously displeased with his task. Who was to blame? Who was there when it happened? She knew what they wanted her to say; she knew herself what to tell them. 'Who was it?' pressed her father. 'This has been going on too long.' 'Who was it?' said the doctor. 'There's queer tales going around, you know, Jinnot!' 'You know who it was,' said the voice in her mind. 'You'll do it, Jinnot, eh?'

'I – I don't know,' she sighed, her eyes drooping, her mouth hot and dry. 'I ... only ...' she put her hand to her head, and sighed. She could almost believe she was really ill, she felt so tired and strange.

After that, the rumours started again. The voice came back to Jinnot, the urgent and convincing warning – 'She *is* like that, like what I said. ...' For her own piece of mind, she wanted to *know*, but there was no one she could ask. She could not trust her own judgement.

It was months before she found out, and the days had lengthened to a queer tarnished summer, full of stale yellow heat. The larches had burned out long ago, and their branches drooped in dull fringes over the pond. The fields were tangled with buttercups and tall moon daisies, but the flowers dried and shrivelled as soon as they blossomed. All the brooks were silent; and the nettles by the hedges had a curled, thirsty look. Jinnot kept away from the duckpond these days. With the water so low, the floating weeds and mud gave off a bad, stagnant smell.

Over the flowers, the bees hovered, coming and going endlessly, to and from the hives. One day, a large bumble, blundering home, tangled itself in the girl's collar, and stung her neck. She screamed out, running into the house, squealing that she had swallowed the insect, and that something with a sting was flying round in her stomach, torturing her most cruelly. They sent for the doctor, and grouped round her with advice. Later, they found the bee, dead, in the lace which had trapped it; but before that, she had vomited up half her inside, with what was unmistakably yellow bees' bodies, and a quantity of waxy stuff all mixed up with wings and frail, crooked legs.

She looked at the watchers, and knew that the time had come. 'It was Minty Fraser!' she wailed. 'It was her! She *looked* at me!' She screamed, and hid her face as the sickness once more attacked her in heaving waves.

They went to the house, and found Minty on her knees, washing over the hearthstone. One of the farm-men hauled her to her feet, and held her wrists together. 'Witch! Witch! Witch!' shouted the crowd at the door.

'What – What—'

'Come on, witch! Out to the crowd!'

'No! No, I never—'

'Leave her a minute,' roared Jack Hyslop. 'Mebbe she – give her a chance to speak!' His mouth twitched a little. At one time, he was thinking, he had been betrothed to Minty, before Beatrice told him ... he faltered at the thought of Beatrice. 'Well, don't be rough till you're sure,' he finished lamely, turning away and leaving the business to the others. Those who sympathized with witches, he remembered, were apt to share their fate.

The women were not so blate. 'Witch! Witch!' they shrilled. 'Burn the witch! Our bairns are no' safe when folks like her is let to live!'

She was on the doorstep now, her cap torn off, her eye bleeding, her dress ripped away at the shoulder. Jinnot's father, pushing through the mob, raised his hand for the sake of order. 'Look, men! Listen, there! This is my house; there'll be no violence done on the threshold.'

T—B

'Hang her! Burn her! A rope, there!'

'No hanging till you make sure. Swim her first. If the devil floats—'

'Jinnot! Here's Jinnot!'

The girl came through a lane in the throng, Beatrice holding her hand, clasping her round the waist. She did not want to see Minty, but her legs forced her on. Then she looked up. A witch ... she saw the blood on the face, the torn clothes, the look of horror and terrible hurt. That was Minty, who cooked her meals and looked after her and did the work of a mother. She opened her mouth and screamed, till the foam dripped over her chin.

Her father's face was as white as her own spittle. 'Take the beast away,' he said, 'and if she floats, for God's sake get rid of her as quick as you can!'

It was horrible. They all louped at her, clutching and tearing and howling as they plucked at her and trussed her for ducking. She was down on the ground, her clothes flung indecently over her head, her legs kicking as she tried to escape. 'It wasna me!' she skirled. 'It wasna me! I'm no' a witch! Aaah!' The long scream cut the air like a blade. Someone had wrenched her leg and snapped the bone at the ankle, but her body still went flailing about in the dust, like a kitten held under a blanket.

They had her trussed now, wrists crossed, legs crossed, her body arched between them. She was dragged to the pond, blood from her cuts and grazes smearing the clothes of those who handled her. Her hair hung over her face and her broken foot scraped the ground. 'No! No!' she screamed. 'Ah, God ...!' and once, 'Jinnot! Tell them it wasna me—'

A blow over the mouth silenced her, and she spat a tooth out with a mouthful of blood. She shrieked as they swung and hurtled her through the air. There was a heavy splash, and drops of green, slimy water spattered the watching faces. If Minty was a witch, she would float; and then they would haul her out and hang her, or burn her away, limb by limb.

She sank; the pond was shallow, but below the surface, green weed and clinging mud drew her down in a deadly clutch. The crowd on the bank watched her, fascinated. It was only when her yammering mouth was filled and silenced that they realized what had happened, and took slow steps to help her. By that time, it was too late.

What must it be like to be a witch? The idea seeped into her mind like ink, and all her thoughts were tinged with the black poison. She knew the dreadful aftermath; long after, her mind would be haunted by the sight she had seen. In her own nostrils, she felt the choke and snuffle of the pond slime; but what must it feel like, the knowledge of strange power, the difference from other people, the danger? Her imagination played with the thrilling pain of it, right down to the last agony.

She asked Beatrice about it. Beatrice was married now, with a baby coming, and Jinnot sat with her in the waning afternoons, talking with her, woman to woman.

'I didn't like to see them set on her like yon. She never done me any harm. If it hadn't been for me—'

'Are you sure, Jinnot? Are you sure? Mind the bees, Jinnot, an' yon time at the barn door? What about them?'

'I – I don't know.'

'Well, I'm telling you. She was a witch, that one, if anybody was.'

'Well, mebbe she couldn't help it.'

'No, they can't help the power. It just comes on them. Sometimes they don't want it, but it comes, just the same. It's hard, but you know what the Bible says: "Thou shalt not suffer a witch . . ."'

She had a vision of Minty, quiet, busy, struggling with a force she did not want to house in her body. Beside this, her own fits and vomitings seemed small things. She could forgive knowing that. 'How . . . how do they first know they're witches?' she asked.

'Mercy, I don't know! What questions you ask, Jinnot! How would I know, eh? I daresay they find out soon enough.'

So that was it; they knew themselves. Her mind dabbled and meddled uncomfortably with signs and hints. She wanted to curse Beatrice for putting the idea into her head; she would not believe it; but once there, the thought would not be re-moved. What if she was a witch? 'I'm not,' she said to herself. 'I'm too young,' she said; but there was no conviction in it. Long before she had been bewitched, she had known there was something different about her. Now it all fell into place. No wonder the village children would not call and play with her. No wonder her father was just rather than affectionate, shielding her only because she was his daughter. And no won-der Beatrice was so eager to keep in with her, with the incess-ant 'Eh, Jinnot?' always on her lips.

Well, then, she was a witch. As well to know it sooner as later, to accept the bothers with the benefits, the troubles and trances with the newfound sense of power. She had never wanted to kill or curse, never in her most unhappy moments, but now, given the means, would it not be as well to try? Did her power strengthen by being kept, or did it spring up fresh from some infernal reservoir? She did not know. She was a very new witch, uncertain of what was demanded of her. Week after week passed, and she was still no farther forward.

She continued her visits to Beatrice, though the thought of it all made her grue. It angered her to see the girl sitting stout and placid at the fireside, unhaunted, unafraid. 'You'll come and see the baby when it's born, eh, Jinnot?' she would say. 'Do you like babies? Do you?' Nothing mattered to her now, it seemed, but the baby. In the dark winter nights, Jin-not made a resolve to kill her. But for Beatrice, she might never have discovered this terrible fact about herself. Beatrice was to blame for everything, but a witch has means of revenge, and one witch may avenge another.

She had no idea how to cast a spell, and there was no one to help her. What had Minty done? She remembered the moment at the byre-door, the upraised arm, and the long, long look. It would be easy. Bide her time, and Beatrice would die when the spring came.

She sat up in the attic, twining her fingers in the fringe of the bedcover, in and out, under and over. Beatrice was in labour. It had been whispered in the kitchen, spreading from

mouth to mouth. Now, Jinnot sat on the bed, watching the
larches grow black in the dusk. She was not aware of cold, or
dirt, or darkness. All her senses were fastened on the window
of Beatrice's cottage, where a light burned, and women gathered round the bed. She fixed her will, sometimes almost praying in her effort to influence fate. 'Kill her! Kill her! Let her
die!' Was she talking to God, or to the devil? The thoughts
stared and screamed in her mind. She wanted Beatrice to suffer
every agony, every pain, and wrench, to bear Minty's pain,
and her own into the bargain. All night she sat, willing pain
and death, and suffering it all in her own body. Her face was
grey as the ceiling, her flesh sweated with a sour smell. Outside, an owl shrieked, and she wondered for a moment if it
was Beatrice.

Suddenly, she knew that it was all over. The strain passed
out of her body, the lids relaxed over her eyes, her body
seemed to melt and sprawl over the bed. When she woke, it
was morning, and the maids were beaming with good news.
'Did you hear?' they said. 'Beatrice has a lovely wee boy! She's
fair away wi' herself!'

Jinnot said nothing. She stopped her mouth and her disappointment with porridge. It did not cross her mind that
perhaps, after all, she was no witch. All she thought was that
the spell had not worked, and Beatrice was still alive. She
left the table, and hurried over to the cottage. The door was
ajar, the fire bright in the hearth, and Beatrice was awake
in bed, smiling, the colour already flushing back into her
cheeks.

'He's a bonny baby, Jinnot. He's lovely, eh? Eh, Jinnot?'

She crept reluctantly to the cradle. Why, he was no size at
all, so crumpled, so new, a wee sliver of flesh in a bundle of
white wool. She stared for a long time, half sorry for what
she had to do. The baby was snuffling a little, its hands and
feet twitching under the wrappings. He was so young, he would
not have his mother's power to resist a witch.

She glared at him for a long minute, her eyes fixed, her lips
firm over her big teeth. His face, no bigger than a lemon,
turned black, and a drool of foam slavered from the mouth.

When the twitching stopped, and the eyes finally uncrossed themselves, she walked out, and left the door again on the latch. She had not spoken one word.

It seemed a long time before they came for her, a long time of fuss and running about while she sat on the bed, shivering in the draught from the door. When she crossed to the window, her fingers probing the webs and pressing the guts from the plumpest insects, she saw them arguing and gesticulating in a black knot. Jack Hyslop was there, his polished hair ruffled, his face red. The women were shaking their heads, and Hyslop's voice rose clear in the pale air.

'Well, that's what she said. The wee thing had been dead for an hour. An' it was that bitch Jinnot came in an' glowered at it.'

'Och, man, it's a sick woman's fancy! A wee mite that age can easy take convulsions.'

'It wasna convulsions. My wife said Jinnot was in and out with a face like thunder. She was aye askin' about witches too, you can ask Beatrice if you like.'

'Well, she was in yon business o' Minty Fraser. Ye cannie blame her, a young lassie like that . . . mind, we sympathize about the bairn, Jacky, but—'

They went on placating him, mindful of the fact that Jinnot was the farmer's daughter. It would not do to accuse *her*; but one of the women went into the cottage, and came out wiping her eyes. 'My, it would make anybody greet. The wee lamb's lying there like a flower, that quiet! It's been a fair shock to the mother, poor soul. She gey faur through. . . .'

They muttered, then, and drifted towards the house. Jinnot left the window, and sat again on the bed. She was not afraid, only resigned, and horribly tired of it all.

When they burst into her room, clumping over the bare boards, her father was with them. They allowed him to ask the questions. Was he angry with them, or with her? She could not guess.

'Jinnot,' he said sternly, 'what's this? What's all this?'
She stared at him.

'What's all this? Do you know what they're saying about

you? They say you killed Beatrice Hyslop's bairn. Is that true, Jinnot?'

She did not answer. Her father held up his hand as the men began to growl.

'Come now, Jinnot, enough of this sulking! It's for your own good to answer, and clear yourself. Mind of what happened to Minty Fraser! Did you do anything to the baby?'

'I never touched it. I just looked at it.'

'Just looked?'

'Yes.'

A rough cry burst from Jack Hyslop. 'Is that not what Minty Fraser said? Was that not enough from her?'

'Hyslop, hold your tongue, or you lose your job.'

'Well, by God, I lose it then! There's been more trouble on this bloody farm—'

'Aye! Leave this to us!'

'We'll question the wench. If she's no witch, she's nothing to fear.'

The women had come in now, crowding up in angry curiosity. The farmer was pushed back against the wall. 'One word, and you'll swim along with her,' he was warned, and he knew them well enough to believe them. They gathered round Jinnot, barking questions at her, and snatching at the answers. Every time she paused to fidget with the fringe, they lammed her across the knuckles till her hands were swollen and blue.

'Tell the truth now; are you a witch?'

'No. No, I'm not!'

'Why did you kill the baby this morning?'

'I – I never. I can't kill folk. I—'

'You hear that? She can't kill folk! Have you ever tried?'

She cowered back from them, the faces leering at her like ugly pictures. She would tell the truth, as her father said, and be done with all this dreamlike horror. 'Leave me alone!' she said. 'Leave me, and I'll tell!'

'Hurry then. Out with it! Have you ever tried to kill anybody?'

'Yes. I tried, and – and I couldn't. It was her, she started telling me I was bewitched—'

'Who?'

'Beatrice – Mistress Hyslop.'

'My God!' said Jack and her father, starting forward together.

'Hold on, there! Let her speak.'

'She said I was bewitched, an' I thought I was. I don't know if it was right . . . it was all queer, and I didn't know . . . and then, when she said about witches, she put it in my head, and it came over me I might be one. I *had* to find out—'

'There you are. She's admitting it!'

'No!' She began to shout as they laid hold of her, screaming in fright and temper till her throat bled. 'No! *Leave* me alone! I never; I tried, and I couldn't do it! I couldn't, I tell you! She *wouldn't* die. She'd have died if I'd been a witch, wouldn't she? She's a witch herself; I don't care, Jack Hyslop, she is! It was her fault Minty Fraser – oh God, no! NO!'

She could not resist the rope round her, the crossing of her limbs, the tight pull of cord on wrists and ankles. When she knew it was hopeless, she dared not resist remembering Minty's broken leg, her cuts and blood and bruises, the tooth spinning out in red spittle. She was not afraid of death, but she was mortally afraid of pain. Now, if she went quietly, there would only be the drag to the pond, the muckle splash, and the slow silt and suffocation in slime. . . .

She had no voice left to cry out when they threw her. Her throat filled with water, her nose filled, and her ears. She was tied too tightly to struggle. Down, down she went, till her head sang, and her brain nearly burst; but the pond was full with the spring rains, and her body was full-fleshed and buoyant. Suddenly, the cries of the crowd burst upon her again, and she realized that she was floating. Someone jabbed at her, and pushed her under again with a long pole, but she bobbed up again a foot away, her mouth gulping, her eyes bulging under her dripping hair. The mob on the bank howled louder.

'See, see! She's floating!'

'Witch! Burn her! Fish her out and hang her!'

'There's proof now. What are you waiting for? Out with her. See, the besom'll *no'* sink!'

So now they fished her out, untied her, and bound her again in a different fashion, hands by her side, feet together. She was too done to protest, or to wonder what they would do. She kept her eyes shut as they tied her to a stake, and she ignored the tickle of dead brushwood being piled round her feet and body. She could hardly realize that she was still alive, and she was neither glad nor sorry.

They were gentle with her now, sparing her senses for the last pain. At first, she hardly bothered when the smoke nipped her eyes and her nostrils; she hardly heard the first snap of the thin twigs. It was only when the flames lapped her feet and legs that she raised her head and tried to break free. As the wood became red hot, and the flames mounted to bite her body, she screamed and writhed and bit her tongue to mincemeat. When they could not see her body through the fire, the screams still went on.

The crowd drifted away when she lost consciousness. There was no more fun to be had; or perhaps, it wasn't such fun after all. The men went back to the fields, but they could not settle to work. Jinnot's father was gnawing his knuckles in the attic, and they did not know what would happen when he came down. Beatrice tossed in a muttering, feverish sleep; and beside the pond, a few veins and bones still sizzled and popped in the embers.

STRICTLY FOR THE BIRDS

Lindsay Stewart

MY NAME is Mason and I have a pretty wife and two children. At least, I had a pretty wife. Now I have only the two children. They, thank God, were too young and innocent to comprehend fully the real horror of what happened in a park in north London last Sunday week. My wife, Elizabeth, now lies in a hospital in Epsom, her face distorted with fear and disgust. They tell me she screams a lot, even in the daytime. They tell me she'll never be pretty again.

We used to live near Regent's Park Road. We've moved now, away from Primrose Hill, away from any park, from any birds. Of course, the children don't understand any of this, or I don't think they do. 'Why can't we go and play on the swings now, Daddy?' they ask. I can never tell them. 'Is it because of that man, Daddy?' they ask. I always make some poor excuse, but I think they notice the beads of sweat on my forehead, they notice that I can't look them in the eyes any more. It's a pity that they should have learned to sense evil so young.

Many of us go through life without ever having to admit that there is real evil in the world until, perhaps, one is shaken by some appalling crime beyond human comprehension. For example, take Christie. Even so, you forget the whole thing until such an evil touches you personally. Then you can never know peace again. This is the story of how my wife found madness and how I learned never to sleep with my eyes shut.

Every Sunday afternoon my wife and I and the children would walk down Fitzroy Avenue, along Regent's Park Road, skirting the gates of Primrose Hill, to the Zoo. After we'd made our customary rounds of the elephants, the goats who ate our hats and gloves, the tigers, the bush babies, Tigger the lynx, Goldie the eagle, and the snakepit, we'd let the children play in the sand, on the swings and seesaws at the foot of Primrose Hill.

Harmless enough, you might think. How could one imagine that on Primrose Hill every Sunday afternoon, with the sun playing among the crocuses, such a repulsive rite was performed? You'll find it hard to believe what I am about to tell you, but it's true. I know, I was there. In fact, I saw it many times. I even joined in, at least until I realized. But let me give you a clue. Have you ever noticed how fat and healthy the Primrose Hill pigeons are? If you have, score one; you're halfway to evil.

We'd been in the park many times before we noticed the old man in his wheelchair, and the valet. The old man was always covered in blankets, wore dark glasses and odd plastic gloves of a peculiar pattern. I thought then that perhaps he had some skin complaint and that the gloves protected his frail hands from the sun and wind. His face was rather pitted, his complexion sallow and wrinkled. Of course, my wife noticed him at once. At three o'clock in the afternoon the old man would be wheeled through the gates by a tall dark man of about forty. They would always rest in one place, the valet standing stiffly behind the chair, the old man fumbling with a bag of what appeared to be bread crumbs, his toothless mouth miming soundless words. Then together, they would feed the pigeons.

Both of them had noticed my wife and me. The old man tried to smile at the children a few times. His red tongue flapped about in his mouth as though he were desperately trying to say something to them. 'Poor thing,' my wife observed.

It was some weeks before we actually approached the old man. I had sensed that something was wrong, though I didn't know what, then. I tried to stop my wife from going near him, but she merely said, 'Pooh!' to me. The valet didn't seem to welcome visitors and discouraged conversation with his silence. The old man smiled: my wife talked about the weather. Then he handed her the white paper bag, indicating that she should feed the clustering throng of pigeons around his chair. She threw a handful of the contents to the birds, and they all rushed towards it, fighting and flapping over each tiny morsel. The crumbs were rather green, very soft and crumbly, like rotting cheese. My wife grimaced when she touched it. It was slimy. With a lift of her eyebrows she asked what it was that the birds were gobbling so ravenously, but the old man only flapped his plastic-covered fingers and crowed with delight. The valet gazed into the distance and said nothing. Then he turned the wheelchair round abruptly and pushed the old man out of the park.

Although on subsequent Sunday afternoons we all helped the old man to feed the pigeons, I was invariably reluctant. I didn't know why. I began to notice that he seemed to be shrinking a little. Old age, senility? Some curious disease? I didn't know. For instance, on the last Sunday in May, I noticed that a corner of the blanket which covered his legs had slipped: he had only one leg. 'Poor old boy,' said Elizabeth, 'There must have been something so terribly wrong that they had to operate.' A few weeks later, the other leg also had gone.

After that, we watched him from a distance. Perhaps we couldn't bear to see him crumble away completely, the victim of a mind and body-destroying fungus, some parasite eating his limbs day by day, spreading a slow death wherever it moved. Perhaps it was the smell of him. It lingered in the air when he had gone. Or perhaps we sensed in our inner minds that something sickening and ugly was taking place. Could it have been that?

On the Saturday night following the incident of the legs, I heard my wife moaning in her sleep. She would fumble with the sheets, cry out a little, turn her body over and over in our bed. I put my arms about her, trying to comfort her. She mumbled something about 'arms', repeated it several times, as though she were desperately seeking an answer to a question. She woke up very suddenly, about four in the morning, crying. I pulled her to me, asked her what was wrong and kissed her. She shivered in my arms, shook her head and fell asleep.

Next day we saw the old man again. My wife seemed obsessed by him. This time she went to him and peered at him closely. He had shrunk a great deal. He seemed to be half the size he had been before. Elizabeth could see black sockets behind the glasses. His arms were wrapped in bandages, strapped around him, covered with a shawl. This time there was no crow of delight, no flapping of fingers: no fingers. The old man was a lump of bandaged, rotting flesh, limbless, eyeless. Suddenly he said something, in a low crackling whisper, the only words Elizabeth had ever heard from him. He said, urgently, 'Feed them, feed them!' The valet said, 'Go away. Don't interfere. He's very ill.'

My wife ran back to me, pausing only to look behind her and see the attendant produce the usual large paper bag of evil-smelling crumbs for the pigeons, who fought wildly around the chair, perching on the back and arms.

After that, Elizabeth's state of mind deteriorated rapidly. I took her to our doctor, who gave her some iron pills and told her she needed rest. She took to sitting in an armchair in the corner of the room, fumbling with her fingers, picking at a piece of thread from a cushion. She said very little, answering questions in a monotone. I meant to take her to a psychiatrist of my acquaintance in Wimpole Street.

On Sunday we went to the park as usual. I didn't want Elizabeth to come with us, but she insisted. The children were playing happily on the swings. Elizabeth sat on the bench, gazing with utter concentration at the entrance to Primrose Hill. I was reading the colour sections. When I looked up from the magazines she had left my side and was standing fifty yards in front of me, facing the gate. I think she was talking to herself. My watch told me that it was three o'clock. This time only the valet came through the gate. No wheelchair, no old man. Only an umbrella, and a bag of crumbs larger than usual. I think I knew what was coming, when my wife turned to me and screamed at the top of her voice. The valet dropped the bag and fled, the soft, green, fleshy crumbs spilling on the grass.

BLOODTHIRSTY

Martin Waddell

THEY SHOOK hands with Henry, slit his throat, attached brown blood and breath bags to his wheezing lungs and dribbling arteries, snapped the bone, cut the remaining sinews and lifted his head clear of his body and straight into a preservation tank.

'Alright?' Miss Phipps asked, and the head managed a grim smile in reply ... it didn't feel like talking for, not surprisingly, it had a sore throat.

With the operation completed they threw the rest of Henry away, and the head nodded sleepy approval. They put it on a special trolley and wheeled it away from the theatre, through the corridor that passed the Memorial Rose Garden and the Cats' Cemetery, to the special room reserved for the Brain.

The Brain in Henry's head ... it thought of itself with a capital 'B' because it was, without a doubt, a first-class specimen ... the Brain in Henry's head was not sorry to be rid of the rest of him. It was used to having his arms and legs and other accessories around it, but just recently most of Henry had been getting on its nerves.

The Brain had not found it difficult to accept that Henry must go. As the Brain saw it, Henry was strictly fifth rate, and an outdated model at that. He had his uses ... you could even say he'd been good for the Brain, but now life in Henry's skull had degenerated to the point where it was just one illness after another. From toothache ... with an element of mystery, for Henry had long lost his teeth ... to sciatica, Burger's disease to bronchitis, poor Henry managed to contract the lot, and the Brain could only sit tight and endure it. Henry was its third body in eighty years, and nothing like as suitable as William or Francis had been ... the Brain had quite lost sympathy with him.

The Brain was not unkind, though it did not allow sentiment to govern its actions. It sent Henry out for a splendid dinner the week before the operation followed by an evening of sensual excess which was almost too much for the poor old chap, but apart from that one gay outing it allowed no let up in its work schedule, which had a high priority Stateside. Henry was for the chop, which was rough on Henry, but there was no reason for the Brain to get upset about it. Take out the brain, it reasoned, and what have you, a turnip, a potato ... and who feels for a turnip or potato when they're peeled and gutted? The Brain, never less than fair, did try to explain this to the rest of Henry, but he couldn't get over his fear, which was to do with what knives felt like and other trivialities. The Brain was a thinking thing, it couldn't cope with the instincts the original owner had planted deep in Henry. ... Henry's original owner had, unfortunately, but not without reason, suspected what they were going to do to him long before they did it.

Henry definitely didn't like it. There was nothing he could do about it, but this did not stop him trying. Once, when the Brain wasn't concentrating, the morning after the Farewell Celebration Dinner, Henry had a quick try at damaging the Brain, but this amounted to no more than dashing his head against a brick wall ... which hurt his head much more than the Brain. Poor Henry wasn't designed for thinking, he could only manage his instincts, and this proved far too great a handicap. The Brain ran rings around him.

The Brain was, of course, very smart. So smart, in fact, that there really were very sound reasons for perpetuating its existence at the expense of the Henrys, Williams and Francises of this world for the Greater Good of Mankind, as it told its friends ... a phrase with ominous overtones. The Brain Must Go On was another slogan it appreciated, but of course poor Henry couldn't go on because the Brain was hard on its bodies. When the Brain was in its first incarnation, Francis, it hit on God Save the Brain but later, when in William, who had religion before the Brain got him, it realized the inherent difficulties in this thesis. If anybody was getting worshipped round the place, it had to be the Brain; so it set up what was left of William as a memorial in the Research Centre. Francis and Henry were thrown away.

The removal of the head was always a nasty stage. Neither William nor Francis had taken it well when their time came, and Henry was no exception to this rule. The Brain, isolated in its preservation tank, found that Henry's head had somehow managed to contract earache, toothache and a second cousin to neuritis in an arm with which it had no longer any connexion. The Brain was supposed to be responsible for pain, but it couldn't cut out the efforts of Henry's head, which was most determined . . . it must have been something bad in the blood.

'How's your old head then?' Roger said, standing by the preservation tank which contained Henry's head, with the Brain still secure inside it.

The head blew bubbles through the Hypernofluid at him.

'Sorry old chap,' Roger said, and put on his long rubber gloves. Then he carefully slid back the tank protector shield and manipulated Henry's head so that the lips were clear of the blood streaked grey liquid . . . it tasted of peppermint, but how Roger found that out is another, disgusting, story.

'This head's giving me hell,' the Brain said, by way of Henry's mouth, which he'd bitten rather badly during the operation . . . Henry's thing about knives lasted right up to the end, for they'd only given him a local anaesthetic because of the Annendrum secretion. Henry's face was swollen now and gave his severed head, otherwise not unpleasant to look at, a turnipoid look. 'Are you sure you have those blood bags stitched on properly? I feel as if I had something stuck in my gullet.'

'You have no gullet,' Roger pointed out.

'Don't get smart with me,' the Brain said.

'Sorry old chap,' Roger said, quite cowed. He had a lot to thank the Brain for, which was most annoying. Any more old guff out of you, he thought to himself, and I'll snip off those little brown bags which pulsate beneath your treble chins ... but it was double chins of course, for one of them had had to go already. Snip the bags, and the Brain would quickly choke on blood streaked grey peppermint tasting liquid, one rasping gurgle and all would be over.

'I don't mind telling you Roger,' the Brain said, once more affable. 'It's been much worse this time. You were a bit hap-handed with that scalpel you know ... very messy. Old Henry had it hard ... but he's getting his own back. I've got pains in his feet now, and God knows where they are.'

'I'm very sorry,' Roger said.

The Brain was about to tell him more when Henry's head ... instinctively squeamish about such things ... managed to twitch and roll under the turgid red and grey liquid in the tank. Distastefully, Roger put his hand inside again ... like burrowing through a vat of melted raspberry icecream, he thought ... and righted the head. The Brain licked Henry's swollen lips and said crossly, 'You see ... he did that.'

'What do you want me to do about it?' Roger said.

'I think you'd better cut me out of this head,' the Brain said.

Which is how the Brain came to be lodged temporarily in a plastic bag without a head to call its own. Henry's head they threw away, in more or less the same direction as his body, though they did not get together ... not in this world anyway.

It was the Brain that mattered. It was the Brain that they carefully slopped into its pink tinged plastic bag ... they demonstrate the technique with the whites of eggs ... the Brain which slithered down to nestle in a poll of denegatoid frog spawn in the bottom of the bag, sightless, deaf to the world around it, but still thinking away for all it was worth.

That was the one thing you could always be sure of with the Brain ... whatever else happened to it, it just kept on thinking, usually about its own comforts.

Who the other body belonged to they didn't know, and to

tell the truth they didn't trouble overmuch to find out. There was time to fill out the compulsory loan form of course, but not to check too carefully on his credentials. In his pockets they found a corkscrew, a small chess set, a black handkerchief and a postcard from Transylvania which didn't help at all. These things must be done quickly and he was, after all, exactly what they were looking for.

He was a fine young man, in perfect mechanical order, vaccinated against all the appropriate diseases and free of the more obvious physical handicaps which might have ruled him out as a carrier for the Brain ... true, his teeth were a little odd, two of them at least were much too sharp and long, but at the time no one paid any attention to that. He had bright red hair and blue eyes and a hole in his head you could put a bullet through, which is exactly what someone had done. Not that the hole worried them ... in the light of what they were about to do with him it was, if anything, an added advantage.

'Quite a mess,' Roger said, surveying the pale newcomer, 'but I suppose we can use him.'

It was Miss Phipps who waxed enthusiastic. Miss Phipps being Miss Phipps, she had every reason to. Though the Brain was very practical it was not above the lusts of William, Francis (though Francis was a bit peculiar) or Henry, and accordingly had allowed itself a relationship somewhat less than strictly professional with chubby fullblooded Miss Phipps. This was very nice for the Brain and also very nice for Miss Phipps ... she could, after all, put it down to patriotism ... but by the time Henry's race was run it had become something of a drag. The newcomer, though a bit pale, looked full of potential.

'Lovely,' she said, patting her magnificent auburn tresses.

'Of course he *might* recover,' Roger said.

'Nonsense,' Miss Phipps said decisively, for that was something Roger should really have kept his mouth shut about. The new young man was going to lose his brain long before he got better if Miss Phipps had any say in the matter. 'The bullet in his head will not allow a full recovery,' she said.

'We are obviously justified in what we're doing, and anyway I've signed the form now.'

'I wonder why he got shot at?' Roger said.

'That is not our concern,' Miss Phipps said. 'We've got to think of the Brain. Think how much nicer it will be for it, going around in a nice young body like this.'

'I'm sure this one would be proud, if he knew,' Roger said.

'Grateful,' responded Miss Phipps, wholeheartedly.

They looked down fondly on the form before them, still breathing strongly despite Miss Phipps' prediction.

'There's a lot of blood,' Roger said, as he traced in the slitting line around the lean white throat.

'Waste not, want not,' said Miss Phipps, and went off to fetch a container for it.

For once, although she did not know it, the joke was on Miss Phipps.

'We've got one for you dear,' Miss Phipps said, but of course the Brain couldn't hear her. It was busy in its pink tinged plastic bag on a pretty piece of theoretical mutation, sure to prove a breakthrough. Miss Phipps didn't know about this; all she could see was the Brain pulsing gently in its pool of denegatoid frog spawn and, quite frankly, she must have seen it through love's eyes, for it was quite revolting.

'It's your Sugarpuss Belinda,' she said, cooing against the plastic. 'Old Brainey come to Mummy.' Having said it she realized that a change in approach would be called for. 'Come to Mummy,' might have done for the Brain in senile Henry, but the new body called for much more effort and originality. After blowing a kiss to the plastic bag she left the Brain's room and went down to the Cats' Cemetery to worry about it.

The Brain wasn't worried at all. It had settled in, quite happily in its plastic bag, free of all distractions of the flesh ... and Belinda Phipps was a considerable distraction, though the Brain blamed her in part at least on old Henry, who had been starved for affection when occupied by his original owner ... the brain he was born with, that is. Yes, the Brain was content, quite certain that its operation would be a success. It had worked twice . . . so why not again? The Henrys of this world might come and go, but the Brain would go on for-ever.

If the Brain pondered at all on where the Henrys and Williams and Francises came from, it did not show it . . . though strictly speaking it couldn't just then, save by slopping from side to side in the denegatoid frog spawn more energetically, for it had no body to show anything with. But it probably didn't ponder on it at all, for it was a happy, happy Brain. It had a nice new body to come, with which it anticipated doing a lot of new things . . . and one or two *old* things . . . better.

They wheeled the new body down through the Memorial Rose Garden, turned left past the Cats' Cemetery and went through the swing doors leading to the operating theatre, where Miss Phipps and Roger took charge, affable smiles on their plump faces. Actually the new body was smiling too, smiling so that his two peculiar teeth, the long sharp fang-like ones, gleamed over the pale pink of his lower lip, one set at each side of his mouth.

If Belinda Phipps and Roger had harboured a little of the romantic in their souls, they might have taken note of this little oddity, and possibly taken it as a warning. But they were not, unfortunately, romantics, though they were superb technicians.

It was as technicians that they set about enlarging the hole in the new body's head, then squeezed out the damaged brain or what was left of it, and threw it away . . . one hopes that, in some sweeter place, it may have encountered the brainless Henry, and come to some arrangement.

The Brain in its plastic bag, perforce incommunicado, somehow sensed that its time was near. It did its best to keep its wits about it, remembering that it was the Brain, and much more important and respected than any other brain it knew. It was all eagerness to get into its new head, now that the old one had been satisfactorily disposed of.

With loving care Belinda Phipps plopped the Brain, soft and slippery, with perhaps a little more ooze about than was desirable, out of its bag and into the newcomer's cavity, where it nestled in comfort as they fitted the little metal plate securely into the bone of its new skull.

If the mouth with the two extra sharp teeth jutting out of it smiled at that moment it was not the Brain's doing, but it may have been an instinctive reaction to the trickle of blood from the work overhead which ran down the new body's waxen cheek and dripped upon its pale lips.

'How do you feel today?' Roger asked the Brain in its new body. Outside the rain lashed down on the streets and people dashed around buying gumboots, with the sole exception of Belinda Phipps who had been to Richard Henry's to get her hair done and was now selecting a nice new frilly night-gown at the Bridal Bar in Harrods.

'Fine,' said the new body, sitting up. 'By the way, you should call me Alexis now . . . Count Alexis.'

'Splendid,' said Roger. 'You're not too cramped in there, or anything?'

'No, this one will do splendidly,' said Count Alexis.

'Anything I can get for you?' Roger asked.

'No thank you,' said Count Alexis, planting his feet on the floor beside the bed.

'You really shouldn't be getting up yet,' said Roger. 'You look a little pale, Count.'

'Nonsense,' said Count Alexis, reaching for his black tights.

Ten minutes later he was on his way round the unit, intro-ducing himself to old friends, not all of whom were glad to see him. Yet his walk seemed to take a lot out of him. As time went by he grew paler, his long black gloved hands began to quiver, his two sharp teeth to grate against the faint stubble on his chin.

It was quite half an hour before he managed to tear him-self away from the Brain's affairs and secrete himself in the Blood Depository.

'Like milk,' said the orderly. 'He was standing there slugging it, like milk out of a bottle.'

'Don't be so ridiculous,' said her friend.

'Dribbling down his chin,' she said. 'Then he looked at me . . . such a look!'

'Maybe he was thirsty,' said her friend, scornfully. 'You don't want to go around spreading tales like that. You know who he is, don't you?'

'He said I could call him Alexis. Then he tried to . . . tried to. . . .'

'He's *the Brain*,' said her friend. 'There now! So it must be all right, mustn't it?'

Belinda Phipps, as befits a top technician, had a splendid home near Sunningdale, surrounded by tall fir trees which obscured the angry moon. It was a hot, airless night and she lay on her large fourposter bed . . . Miss Phipps collected antiques . . . in her splendid new Bridal Bar nightie, lustrous hair curling on her shoulders and the white monogrammed pillow, dark eyes a-glitter in the candlelight . . . she found candlelight romantic. She was restless and full of petty frustration.

'You can call me Alexis,' he had said, showing her his new black velvet cloak . . . but where was he? Apparently with the Brain's new body, punctuality was not important. Transylvanian Count or no Transylvanian Count, she'd soon knock that out of him. Belinda Phipps was nothing if she was not businesslike, and an arrangement was an arrangement, a form of contract, even if it was for a night of passion.

Somewhere in the tall trees outside an owl hooted . . . or was it an owl? It could have been the call of a lost soul . . . but Belinda Phipps didn't take it that way, she was far too rational. The skeletal arm of a tree rapped the pane, a distant dog howled, but she lay on undisturbed, a superb technician to the end.

It was the technician in her that had her up counting the seconds between the thunder claps and charting them at the little desk in the corner of her room, when the window unaccountably burst open. She turned, auburn tresses flowing on her white shoulders, bosom all a-heave, locket trapped in her cleavage, to find a black figure outlined against the drapes, fierce eyes upon her. He strode forward, seized Miss Phipps and bore her to the bed.

'Alexis,' she cried, 'Count Alexis . . . Brain . . . what are you. Aaaaaghaaha!'

His fangs cut her throat, ripped the soft white skin, milked the pumping blood from her veins . . . so much better than the bottled variety. When he rose from her the pillow on which she lay was awash with blood, her Bridal Bar nightie in tatters. Miss Belinda Phipps lay ravished in the moonlight as the Fiend, sated, drew his black cloak around him and fled amid the gaunt trees.

He exited splendidly, though there was no one to see him. The hearse he had had to hire from a company which specialized in such things, but he drove it with the verve of an expert, long cloak flapping about him as the four black horses drew him away down the drive. An hour later he was home in Hangman's Hall, Clapham, clambering into the great big black coffin in the cellar.

The Brain was very very happy. In the past Francis' peculiarity had been awkward, Henry's senile decay a bit of a bore . . . but Count Alexis' technique was a revelation. As usual, the Brain had done superlatively well . . . much better than the original owner who'd had to make do without most of the trimmings because of his social position, something which did not inhibit the Brain one bit. Count Alexis' satisfied senses told him he had done well . . . but then the Brain was always best at anything he put his mind to.

Count Alexis lay back in his coffin, drew his cloak around him, settled himself in comfort against the silk accessories, and pulled down the lid, a pleasing prospect of bloody days before him.

He was destined, after all, to be the smartest vampire in Christendom.

AN APPARITION AT NOON

Adobe James

INEXPLICABLY, the dogs died.

Within seconds of each other!

I had been watching them from my vantage point on the cot which I take to more and more often these days – my refuge from that miserable African sun which can be compared to an atomic blast furnace this time of year. Bloody sod of a place, this whole rotten country.

But the dogs!

First one – then the other – had risen, sniffed, and wagged his tail as though a friend or something to eat were approaching him. A moment later they had stopped in fright, howled once, twitched, and then lay down to shudder their lives away in the dried grass of the *vlei*.

Fifteen years ago, I would have suspected Kenyatta's Mau-Mau.

Not now. His Kikuyu bandits and assassins have gotten what they wanted – everything! Now they are all Gilbert and Sullivan Major Generals in their own black armies – politicians robbing the *natives* now. Nothing else left to take from us, the whites. Nothing except a little patch of red dust here and there – like mine ... green only when the rains turn the *vlei* to swamp. Wretched god-forsaken place. Lonely.

Very lonely.

Especially since Kathleen died five years ago.

I got up from the cot, mixed myself number five for the morning, and went out to do my Christian duty for the dogs – those poor dumb brutes. I owed that much to them; they were my only friends. Besides, they'd start stinking like hell within the hour if I didn't get rid of them.

I buried them beneath the flame trees at the far-edge of

the *vlei*; one dog on each side of Kathleen. Guards, you might say. Mastiffs to protect her from the hounds of hell.

I pounded the last of the earth down on the graves, rolled some rocks over the top, and sprinkled arsenic all around to keep the baboons away. The exercise – the first in weeks – left me winded, but had helped clear my head a bit; I began thinking in earnest.

Odd, you know, how the dogs had died. Just like that! No one in miles. Damned mysterious, if you ask me.

I wiped the perspiration from my face and neck, and started walking back through the brown long grass towards the house. I was halfway there when I abruptly began thinking about the roosters and the hens. Something wrong . . . odd.

Then I remembered. Of course, there had been something. A noise, I think. Last night or early this morning. I had been awakened by their sounds. They had all been squawking as though they were fighting over kernels of corn, and then . . . a note of panic . . . yes, frantic it was, in the darkness . . . and, suddenly, silence.

I hadn't worried particularly at that time; the dogs were capable of handling anything up to and including a lion or the smartest baboon. I hadn't even bothered to get up and investigate. Should have, I suppose, but the nightcaps had made me lethargic and uncaring.

I stood there in the dried grass for a moment, trying to decide whether to check on the chickens or go back to the house for a drink first. 'Well,' I muttered, 'do it now and get the blasted feeding chores done with at the same time. That way we won't have to come outside again today.'

I turned and marched towards their coop. No rooster strutted, no hen clucked or scratched the ground. You know, I'm slipping – truly slipping – I really should have noticed all this earlier this morning.

I opened the wire mesh door of their pen and went in. Only silence greeted me.

I peered into the dimness of their coop. Then I crouched down, went inside, and stood upright again, looking down at the poor bastards. Dead. All dead. Just as though they had been gassed. Unnerving. And another oddity! Ordinarily a dead thing in this area of the world is covered with black flies and white ants within seconds of death – some subtle jungle telegraph communicates the news, I suppose. But not here. Not now. The only thing moving in the coop was the rapid rise and fall of my chest . . . and one tiny white fluff of feather that waved to and fro on the tip of my boot.

Quickly, I scrambled outside. The sun, like a hammer between my eyes, caused an immediate headache. That was unimportant, though, for I had been struck by something else – the absence of all sound! That sinister, unreal silence was even more startling than a thunderclap! No cicadas. No birds. Quiet. So quiet. Unearthly quiet.

I have lived in this green and red hell long enough to know danger. Danger has a smell all of its own. Unique. Acrid, and also arid. There was that odour now. A smell plus the instinctive feeling that I was under observation. I could feel eyes – a tingling sensation in my skull – as though someone or something were trying to ascertain my course of action.

My scruff was crawling. The adrenalin surged and roared through my veins. Fright. I recognized it. Fright! My God, I was actually scared!

And the reason lay one hundred fifty metres away. I could see it. A burned area . . . the erythrinas with their blossoms the colour of blood were gone, snapped off at the ground. In the middle of that scorched area . . . heat waves – at least they looked almost as if they were heat waves – shimmered and quivered like a huge mould of plain gelatine.

I forced myself to move; believe me, it took courage to begin walking. There was something monstrous out there beyond that curtain of heat – something alien to me and my senses. Only one thing was certain: I was the hunted – it the hunter.

Expecting the attack to come at any second, I began making my way slowly back towards the house. I was unarmed; frankly, I didn't expect to make it. I willed myself not to look behind me. My heart was lunging around like some poor tethered sacrificial goat as the lion approaches. I made a detour around two white and grey doves lying in the path. They were dead.

You should know that I have attempted suicide twice in the past. Half-heartedly, I suppose, or I wouldn't have botched the job. During the last five years I really haven't cared if I lived ... or not. But now ... I feared death! It was all I could do to keep from sprinting the last fifty metres, but I was able to maintain my outward composure and dignity.

I climbed the four stairs to the porch. I opened the screen door. I went inside. I closed the door behind me ... and, breathing hoarsely, collapsed against the wall. My knees were quaking. A drink, I thought frantically, I need a drink. And my voice, like the croak of a dying raven, came, 'No ... not now. No alcohol. Don't dull the adrenalin reflexes. Keep the edge on. You'll need it.'

The gun I wanted was on top of the mantle; it hung just above the discoloured and fading old wedding photograph of Kathleen and me.

I took the gun down and broke it open.

The shells were in the pocket of my bush jacket.

Insert one shell – hands trembling, and not from alcohol this time – into the smooth tube ... another shell into the adjoining chamber. Click ... the barrels are locked in place. Click ... click ... the heavy firing pins pulled back and cocked.

For just a moment, I stared with unseeing eyes at the weapon in my hand, and then took a deep breath and stepped outside. I stood in the noonday shadows of the porch and looked towards the burned area. I waited. Silence. No wind. The world was holding its breath – waiting with me.

Suddenly the feeling of fright left me ... along with that cold and hostile presence that earlier I had imagined to be in my mind.

There was a slight puff of wind, and the tufted papyrus fluttered like soft white feathers on a baby chick. Down by the scorched area, the heat waves swirled in a little cyclonic movement ... and solidified.

Out there, the shimmering curtain parted – and something emerged.

I lowered my gun and blinked when I saw what was coming towards me.

Kathleen? I must be going insane. Kathleen?

Her négligée was half open – revealing that golden body, its ripe full moon breasts, its ivory belly, its pungent spice valleys.

She came across the *vlei*. Smiling at me, that's what she was. Smiling – with love and desire. That sensual smile I knew so well. Kathleen!

'Kathleen?' It was croak, a lament – an unbelieving whisper of hope. A miracle? God, could it really be? 'Kathleen?'

She stopped. Her eyes were locked with mine. And casually, but with great feeling, she dropped the négligée and stood naked before me. A goddess. My goddess!

She reached up; I saw the familiar blonde nest beneath her armpit . . . and she removed the ribbon which held captive her long golden hair.

Oh, dear God, she is so lovely . . . and I have been so lonely without her.

She ran slender fingers down across her breasts and belly. And she moaned. It was her moan. She was alive! I had been mistaken all these years. She lived. She lived!

'Kathleen . . .' My earlier disbelief had vanished – replaced by a desire which was sweeping like a raging *veld* fire through my groin. I took a faltering step towards her.

Now, slowly, she walked towards me. Ten metres away she held out her arms and spoke for the first time . . . and it was her voice! Truly, it was her voice!

'Oh, Charles,' she said. 'I want you so.'

I raised my gun and fired. First one barrel, then the other, roared out in an orgasm of fire and lead and death. If there had been a third and fourth barrel, I would have used those on her too!

Before me, Kathleen dissolved in a shimmering swirl of silver flame that writhed and convulsed as though in silent pain. Soon, all motion stopped; and the silver fire dimmed, turned grey, and fell like unchaste snow to the red African earth.

I stared at the thing on the ground.

It is the only name to describe it. A being. An alien thing. Repulsive. Blue-green. Fly-like wings with great green veins from which oozed thick pus-like blood. Antennae. Many eyes. And dead. Very dead. An extremely dead and loathsome thing a long way from its home.

An intelligent thing, though. It must have read my mind, just as it had the minds of the dogs and the chickens . . . and it knew about the things we loved most – feared least. The dogs and the chickens loved food. Me? . . . Kathleen, of course.

And it had materialized these things for us in order to get close enough to kill us. It had reproduced my love for me – just as I remembered her best. That night five years ago when she had come across the room, removing her négligée as she walked. Her green eyes ablaze like jade beneath an African moon. Her alabaster body taut with lust. Her nipples erect. And moaning her desire.

She had said that night, 'Oh Charles. I want you so.'

And, I had stuck my shotgun inside through the window and shot both her . . . and Charles, the rotten black sod!

THE BABY MACHINE

Rene Morris

IT WAS a beautiful machine – everyone said it was, and there was never any doubt as to its capabilities, for was it not the most advanced machine of its kind – and the most expensive? But then, Malinda had always expected the best, and married as she was to an electronics engineer, and a leading figure in his field, there had never been any doubt that she would own one when the baby came along.

Now, as she moved, smiling, among her guests she felt completely at ease; she felt free, so free that her heart sang inside and her conversation positively sparkled. Once again she was the centre of attraction, and as she sipped her wine she knew that all eyes were upon her, and her happiness was complete.

Malinda loved her baby almost as much as herself, but her maternal instinct was mainly one of pride, and she cared very little to be inconvenienced by the more wearisome side of motherhood. But the machine had relieved her of all that was distasteful to her, and now she was free again to enjoy herself.

'Malinda darling,' Ann said urgently, 'I've just come past the nursery and little Paul is crying. Do you think we should go up? He sounded most upset.'

'No darling,' Malinda said confidently. 'The machine is there and we would only be in the way.'

'But please,' Ann said wistfully, 'couldn't we just take a teeny weeny peek, just to see that everything's all right?'

Malinda sighed. 'Oh very well, but really there's no need. Little Paul is quite all right, you know.'

Ann led the way to where the white staircase spilled into the blue and gold hall, and together they climbed the richly carpeted stairs and along the white balcony above, adorned so beautifully with its delicately carved corbels. There was no sound as Malinda quietly opened the nursery door, only the tinkle of Malinda's bracelet as it slid down her soft, white arm and barely touched the door handle.

'Can we go in?' Ann whispered, 'just for a moment.'

Malinda sighed again, and nodded. They tiptoed over to the cot, so pretty with its white lace folds falling to the floor, and the little blue ribbons that caught it up around the hem. Ann leaned carefully over the sleeping child, pulling back the coverlet gently that she might see him better.

'Isn't he a little darling? See how he lies with one little hand beneath his head. Oh Malinda,' she breathed pitifully, 'how could you ever trust him to a machine?'

'It isn't just *any* machine you know,' Malinda said indignantly. 'It's capable of the most sensitive movements. Peter helped in the making of it. It even has a danger system to stop anyone from taking the child from the room. I only turn it on when we go out for the evening. It really is the last word in baby care. Look, I'll show you just how clever it is.'

Malinda pulled back the covers until the child's other hand could be seen, then stepped back motioning Ann to do the same. In the corner behind them, the pale green eye came suddenly to life. The machine moved silently towards them across the carpet, its thick rubbery arms outstretched and the round, glassy head bent towards the cot. It stopped, its pincer-like hand smoothing back the covers and neatly turning in the edges where the child had started to chew them. The child stirred, his little hand pushing upward then falling limply back on the pillow. The green eye flickered, and the rubber arm took the tiny hand and gently pulled it down snugly beneath the covers, turning in the edges as before. Then, seeing that all was well, backed away into the corner from whence it had so noiselessly come.

'It's wonderful,' Ann breathed. 'I've never seen anything like it.'

'Well, I *did* tell you, darling, didn't I? I must admit though, at first I was a tiny bit afraid that Martha – that's what we call it – might drop him or something, but I soon found that there was no need for anxiety. There isn't a thing that Martha can't do. Peter's tried all kinds of tests on her, and he adds to her knowledge all the time.'

'You are a lucky one, Malinda,' Ann sighed. 'You have a lovely home, a wonderful husband, and the sweetest baby I've ever seen. Why do you treat him so?'

'Peter's happy enough. He *is* older than I am, darling. He doesn't like parties and things, and I do. He doesn't mind my going out and about. I like to enjoy life, and he likes to see me happy.'

'Do you still see Clive, or did you give him up as you said you would?' Ann asked quietly.

'Of course I didn't give him up, darling. Whatever made you think that I could? After all, he loves me. It wouldn't be very kind to him would it? I'm not a robot you know – not like that monster over there. *Really*, Ann. I'm a good wife to Peter – good for his business. I entertain for him, don't I? I run his home perfectly. What more can I do?'

'I'm sorry, Malinda,' Ann sighed. 'I shouldn't have asked you. It's just that I thought that things were different now that you had the baby to think about. A woman settles down when there's a baby.'

'I also have Martha,' Malinda retorted coldly.

'We had one of the earlier models. Do you remember it, Malinda?' Ann said soothingly. 'It wasn't much of a baby nurse at all, was it? It sounded alarms mostly, but it couldn't cope by itself. In a way, I was glad. I *liked* doing everything for Wendy . . . she was so small, and forever wet, or hungry . . .'

'We'd better go down, darling. People will wonder where on earth we've got to, and I hate missing coffee.'

Martha's green eye flickered into life as the door closed upon them. Down below she could hear the sound of laughter, and then the child turning in the white lace cot. He was dreaming of his mother, and Martha's fine tuner beam picked up the dream and stored it away with so many other dreams and thoughts that had needed her attention. She moved silently towards the cot, the long arms reaching for the child, as gently she gathered him close to her soft rubber breast, rocking him deeper and deeper into a dreamless sleep.

Malinda stretched luxuriously in the ivory satin bed, then listened for the usual plaintive wail from the nursery. Little Paul started to cry, then stopped. Malinda smiled, then turned over happily knowing that Martha had everything under control. It really was a blessing, that wonderful machine. Reaching under her pillow, she drew out the letter and opened it. It was from Clive, and it asked that she should meet him tonight at The Blue Grill. Malinda heard Peter's heavy step outside the door, and she quickly pushed the letter back under the pillow out of sight. He looked tired as he entered, and she guessed that he had worked well into the night, for he seemed distant to her lately as if his mind was deeply solving some new mystery.

'Darling,' he said without his usual smile, 'see to my tie for me, will you? I've tried, but I seem to be all fingers and thumbs today.'

'Is that all you've woken me for?' Malinda pouted.

'Now who else could tie it for me the way you do?'

'There's Martha,' Malinda said in a tired voice.

'But Martha's busy with the baby at this time in the morning. And I didn't buy her to do jobs for me. It was for the baby's sake that I let you have her.'

'So you don't think I'm capable of looking after my own child then?' Malinda said hotly. 'I didn't think you felt like that about it. If you like, you can get rid of the blasted thing and I'll cope by myself.'

'Well, I didn't mean it like that, Malinda, but while we are on the subject, don't you think you should spend more time with Paul? I don't mind you enjoying yourself, but the child hardly knows you. You don't see him from one day to the next.'

'Don't be so ridiculous. He's my child, of course he knows me. Every child knows his own mother.'

Peter lifted his hand. 'All I am saying is that he should be given more opportunity to know you better. He knows Martha better than he knows you, and you must agree that this isn't right. I tell you what we'll do darling. We'll both spend

T—C

an hour or so with him every night. I've been worried about the boy, he doesn't seem to want to learn to talk. You do want him to develop properly don't you?'

'Yes, of course I do.'

'Then I'll see you both tonight?'

'I can't, Peter. Not tonight.'

'Why not?'

'I'm sorry, darling, but I have to go out.'

'Well, you can damn well put it off. I don't ask much of you, God knows. Who is it this time?'

'I'm going over to Ann's. I can't let her down.'

'No, but you'd damn well let *me* down wouldn't you? There's the telephone. Ring her. Tell her your husband has booked an appointment with you. It looks like it's come to that. Anyone except me.'

'What do you mean, Peter, anyone except you?'

He went quickly over to the dressing table and tore open the top middle drawer. When he turned to face her he held up a small spool of tape. The kind that she had seen him feed into the baby machine.

'You didn't think I knew, did you, Malinda? And I wouldn't have found out if I hadn't listened to this tape.'

'What tape?'

'The one I fed into Martha to see if our son has learned to say anything. And he hasn't, has he? But my God, Malinda, you had plenty to say, didn't you? Yes, it's all on here, your conversation with Ann. I am disgusted with you – and tired of being laughed at. You'll phone him now and tell him it's all off – or you will leave my house.'

Malinda could not speak. So deep was her fury that there were no words. She reached for her cigarettes while Peter stood beside her, his face pale but determined.

'The phone, Malinda.'

'I will not be treated like a child. Be rational, Peter.'

'Rational? *You* ask me to be rational? Haven't I given you everything? You will phone now, or be out of this house before I come home this evening. That's all I have to say to you.'

'All right,' Malinda screamed. 'I'll go. See how you get on without me to play hostess for you. I'll be glad to go.'

Peter walked slowly to the door, half hoping that there was still something he could say to her to make her stay; but his temper had robbed him of words, and his world had suddenly crashed about him, and there was nothing ... nothing except the baby. He stood in the doorway, he looked beaten and Malinda waited for him to beg her to stay.

'You will not take my son with you. This is his home and he will stay here with me.'

'Paul goes where I go,' Malinda shouted. 'I am his mother. He cannot be without his mother, he needs me.'

'Paul has Martha. He doesn't need you. He stays. I have seen to it that he stays. I do not advise you to try to take him from this house. Will you telephone Clive and put an end to all this? A man can only take so much.'

Malinda reached for her shoe and flung it at the door. It cracked against the panelling and fell to the floor. The door closed quietly behind Peter, and then she heard his measured step along the hallway, and then, downstairs, the click of the front door.

She reached for the telephone and dialled frantically, her hands trembling with fury.

'Hello, darling. Is that you, Clive? Oh darling, he's found out ... yes ... that's right ... it was that blasted machine ... yes ... he taped a conversation between Ann and I ... No, darling, I know he wouldn't do a thing like that on purpose. It was to hear the baby ... yes, darling, the baby. Will you come over for me? ... Thank you, darling ... yes ... in fifteen minutes ... yes, I love you too ...'

Malinda dressed quickly, throwing a few clothes into a suitcase she ran down the stairs still trembling. She pulled on her coat, then hurriedly pulled it off again, and running back up the stairs she flung open the door to her closet and took out the expensive fur that Peter had bought her 'for being a good girl' and pulled it on. In the corner stood the baby's night bag. She snatched it up and ran to the nursery. Flinging open the door she rushed inside and quickly gathered up the baby's clothes and his immediate requirements and flung them into the bag. Martha stood in the corner, and as the baby started to cry her pale green eyes flickered into life. Malinda ran past her and down the stairs, putting the night bag along with the other. Martha heard the hurrying footsteps, and was aware that something was wrong ... felt that the child was in some kind of danger. She heard the footsteps hurrying back up the stairs and moved halfway across the room towards the child, her arms outstretched protectively. The child stood wide-eyed in its cot, then started to cry again as Malinda ran back into the room.

Malinda stopped. Peter's words came back to her ... 'I do not advise you to try to take him away' ... She stood still for a moment. There was a small button at the base of Martha's neck ... it would, once pressed, immobilize her completely. Martha stood quite still, trying to analyse the strange pattern of signals that whirled round and round inside her brain. She felt confused, uncertain as to what action she would be called upon to make. Malinda smiled at the machine, then walked casually over to the child. Quickly, she picked him up in her arms and carried him over to Martha, and placing him in the soft, rubbery arms she waited for Martha to take the child back to his cot, or set him down on the floor. If she would just bend over ... she could just reach the button at the back of Martha's neck ...

Martha held the child, her head turning this way and that, until she finally decided to return the child to its cot. She pulled back the covers and set the child down ... Malinda reached for the button and pressed it hard. Martha straightened up, and in a flash Malinda had the child in her arms and was running to the door. Something grasped her shoulder with a grip of iron. She let go the child and it fell with a scream on to the soft carpet. Malinda fought desperately to free herself, but the vice-like grip drew her slowly back into the room, nearer and nearer to Martha's soft rubber breast. She couldn't breath ... she was suffocating ... there was no air ... She tried to scream, but the soft rubber filled her nose and mouth ... everything was black ... black as death as the rubber closed about her ...

Something inside Martha clicked, and slowly she released the tension and the rag-like thing she was holding fell to the floor . . . Martha's eye saw the child tumbling towards her, his little arms reaching up for her. Lovingly, and with great gentleness, Martha bent down and gathered him close.

'MMM. . . Mmm . . . Mmomma . . . Mmm . . . Momma . . .'
Martha heard the small utterance . . . and felt strangely moved.

THE BEST TEACHER

Colin Graham

'MORE WINE, sir?'

'Thank you.'

An anonymous, white-coated arm reached from behind him and gently refilled his glass. Then it withdrew and passed on the wine to the next man. Reaching slowly for the replenished glass, Gareth Gwynne wondered if he was still being watched. He took a measured sip and looked carefully down his nose at the man whose presence had irked him all evening. But the other was chatting amiably to a fleshy woman sitting at his side who was drawing heavily on a cigarette.

Gareth Gwynne, celebrated writer of countless horror stories, was the guest of honour at the annual dinner of a writer's circle taking place in a large town in the south of England. He sat at the top table with the circle's minor celebrities while before him stretched two long tables at which sat the members.

The man who had caught his attention was seated halfway down the table on his right. Every time that Gareth Gwynne had looked up during the meal he had found the other's eyes upon him. In normal circumstances, this would not have bothered him for wasn't everybody looking from time to time at the guest of honour? But there was something distinctly odd about this particular gentleman.

He was in his sixties, well built with thick black hair and equally black eyes that held an expression Gareth would have interpreted in one of his tales as malicious jealousy. Or was it? Perhaps he was being over dramatic.

'Ladies and gentlemen,' called the chairman – they were not in a financially attractive position to afford a toastmaster – 'Ladies and gentlemen,' he repeated in a stronger voice, 'we are exceptionally privileged tonight to have with us a man you all know from his work in books, magazines and newspapers. He has graciously come along to tell us all about his work and . . .' etc., etc.

Gareth Gwynne attempted to hold back the smile of conceit and pride that was trying to force itself on to his face, but he failed. When the introduction was finally over, he rose to his feet and proceeded to put his audience in the right mood by recounting a couple of jokes copied from a woman's magazine. Then he turned to the more serious business of writing.

'As you all know,' he said, 'I have been writing horror stories for many years, more than I care to recall, in fact.' Polite laughs. 'This type of writing has its advantages but it also has its drawbacks. There is always a ready market for this kind of tale and, of course, you are quite entitled to think of its devotees as cranks and morons but I should like to assure you that people from all sections of the reading public and from all walks of life buy and avidly devour any books, whether fact or fiction, on man's inhumanity to man.'

Here, Gareth went a little farther into the subject before returning to the drawbacks.

'There is really only one of these,' he said. 'As writers, you will doubtless appreciate that the best way, in fact, the only way, to achieve reality and life is to place yourself in the position of your character. You must see what he sees, you must place yourself in the same situations and try to visualize how you would cope with them. In short, you must be your own character and write from experience. You will then write with conviction.'

Gareth paused for a drink to wet his dry throat and to collect his thoughts. It seemed to be going down well and with a little more self-assurance he glanced casually across at the man who had been watching him so closely. Naturally, he was still watching, but so were the others. He was surprised, however, to see that the look in the other's eyes had now become one of acute concentration. It was as though he were drinking in every word the speaker uttered. The eyes were cold and, apart from the attentiveness, they were now expressionless.

Clearing his throat, Gareth Gwynne continued.

'Now I come to the drawback. This is not so obvious to those who have never written horror fiction but it is, quite simply, experience. Perhaps I should say, it is the lack of experience.

'We can all write about things that have happened to us but how do we tackle something we have never known and may be beyond our conception?

'How do we place ourselves in the position of a demon incarnate and see life through his eyes? Or, to take extreme examples, in that of a man undergoing torture by having his eyes put out' – he thought of the black eyes on him at that moment – 'or someone being slowly racked or having a limb cut off?'

He looked round with pride at his enraptured audience, carefully avoiding the black eyes.

'That is the most difficult part of this type of writing and I'm sorry to have to admit that I have no ready answer to that question. We have all suffered physical pain, usually only of a minor kind, although we thought the world was coming to an end at the time.

'This is where imagination comes into play. We must take this pain, whether it be toothache, earache or a broken limb, and magnify it as much as possible. We can study actual accounts by people unfortunate enough to have suffered in terrible ways but it still boils down to the one thing – imagination. We have no mental guidebooks to help us and must do the best we can.'

Gareth Gwynne continued for a few more minutes before finally resuming his seat amid much applause. He smiled gratefully and not without a little conceit.

It had certainly gone down well. And to think he had nearly refused their invitation as being beneath his dignity. Ah, well.

Shortly afterwards, the proceedings ended and, to his chagrin, Gareth Gwynne found himself being introduced to the owner of the black eyes. It transpired that the man's name was Sadelim and he was particularly interested in horror fiction.

They chatted for several minutes while Gareth was itching to get away as quickly as possible. He had always felt a particular revulsion for those with deformities and the empty sleeve of Sadelim's dinner jacket hung idly by his side. Gareth thought it odd that he had not previously noticed that the man had only one arm. He was glad he had not seen it before and even more glad when the chairman came across and joined in the conversation.

With rescue at hand, Gareth glanced casually at his watch then made a great play of only just noticing how late it was and said that he had to get to the station if he was to catch the last train back to London. That was his biggest mistake for Sadelim immediately volunteered his services and his car and no amount of refusal could shake him off. With the pressing of the chairman, whom he had taken for an ally, he was finally persuaded to accept the offer.

Five minutes later, he was speeding through the darkened town in a Mercedes specially altered for its owner's requirements.

Sadelim talked about horror stories and admitted he had written a number himself which had never been published. He wondered if Mr Gwynne would be kind enough to read them and add his comments. Gareth was almost afraid of his companion and having no wish to offend him, particularly when he noted the skill with which the car was handled, he accepted.

A note, almost of grim glee, entered Sadelim's voice as he thanked his passenger, slowed the car, changed gear and turned off to the left.

'Where are we going?' inquired Gareth anxiously, sensing rather than realizing that they were no longer heading for the station.

'I just thought you might like to take them with you,' came the reassuring reply. 'They're at home and not only will it save me parcelling them up it will also give you something to read on the journey.' The master-pupil relationship was slowly being reversed and it was with great hesitation that Gareth replied that he hoped they would not be too long.

'The train goes at 11.33,' he said, 'and I'm stranded if I miss that.'

'Nonsense,' replied Sadelim, 'you must have looked at the

weekday timetable. The last train on Saturday leaves at 12.03. That gives you an extra half hour.'

Although Gareth was certain he had not made a mistake, Sadelim's assurance set him wondering. Perhaps he was wrong after all.

Soon, the lights of the town were behind them and apart from the road immediately ahead, darkness was all around. Along winding country roads they sped with the hedgerows bathed in the ghostly glow of the headlamps and occasionally, Gareth glimpsed the black expanse of fields behind them.

Two luminous eyes were suddenly picked out on the road in front as a rabbit froze at the appearance of this huge monster bearing down upon it. The creature was hypnotized. When Gareth thought about it afterwards, he was certain that Sadelim had not accelerated, but the car surged forward with the eyes growing nearer, nearer, nearer – then bump! It had passed beneath the machine and those who used the road next morning would see a bloody, furry mess squashed against the surface.

Shortly afterwards, the car turned off the road and up a narrow driveway. Sadelim slowed down and Gareth could hear pebbles scrunching under the wheels. They finally came to a halt. Although the headlamps remained on when they stepped out into the cold night air, Gareth could not estimate either size or style of the house. It was large, that much he could see, but not a single light shone anywhere. He guessed it was the only building for miles around.

They passed in darkness through the hall and into a room at the front. As soon as the light went on, Gareth was struck by the small effect it had.

The room was furnished with the darkest and drabbest of fittings and the ceiling was painted with a black emulsion. The single bulb burning beneath the brown shade could not have been more than forty watts and, consequently, the farthest corners of the room remained unilluminated.

Sadelim busied himself with drinks at the cocktail cabinet while Gareth stood looking curiously around. He wondered if he was dreaming for here, recreated before his eyes, was the setting of the last story he had written. It was as though he had stepped into the pages of his own book and the fear he was experiencing was quite unlike anything he had ever known before. He bitterly regretted not having met Sadelim before but comforted himself with the knowledge that he could turn this 'experienced fear' to good advantage in his next story.

Sadelim handed him a glass of whisky.

'Different, isn't it?' he said. Gareth started. Surely they were not thinking the same thoughts. No, he must be referring to the whisky, decided Gareth, and took a sip. It burned his mouth.

'Yes, it is,' he replied truthfully.

The other smiled slightly. 'I didn't mean the drink,' he said. 'The fear,' he added, 'it's not the same as you had imagined it would be, is it?'

Before Gareth could reply, Sadelim hurried on, apparently oblivious of the other's uneasiness.

'I won't keep you a moment. I'll just go and fetch those stories I was telling you about.'

He left the room and Gareth took another sip. The whisky tasted good and he certainly needed it. His nerves felt as though they were strained to breaking point and, for all the experience in the world, he wished he had never accepted Sadelim's offer of a lift. Still, I'll soon be on my way now, he thought.

His legs suddenly lost their power and a feeling of exquisite fatigue overcame him. Everything before his eyes blurred and his head was swimming as he staggered for the nearest chair. White lights popped inside his head and the hand holding the glass relaxed. In his dim consciousness, he heard it strike the floor and break, but it seemed miles away. Then he fell.

'Damn!' he swore. 'Where's that . . .' But his mouth fogged and his tongue became as limp as his body.

Gareth Gwynne was smashed out of his subconscious state by a sharp blow across the face. At first, he did not open his eyes and was content to drift in the light-headed condition that often comes before full awareness is reached.

Cold air blew across his body and he attempted to curl into a tight, warm ball but however hard he tried his brain could not force his arms and legs to move. He shivered, then finally gave up trying to shift his position. He would go back to sleep. Yes, that's what he'd do.

'Open your eyes, Mr Gwynne.' A cold, hard voice interrupted his dreams. The first thing he saw when he obeyed the command was the pair of black eyes. Surely not, he thought. I must hurry or I'll miss that train. Then he remembered his collapse and began to think clearly for the first time.

'I fell . . . I think,' he said slowly.

'That's right. Your drink was drugged.'

The black eyes never left him for a second. Gareth did not fully accept what had been said at first and attempted to rise, hoping his brain had cleared. But nothing happened. Then he lifted his head and looked down at his body. No wonder he couldn't move: he was bound with thick leather straps to a long metal table whose polished surface reflected light from the bulb above his head. Sadelim towered over him.

'What's going on?' he muttered thickly, trying to tear his gaze from the eyes of his captor.

'You are my prisoner,' said the noncommittal reply.

'Why? I've got a train to catch,' he said, not fully realizing the import of the other's remark.

'You won't be catching any more trains, Mr Gwynne.

'I've waited for this moment a long time and I'm not going to let it slip through my fingers.'

Although he still had no idea what Sadelim wanted, the horror and extreme danger of the situation finally got through to the bound man.

'Look, what the hell are you up to?' he asked, trying to appear less concerned than he really was.

'I'll tell you, Mr Gwynne,' Sadelim replied softly.

'I've been reading books for many years, particularly pornography and the type of fiction you write. I regard these books as undesirable and have nothing but loathing for the type of person who can conceive such rubbish. You, in particular, of all these authors produce work calculated to undermine public morality and create sadistic ideas in the minds of weak-willed individuals who would not otherwise have them.

'I have seen with these very eyes' – at this, they blazed even more furiously – 'what your books can do to people. It is disgusting, even more so when one considers that you do it for one reason only – money. You are a canker on humanity and, as no one else will remove you, then I must do it myself.'

'You're mad!' hissed Gareth Gwynne, trying to stem the tears of anger, humiliation and fear.

'Quite possibly, Mr Gwynne. That we shall see. But in the meantime I intend to put an end to the cause of such suffering and when you learn how, I am sure you will not be quite so angry.

'I fully realize that I cannot remove all the rubbish that is on the market, or its evil perpetrators, but even one will satisfy me, temporarily. That is why I have chosen you, the worst, to take part in a little venture I have planned.'

The eyes sparkled merrily. Gareth Gwynne said nothing. It was now apparent to him that no amount of argument could sway this madman. A trap had been laid for him and his vanity in accepting the invitation to speak had been his downfall. Sadelim had obviously prepared for this meeting for some time and all he could hope for was that it would all happen quickly, whatever it was.

'Before tonight,' continued Sadelim softly, 'I had merely planned to ... er ... shall we say, remove you? But your talk gave me another idea. You mentioned experience, or the lack of it. Well, now I am going to show you what it is like to undergo the pleasures you have devised for your characters.'

Gareth saw a way out. 'I shall never be able to use them, though, if you kill me. How would I ever write about it?'

'Let me finish Mr Gwynne. No, you will not be able to write about it. But you also mentioned a mental guidebook. Between us, we are going to go even better than providing a mental guide; we are going to produce an actual guidebook for horror writers. Then, if they are to write this kind of rubbish, they will at least be able to write correctly.'

A triumphant look appeared in the eyes, then Sadelim

moved out of Gareth's vision and a few seconds later he twisted his head round to see his captor putting a microphone on a stand within a few inches of his head.

'What's that for?'

'Wait and see.'

Sadelim made other arrangements that Gareth could not see and stripped his prisoner bare to the waist, not without some difficulty. He went to get something and when he re-appeared stood beside Gareth. But Gareth did not look at him. He was looking at the hacksaw in Sadelim's one hand.

'I'm going to saw off your arm,' said Sadelim casually. 'The tape recorder is on and all you have to do is say what it feels like. You can start now if you like. The build-up, the suspense, is all part of the story, isn't it? As we go along, I shall give my own commentary on what is happening. Scream as much as you like and talk as much as you like. But I do ask one thing – try and be coherent. I don't want it all wasted.'

'You callous madman!' shouted Gareth. 'You're not really going through with it, are you?' Events had become so ludi-crous that he began to wonder if Sadelim was joking.

'Of course I am,' came the hurt reply.

With that, he rested the blade on Gareth's left arm, near the top.

'Describe it,' said Sadelim.

'It's . . . it's cold . . . and . . . and the points are biting into my flesh. Aaaaaaahhhhh!!' The scream was wrung from his lips. Sadelim began his commentary.

'The blade is having a little difficulty cutting through the flesh of the arm. I shall have to draw it faster. Blood is pouring out, from a severed vein, I suppose. Tiny pieces of white flesh are sticking to the blade which is already covered with blood. I am now about to make the second stroke.'

'Aaaaaaaaahhhhh!!! Stop it! Stop it! Please! I'll give you anything! I promise you everything! Aaaaaaaahhhhh! It's hurting! Please! You're killing me!'

'The subject's face is terribly contorted. Tears are stream-ing from his eyes and his mouth is wide open. I can see right down his throat. He's writhing and struggling with the force of ten men. The blade went a little easier that time. Already, I can feel it cutting into the bone as the handle jarred when it first struck it. There's blood everywhere, much more than I had expected. The subject's face is white. I shall now make the third stroke.'

'Aaaaaaaaaaaahhhhhhhh!!!!'

'You will note that this time the pitch of the subject's scream has risen. He appears to be nearing breaking point. When I have sawn this arm off I shall wait till he recovers consciousness before proceeding further. I had to put more force into the last stroke to get into the bone. I shall no longer list the individual strokes of the blade.

'There. That's the fourth. Now the fifth. It's rather like sawing wood except that it makes a crunching noise which I hope can be heard above the screams. Now the arm is just hanging. One more hack. There. It's off and lying on the floor and looking quite white as all the blood has drained from it. As I expected, the subject has fainted.'

It was the pain that caused Gareth Gwynne to faint and it was the pain that brought him round, nagging and tearing at his mind.

'I shall now put out one of his eyes.' Sadelim took a poker which had been slowly heating and lowered it slowly into the screaming skull. Hissing and bubbling sounds were all that were recorded.

Throughout the night, Sadelim worked. He cut off Gareth's other arm, waited till he was conscious again, then started on a leg. Soon, two arms and two legs lay in a haphazard pile where they had been thrown. The bleeding torso became even bloodier as Sadelim worked on. The floor and everything within spitting distance was covered with blood and a couple of times he nearly slipped in it.

He continued with his commentary and was constantly having to stop and change the tape. Bloody fingerprints were left on the thin strips of celluloid, the plastic discs and the machine.

Occasionally, and without intending to, Gareth screamed a description of his pain and, when the screams grew weaker, Sadelim moved the microphone still closer.

Four o'clock struck as he cut out the second eye with a specially sharpened kitchen knife. He then slit open the stomach to examine the contents.

The next time Gareth Gwynne fainted, Sadelim cut around till he found the heart and felt it. He could see a gentle pulsation as he peered into the chest and this communicated itself to his hand.

As dawn broke through the windows, Sadelim decided to finish the job completely. With one stroke, he cut Gareth's throat and held the microphone close as the remaining blood gushed out.

When Gareth was finally dead, Sadelim slowly sawed off the head, described it and concluded his commentary. He then changed the tape and attempted to list the feelings and thoughts he had had during the evening but which he had previously omitted.

Then he tidied up.

FOOTNOTE: The tapes were transcribed, printed and privately circulated to writers of horror fiction by Sadelim. Although a number of authors who took their subject seriously and thought it a practical joke threw the book into the wastepaper basket, others placed it in a prominent position in their libraries where it has now become a standard work of reference.

Some of them may even have used it for tales included in this book. . . .

STICK WITH ME, KID, AND YOU'LL WEAR DIAMONDS

Walter Winward

HE STOOD well inside the doorway, in the shadows, hatless, his shabby fawn raincoat buttoned up to the neck. It was raining. November rain: cold, cheerless, heavy with dirt. The time was almost midnight and, apart from the distant miaowing of a lonely tomcat and the occasional swish-swashing of motor-car tyres on tarmac, the street was quiet. He had known it would be. That was why he had waited.

Across the street a solitary light burned in a shop window, and once in a while a man's silhouette was seen. A busy, fussy silhouette: now bending over what appeared to be a ledger, now scrutinizing something carefully. Above the window a name was painted in faded gold letters. It was impossible to read the name from where he stood, but the man in the shadows knew it said *S. Hyman, Jeweller and Silversmith*. He had worked for Hyman for close on thirty years.

In some ways they had been thirty good years, he thought, putting a match to a cigarette and concealing the glowing end between his cupped hands. He had always been paid regularly, if not very generously, and his two weeks' annual holiday had never been refused, even though Hyman had often grumbled that in his young day an employee who was absent did not get paid. In many other ways, however, they had been thirty disappointing and trying years.

He remembered the youthful promise, boast, he had made to his wife the day they were married, just a week after he joined the one-man firm of S. Hyman. 'Hyman says there might be a partnership in it for me before long, but I won't wait around for that. As soon as I've got enough saved, I'm going to open a place of my own. Then we'll really make some money.

Stick with me, kid, and you'll wear diamonds. Promise.'

And he had meant it, every word, but somehow it had all turned sour. There had been no partnership and household bills had simply eaten his wages. At the end of ten years he had saved nothing. It was then that his wife really started to complain.

'Why do you have to be a jeweller's assistant? Why not get a decent, well-paid job? You could earn twice as much in almost any other business I can think of.'

'But I like my job. It's the only thing I know.'

'Learn something else.'

'I can't. And why should I? I'm a damned good jeweller. I'm a craftsman.'

And it was true. He *was* a craftsman, a damned good craftsman. There had been many occasions when a lady or a gentleman had entered the shop with a badly-chipped ring or pendant. And Hyman never failed to say: 'Leave it to us. My staff are the best in London.'

Hyman's staff. One man. One damned good craftsman who did all the work while Hyman collected and banked the profits. It was unfair. A craftsman deserved recognition.

After fifteen years of marriage the complaining graduated to fighting and bickering. He, himself, was not a violent man, but sometimes he was goaded beyond endurance.

'You promised me we'd have money,' his wife used to say. 'You promised me I could have everything I ever dreamed of. And now look at us. No children, still in the same dreary little house . . .'

'Shut up, for God's sake. It's not my fault.'

'Well, it certainly isn't mine. I didn't make all those promises, did I? I didn't make all the mistakes. I only made one mistake, and that was marrying you. I could have had my choice, but I chose you. More fool me.'

'Shut up, damn you!'

'Don't you raise your voice to me!'

Once or twice he was driven to the point of striking her, but afterwards he was always filled with remorse.

'I'm sorry, dear. I really am sorry.'

'How could you hit your own wife! How could you!'

'I didn't mean it.'

'You don't know your own strength.'

'I'm sorry. I said I was sorry. Forgive me. I love you.'

And he did love her. As she said, it wasn't her fault. He had made a promise and he had broken it. A man should keep his promises. That was part of being a man.

Once he had thought seriously of leaving Hyman, but the jeweller had offered him a ten-shilling rise, and that had been sufficient to keep him. Besides, he would be no good at any other work. Diamonds were his world. Rubies and sapphires were too, of course, but he loved diamonds particularly. He would look at them for hours, fondle them. He understood them. He knew instinctively what would match and what would not, and he could sense a stone's worth at a single glance.

Twenty years of marriage passed, and twenty-five years. He had resigned himself to his fate as a jeweller's assistant, to the long walks from home to the dingy shop, to the moans and constant groans of his employer. But his wife had grown more bitter with age. *Look at the carpet. We need a new carpet. And the curtains. My God, the curtains. And this terrible house. I'm ashamed to tell anyone I live here, do you know that? I'm actually ashamed. Promises! Good God, if only I had my life over again. I'd be wiser. I'd have married someone else....*

That, he thought, puffing furtively at his cigarette, was a dreadful thing for his wife to say. He loved her in spite of everything. Why on earth couldn't she love him on the same terms? To say that she would rather be married to someone else was awful. But she had said it, and she kept on saying it. She had said it almost every day for the last five years. She had said it, and worse, that very night.

Their thirtieth anniversary was a fortnight away, and he had planned a surprise. For the past year, in preparation, he had foregone part of his regular lunch and hoarded the money he saved. It was not much, but over the year, allowing for holidays, it amounted to almost fifteen pounds. With it he had bought an eternity ring. Mr Hyman had even allowed him a small discount.

That evening, when he arrived home from work, his wife had been in a worse mood than usual. It was the curtains again, or perhaps the carpet – he could not quite remember. But to placate her he hinted that he had a small gift for their wedding anniversary.

'What is it? Can I have it now?'

'No, not for a fortnight.'

'Oh, please, please.'

She pleaded so hard that eventually he relented. It did not really matter when she saw it. It was hers.

He took the tiny box from his pocket and gave it to her. She snatched it and opened it eagerly.

'It's an eternity ring,' he said helpfully, puzzled at her silence. 'Diamonds.'

For a second he thought she was crying, but then he saw that it was laughter. Uncontrollable laughter.

'You call these things diamonds,' she gurgled. 'You call these pitiful, tiny shavings diamonds. Oh my God, you are a fool. If only I hadn't married a fool.'

'They *are* diamonds,' he insisted.

'But the size of them! You can scarcely see them. I can't possibly wear it. I'd be the talk of the neighbourhood. My husband works for a jeweller and all he can afford for our anniversary is a cheap little ring.'

'Shut up,' he said. 'Shut up, damn you.'

But she continued to laugh.

'My God, you're so pathetic. You're so damned pathetic. You and your promises of diamonds. Stick with me, you said . . .'

'Shut up, shut up, *shut up*!'

She had been right, though, he thought, stubbing out his cigarette. They were quality stones but they were very tiny. And she knew nothing about quality. Still, he would make it up to her. He would keep his promise. Everything would be different from now on.

He checked his watch, peering squint-eyed at the luminous numerals. It was two minutes to twelve. Time to go. Hyman always locked the safe at midnight.

He crossed the street, head bent against the driving rain, and knocked on the door of the shop.

'Who's there?'

'It's me. I forgot something, Mr Hyman. Let me in.'

He heard the sound of bolts being drawn and a key turning, and the door swung open.

'Don't you know it's midnight?' growled Hyman. 'What the devil did you forget?'

'It's in the back room. I won't be a minute.'

He left Hyman muttering irritably, and went into the back-room. He fingered several potential weapons thoughtfully before settling for a heavy silver candlestick.

'Mr Hyman,' he called.

'What is it?'

'Come here a moment. There's something I think you should see.'

The old jeweller, muttering continuously beneath his breath, hobbled into the back room. The silver candlestick descended with a sickening crunch on the fragile white head. And then again and again.

'Serves you damn well right, Hyman,' said the man in the fawn raincoat, and returned to the main shop.

The safe was unlocked and bulging with uncut diamonds and polished diamonds, rubies, emeralds and sapphires; some loose, some made up into necklaces, pendants, tiaras. He selected only those items that were composed exclusively of diamonds. That was the limit of his promise.

It was a quarter of an hour before he was satisfied with his collection, which he stuffed into a paper bag. His final act on leaving the shop was to switch off the lights and snap the front door catch.

Outside he walked quickly in spite of the rain. It had taken him thirty years, but his wife could no longer complain.

He was drenched when he arrived home, and he shook his raincoat in the hall before going into the sitting-room. His wife was where he had left her, lying face up in a pool of blood and staring at him with lifeless eyes. The knife he had used to stop her laughter was beside the still warm body, and he kicked it under the sofa. Then he bent down, took her by the shoulders, and levered her into an armchair. Her head hung curiously to one side, unhinged by the dozen slashes he had taken at her throat.

Necklace first, I think, he mused, and selected one from the paper bag. Somehow the congealing blood and the diamonds went well together. Now a tiara, he thought. Oh yes, very pretty. Very pretty. And now a bracelet. Perhaps two. Yes, two. Why not.

He chuckled.

'My, you look nice,' he said aloud, when he had finished. 'My goodness, what diamonds do for a woman. Pity about the angle of the head, though. Here, I'll help you straighten it up.'

He placed his hands on either side of her head, and tilted it slightly. There was a squelching sound, like an éclair after the first bite, and he wiped his wet fingers on the hem of her dress.

Yes, very attractive, a real craftsman's touch, he thought, and went into the kitchen to make a cup of tea. It was some minutes before he realized that tonight, for the first time in years, he would only have to make one cup.

THE HAPPY RETURN

Dulcie Gray

SHE WAS sixteen when he first seduced her, and seventeen when she had her unwanted baby. A boy, whom she named Arnold, after its father. During that year her nature changed completely.

She had been a sensual but romantic little virgin, and when he seduced her, she fell for him completely. He had promised her marriage, but from the moment he heard about the baby, he faded out on her; simply didn't want to know. She threatened to tell her family. He advised her to go ahead, and nothing that she or they could do made the smallest impression on him. He just moved out of her life.

She had a hideous time having the child. She was desperately in love with Arnold still, and was nearly out of her mind with depression and shame. Also she hoped with all her heart to see him again. And there were complications in the childbirth itself.

When the baby was finally put crying, into her arms, she turned her head away with a look of disgust, and refused to take any notice of it.

The nurses at the hospital were shocked, but the psychiatrist was sent for, and a series of weekly sessions began.

The psychiatrist was unable to make much headway, and when Diane was sent home, she was also told to continue with the sessions.

She remained at home, sitting almost in silence for several weeks. A nurse sent by the health service, and her mother, saw that the baby was fed, as Diane refused utterly to take care of the child, and her mother was seriously considering sending her to a home. One morning early, Di took the baby away, and as far as her parents and friends were concerned, was never heard of again. In fact she changed her name, bought herself a tumble-down bungalow miles from anywhere which was going for a song, and began the appalling scheme she had formed in her mind to revenge herself on her former lover.

She had been a clever child. History had been her favourite subject and the Middle Ages her special period. From this now sprang her inspiration. She remembered reading of helmets which children were made to wear from earliest infancy, when the cranium is still soft. She set about making detailed drawings for such a helmet, and when completed took them to the nearest blacksmith. The blacksmith who naturally had no idea what he was making, was very interested when Diane told him he was making the top part of an unusual mediaeval suit of armour, and he took enormous pains with his job. When it was finished Diane took the mask home, and fitted it carefully over the head and face of her crying baby.

With the cunning of obsession, she managed to keep the fact of the baby quite secret from her neighbours. She bought the baby-food at a town some distance away, and kept the child itself locked in a bedroom at the back of the cottage. She became very clever with her hands, and soundproofed the room herself.

When the baby grew into a child, she still kept it locked in the room, which it never left, wearing its horrifying headdress.

Days, weeks and years passed, and the mask was never removed. The child was used to wearing it, and caused no trouble in its lone practically silent existence. It never seemed to get ill, had a healthy appetite, and managed to learn a few words of speech. 'I'm quite well thank you. I've finished my food thank you,' and 'Goodnight'. It also said 'Daddy'. It spoke in an utterly monotonous voice, and because of the lack of exercise it was rather fat. Otherwise except for the contraption on its head it was normal.

After breakfast which she made for them both, Diane went out to work every day as a dentist's receptionist and among other things made enough money to buy herself a station waggon. At night she cooked for both of them, put Arnold to bed, locked him up, then went downstairs and either read or sewed. It was a tranquil life. Her only real contact with the outside world was that she kept a distant watch on her ex-lover. She had reports sent to her by an agency, care of a box-number in a town fairly near, where she never shopped, and was unlikely to be recognized. She learned that he had married a girl who had been at school with her, and that the pair were very happy. She remembered this girl well. She was a timid little creature, and very pretty. Naturally Diane hated her.

A fortnight before Arnold's seventh birthday, Diane gave in her notice to the dentist in order to put her long formulated plan into action. She woke, very early indeed, gave Arnold his breakfast, then a sleeping pill, unlocked his door when he was so sleepy that the excitement of leaving his prison hardly registered – put him in the back of the station waggon on a mattress, and drove him, sleeping soundly, to the village of her birth. It was four-thirty when she arrived at her lover's house, a charming little place some way beyond the other houses at the end of a long lane. She wrapped Arnold carefully in blankets, laid him gently on the doorstep, and saw to it that the label round his neck was the right side up. On the label was written 'Arnold Ransome, son of Arnold Ransome, aged seven years. Hullo Daddy. It's my seventh happy birthday.'

She then got into the station waggon, and left for London airport, where she had booked a flight on an early plane to the South of France. She had a false passport in a false name, and an excellent blonde wig, which with the aid of a complete change of make-up, and a newly-bought wardrobe of clothes completely altered her personality.

Her only thought other than revenge when she left Arnold, was that she was glad his birthday fell in June when he wouldn't die of cold at being left out in the open. She was also for his sake, glad it wasn't raining.

It was Arnold's wife who discovered the boy and finding him too heavy to lift ran into the house utterly amazed to wake her husband to tell him what was on their doorstep. She suggested that she send at once for the police but her husband realizing that if they did, there was bound to be publicity, said that they had better deal with the situation themselves.

He realized immediately on seeing the name tag that it was Diane's child and carried the little boy indoors. Both he and Mary his wife were horrified at the headdress, but not having studied mediaeval history had no idea what they were in for, when they carefully unscrewed the mask.

The child's head had grown into every nook and cranny of the fiendish device, and his deformity was so horrible and obscene that Mary fainted, and Arnold found himself trembling as though in a fit. The child held out its arms to Arnold, and in its flat monotonous voice said 'Daddy', and Mary who had just come to, went into screaming hysterics, while it was all Arnold could do not to leave the house.

Mary never recovered from the shock and became a prey to depression. Arnold put the child in a home, and took to drink, and Diane took up the job she had already arranged in the South of France, of looking after a charming little boy, aged by a curious coincidence, seven years.

FATHER FORGIVE ME

Raymond Harvey

A HOST of slim shafts of sunlight beaded their way through the perforated partition on to Father O'Neil's perspiring face. Tiny particles of dust swam aimlessly from beam to beam. This hot Irish summer was dragging on one monotonous hot day after another. Father O'Neil was finding life hard these days, his black clothing always sucked the sun's heat to his body as he trudged along the dry dusty streets of his village and it was always a relief to him when he could shut himself away in the comparative shade of the confession box. He dabbed his moist handkerchief lethargically from one part of his glistening face to the other. It got so stifling in this confined space after a while and when you had to sit and listen to Mrs Casey holding forth in the adjoining booth it made you feel that you'd already spent a lifetime there.

'It's not only that, Father,' her thin voice prattled through 'but I've told him and told him six children is enough for me so it will have to be enough for him. Now I ask you, Father, haven't I done my bit? . . . Father, are you still there?'

Father O'Neil straightened himself quickly from his drowsy slouch, normally one didn't get the opportunity to say much with Mrs Casey and he had been caught unprepared.

'Yes, I'm listening, my child,' he assured her thinking to himself how ridiculous it sounded, he merely thirty-two years of age calling this mother of six, his child.

'I know it's difficult but remember we are here for a purpose – to multiply that is God's wish . . .'

'Multiply, is it, indeed?' she cut in. 'I'll tell you this for nothing, Father, it's all right for you young single men to talk but as far as I'm concerned moi multiplying days are over and that's a fact. Good-day to you, Father.'

He watched her thin black silhouette against the mesh as she stood to go. He hadn't handled that one very well but with Mrs Casey it was always best to leave her to go her own way so he had discovered in his eighteen months here at Kilenmore. In the end whatever Mrs Casey said went, so to disagree was usually as effective as Canute's attempt to stop the tide. The thumping shut of the door as she left, stung his tired nerves. He poured himself half a tumbler of water from the glass bottle. The water tasted stale and was lukewarm but he didn't pause until he had drained the glass. He wondered if there would be any more for him. One advantage of being in a village as small as Kilenmore was that tedious duties were soon over because of the low numbers. Ah well, he'd rest here in peace for another ten minutes or so and then go on his way.

He had just closed his eyes and rested his head against the wall when his nerves jolted to life again as a result of the same offending door. By holding his head well back from the mesh at a slight angle he could always make out enough of the person's features to know who was there and Father O'Neil like the boy scouts always wanted to be prepared. He squinted inquisitively at the screen, oh no, that's all he needed – first Mrs Casey and now John Flynn. He knew within his heart of hearts that he should have compassion for this poor creature. Due to a prominent purple birth mark John Flynn's face could only be termed as disfigured. The blotchy stain had made such an impression on O'Neil's brain when he first saw it that he could picture it quite clearly now in the next booth despite the partition.

John Flynn was about three years younger than himself and as a result of the branded appearance of his face needless to say he had been unable to attract or impress any members of the opposite sex. As a result John had now accepted that for him the only sex experience he would ever have was that which he practised with a few of his own sex in the village. Unfortunately, John Flynn interpreted Father O'Neil's celibacy as a good omen and had the embarrassing habit of pressing his case whenever an opportunity presented itself.

'Are you there, Father?' John's thick voice oozed through the mesh.

'Yes, my son,' he answered cautiously.

'I have a great confession to make, Father.'

'God is merciful to all that are repentant,' said Father O'Neil striving to give his own voice the note of authority he knew he needed when dealing with John's infatuations.

'I love you Father O'Neil, and I can't go on much longer without . . .'

'Stop that this instant,' O'Neil cut in, 'you must stop this fetish of yours. You . . .'

'But I can't stop it, Father,' he hissed back through the tiny gaps.

'You must, you must,' Father O'Neil realized his own voice was rising as a trace of panic crept into it. 'Find yourself a woman to love, my son,' he continued struggling to retrieve some dignity into the conversation. 'God wants you to marry, have children and live a good life.'

'Marry? Marry? Me, marry?' he squawked back in disbelief. 'If he wanted me to get married why did he give me this face, eh? Answer me that if you can?'

Father O'Neil ducked his head back sharply from the mesh to relieve his nostrils from the putrid smelling breath that had seeped through as a result of that outburst.

'Control yourself,' he said keeping his head turned as he spoke. 'Who are we to try to understand God's reasons.'

'If he'd wanted me to marry a woman he wouldn't have given me this face. He meant me to love you and want you, I know it, I can feel it.' John's thick dirty fingers scratched against the mesh as he pleaded for recognition.

'Please Father be kind to me. You must know what I'm going through, you must be lonely yourself. I could do wonders for you, Father, honestly I could. Give me the chance and I know you will get to feel the same way about me and then you won't miss not having a woman either. Please Father, please help me?'

The poisonous stench in the hot stale air and the scratching nails had driven Father O'Neil back against the farthest wall in his cramped cell. He found the remarks as obnoxious as the foul odour. He was at a loss for words. He merely cowered back in his corner waiting for the attack upon his senses to cease. But there was more to endure.

'Aren't you supposed to help your parishioners by administering to their needs? Well then what about my need? Why am I to be left unfulfilled?'

Father O'Neil made a determined effort to end this fiasco. 'My son, God cares for all his children, you must have faith. Now go and reflect upon what I have said.'

'But I want . . .' burst back the voice but Father O'Neil was adamant.

'Go and reflect,' he repeated sternly and held his breath hoping and praying that he had commanded sufficient authority in his voice to subdue John Flynn.

The banging which he had found so irritating earlier was like music now as the noise of the slamming door in the adjacent box reverberated in his ears. He waited until the clopping footsteps faded in the distance before he exhaled his own sigh of relief. What a day he was having! Still these things are sent to try us, he thought profoundly. The trouble was they made such a good job of it. He wriggled his swollen feet painfully back into his pinching shoes and loosely tied his laces. That was as much as he could take for now and as all seemed silent around him he decided to leave his prison for some fresh air.

He was in the act of pulling to the rust-infested gate when he caught sight of a solitary figure waiting at the corner of the church wall which he had to pass on his way home. The blue smudge on the distant white face immediately placed him on his guard. He lingered where he was on the pretext of fiddling with the brown coated chain on the gate. What should he do? If he went on his normal way, John was bound to accost him and an unpleasant scene would invariably follow. He no longer had the sanctity of his church to protect him. He would open the gate and return to the church as if he had forgotten something, but then the chances were John would still be there when he came out again later. But at least such a move would give him more time to try to solve his predicament. On the other hand he could go in the opposite direction to avoid the waiting figure. It would mean a longer and wearier route through the blazing heat, but that would be the lesser of the two evils. His fingers trembled with the rattling chain as he summoned up his courage to execute whichever decision he conceded to. The prospect of going the other way was the more attractive apart from the risk that John may decide to follow him and make a fresh onslaught when he had reached a lonelier spot.

'Are you chaining yourself to the gate now, Father?' he swung his head round to see where the voice came from. To his relief it was Mrs Casey's eldest daughter Mary who stood there smiling at him.

'Oh Mary, it's you,' he said. 'Forgive me, I was deep in thought I didn't notice you coming.'

'Is it my mother that's been after giving you so much to think about then?' she asked cheekily.

'No, no, of course not, my child, how lucky we all are to have such a good woman like your mother to sustain us all – indeed yes a fine woman, er, you're not going my way by any chance, Mary, are you?' he asked trying to keep the eagerness from his voice.

'As a matter of fact I am Father. Why? Do you fancy taking a walk with me then?' she teased.

'Now, Mary, behave yourself. A young girl like you should know better than to say things like that to me,' he said strategically moving to one side of her before they started walking towards the waiting John.

'Oh come off it now, Father, you're as much a man as the rest of them under your clothes. Maybe more so!' she said raising her eyebrows wickedly. But Father O'Neil was too busy concentrating on trying to look relaxed and natural as they walked alongside the church wall, to be shocked by anything his life-saving escort had to say.

'Good day, Father,' said John looking directly at him as they passed.

'Good day to you, John,' he answered quickly diverting his

eyes from the crescent mark on John's left cheek to Mary's gay yellow mini dress.

'Hello Mary,' added John also admiring the yellow curves, 'I like that dress you're wearing.'

'Huh, I suppose you mean you like what's inside it, don't you, John Flynn?' she answered with disdain.

John's face hardened with a glare of hatred. His slow brain struggled for an apt rejoinder to the taunt but as no sound emerged from his working mouth, he contented himself by pouring his enmity through his eyes at her departing back.

'That was not a very charitable thing to say now was it, Mary?' said Father O'Neil when they had moved out of ear-shot.

'Come off it, Father,' retorted Mary hotly, 'you know what he's after as well as I do, so don't play the innocent with me.'

This sudden broadside shut him up completely. He contented himself to walk along in silence at her side thankful that her presence had solved his predicament. He glanced over his shoulder and saw that John was rooted to the same spot but still following them with his eyes. He was always amazed that Mrs Casey had succeeded in producing something as attractive as her daughter Mary had turned out to be. But he was also worried that this girl of a mere seventeen years should be so worldly and brazen about sex and life. She glided along beside him, her long copper-coloured hair flaming in the sunlight, her head held erect and fearless. She was already a mature woman physically and he could easily understand why she was so sought after by all the males in Kilenmore.

They turned off the road and followed the baked mud path through Highfield woods.

'Now you're not pouting, are you, Father?' Mary asked suddenly looking at his frowning face.

'Pouting? Me? Glory be, no, Mary, whatever gave you that idea?' he asked.

'You know, Father,' she said speculatively 'the trouble with you is that you take life far too seriously. You should try and let yourself go more.'

He laughed at the very idea.

'No, I mean it, Father,' she persisted. 'Look at yourself. You're still a young man, you should get some enjoyment out of life before it's too late.'

'And what makes you think I don't enjoy life?' he asked still smiling.

'I don't think, I know you don't. How can you? You can't go out with a woman.'

'Ah but my vows,' he interrupted.

'Oh you and your vows. You're just developing into an old maid going round dressed in black with everybody calling you Father. Now let's face it, is that your idea of letting your hair down and enjoying life, well is it?'

'But you see I'm here for a purpose, Mary . . .' he began in earnest.

'Oh, yes and what purpose is that, Michael?' she stopped and leaned against a tall pine tree to watch his reaction.

'Mary,' he said his voice riddled with shock, 'You must call me Father O'Neil not er . . .'

'Not Michael,' she helped out. 'Oh, come on, everybody knows you're Michael O'Neil and we're alone here aren't we? I'm not embarrassing you in any way, so where's the harm?'

'Well there is no harm I suppose,' he said hesitantly.

'Well then, that's settled,' she said. 'Whenever we're alone I'm always going to call you Michael, it'll be our secret,' she whispered as if it was all part of a conspiracy. 'Have you heard the one about the nun in the convent?' she continued leaving the tree and trudging on. 'One day she went to the Mother Superior and said I've been sleeping with Saint Michael.'

'Mary, is this some kind of joke?' he burst in sharply.

She turned and looked at him. 'Well, if it isn't things are beginning to look up for the nuns aren't they, Michael? Anyway, the Mother Superior is shocked just like you are this minute Michael, and she says I don't believe you. How do you know it was Saint Michael? So the nun says when the morning bell went he left in such a hurry he forgot his underpants and here they are. See they've got St Michael on the tab inside them.'

T—D

Mary laughed happily at her own joke and the sight of her laughing along with the farcical joke forced Michael to smile back at her.

'I don't know what I'm going to do with you, Mary Casey,' he said shaking his head.

'Mm promises. Nothing but promises,' she said skipping away from him smartly as if she were expecting him to retaliate.

She plopped down on the prickly pine needle carpet around a tree and lay back against it. 'Phew it's so hot,' she complained. 'Let's have a rest for a few minutes.'

He sat down alongside her and mopped the beads of sweat off his face with his handkerchief.

'I thought you'd be more of a gentleman than that Michael,' she said just as he was beginning to get comfortable. He looked at her in bewilderment, what on earth was she talking about he wondered. The puzzled look on his face prompted her to continue.

'Now, don't you think it's unkind of you not to offer a poor girl your coat to sit on to protect her young flesh from all these prickly needles?'

He struggled instantly to his feet. 'My dear Mary, how thoughtless of me,' he said peeling off his jacket. 'Allow me to offer it now.' He laid it on the floor and watched the golden hairs on her bronzed legs twinkle as she squatted upon it.

'Ah, that's better,' she sighed. 'Thank you, Michael.'

He settled down again feeling spiritually uplifted for the first time that day by his helpful deed, but also feeling a little apprehensive at the effect Mary's weight and the needles would have on his best black jacket. Still a good stiff brushing would do the trick. It would have to because it would be a long time before he could afford to buy himself another. But this was being materialistic which would not do at all, so he lay back infusing his brain with the feeling of satisfaction at his Christian act. He put his hand behind his head but quickly changed his mind as the smell of sour sweat wafted from the patches of stained shirt at his armpits. He sat up and propped his back against the tree with his arms folded self-consciously in an effort to smother the smell.

His efforts were interrupted by the crisp rip of Mary's zip. He looked to see what she was doing and was rather taken aback to see that she had lowered the zip that ran down the front of her dress a good nine inches.

'Mary!' he said aghast, realizing from the amount of her breasts he was able to see that she had nothing on under her dress.

'What is it, Michael?' she asked purposely displaying a mask of innocence.

'Your dress, Mary,' he said turning his eyes away as if to protect himself from corruption.

'But it's so hot, Michael,' she answered, 'now you wouldn't begrudge me a little cooling air would you.'

'Not at all, Mary,' he said still looking at the taut laces of his left shoe. 'But – um – do you need quite so much?'

Her gurgling laughter unsettled him even more than her sudden un-zipping. He was now beginning to feel just a little uneasy in the presence of Miss Mary Casey.

'Oh, you're a real card, Michael, and that's a fact,' she said stretching her body taut in the shade of the tree. 'Well I must be getting on my way now,' he said nervously beginning to clap away the dead clinging needles from his trousers.

'No not yet,' she said sharply sitting up and eyeing him calculatingly. 'What I mean is you can't go just yet because well, you haven't heard my problem have you?'

'Problem?' he repeated looking at her then quickly averting his eyes as they alighted on the cleavage of her smooth breasts. 'What problem could you possibly have Mary?' He heard the rustle of the needles as she lay down again.

'Well, Michael, let's pretend – just pretend now mind you that I was pregnant,' she said carefully.

'Pregnant?' he echoed, his voice sounding an octave higher than normal. 'I mean,' he cleared his throat and regained control of his voice, 'pregnant, did you say, Mary?'

'Yes,' she affirmed. 'Now if that were the case how do you think my mother would react to the news.'

'Well. Oh yes – well I think she'd – oh dear, I don't know

what to say,' he stumbled for the right words. 'Well, Mary, it's difficult to say really I . . .'

'And suppose,' Mary cut in 'she was told that the father was not a Catholic, what then?'

'Not a Catholic?' he realized he was beginning to repeat everything she said but seeing as she kept coming out with such outrageous remarks then it wasn't really surprising. 'Well, if that were true, Mary, then I think she would be very – well – annoyed with you,' he ventured hesitantly.

'I would say she'd give me hell. Oh, forgive me, Father, but, oh, you know what sort of treatment I'd get. I'd be shown the door on the spot and then what?' Mary's voice was becoming quite excited as she envisaged her mother's uncontrollable temper in the situation.

'Yes, I know, Mary,' he said looking at her flushed face. 'So let it act as a further deterrent to stop you doing anything so foolish.'

She propped herself up on one elbow and looked him straight in the eye. Then in a voice that was little more than a whisper she said, 'But it's too late, Michael, it's already happened.'

He could think of nothing to say. He just stared blankly back at her as she toyed with the brass ring on her zip.

'So you see, Michael, you're my only salvation', she said looking as if she was sorry for him, not for herself. 'I know it's going to be terrible for you but – well that's me. I'm afraid I'm a very selfish person and I worry about myself first and it's not my fault that I've got such a tyrant for a mother, is it?'

'I don't know what to say Mary,' he said still in a state of shock. 'If I thought anything I could say to your mother would help you, well I'd try of course – it would be my duty – but well she is such a difficult woman at times that well, you know what I mean.'

'Oh I know only too well,' she said slowly sliding her zip down a few more inches. But this time he made no protestations he merely observed the augmented view as his brain wrestled with this latest dilemma. The zip had now crawled slowly down even farther allowing her yellow dress to yawn open. He could only sit there transfixed as her young proud breasts were unveiled before him. Even her voice was unable to break the trance her beauty held him in.

'Do you like what you see, Michael,' she coaxed.

'Yes, Mary, I think you have a wonderful body,' he croaked weakly.

'Would you like to see more?' she said easing the zip lower still until the edge of her thin black nylon panties emerged to break the line of her bare brown skin.

'Oh, Mary,' he gasped, completely overcome by the vision of beauty before him.

'Well, you've done enough window shopping, what about coming in for a free sample,' she invited taking the zip to the very bottom of her dress.

For years his masculinity had been bottled inside him under a cover of controls and vows and restrictions until now suddenly this touchstone had erupted before him. His moist palms itched to smooth and fondle their undulating way all over her. The beads of sweat that trickled into meandering rivulets on his face were now a result of the nervous strain as well as the heat.

'Come on, Michael,' her voice was a smooth whisper, 'I'll help you, don't be afraid.' She slid her thumb between her skin and the top of the black gossamer nylon and tantalisingly dragged its wrinkling form a little lower. 'Come on, Michael,' she urged, 'you do it for me.' His right hand had already left his knee and was travelling hesitantly towards hers when a wave of cold fear flushed some of the hot thumping blood clear of his head. His hand wavered short of the target as another icy spray lashed a fresh attack upon his confused brain.

His whole body froze, he hesitated in his purpose, the hot sweat seeming to chill all along his back.

'My God, what am I doing,' he hissed desperately. He smacked his hands together and locked his thumbs between his teeth. He shut out all further temptation by jamming his eyes shut tight. Helpless whimpering gulps escaped between his trapped thumbs. He tried to shut out her voice as well as everything else so that he could do justice to his prayers pleading for help and strength.

'You pathetic little worm,' her voice raged in his ears. 'I bet you don't even know what to do, you're given it on a bloody plate and look at you – just look at you!' She glared at the sitting statue before her. 'You don't think meeting you and getting here was pure chance, do you? Well, do you?' she roared at him but got no reaction.

'If you only knew how much I've worried and how many sleepless nights I've racked my brain for a way out of the mess I'm in. But it's nearly over for me now and believe me it's just starting for you, do you hear me?' she screamed at him. But the blind mute did not move.

'Wake up and listen, will you?' she shouted cracking her open palm across his head, but this merely provoked a fresh flow of whimpering.

'Holy Mother, will you look at him,' she grated through her clenched teeth. 'Open your eyes, will you, and look at me?'

This request obviously registered because he shook his head violently.

'Right, have it your own way but remember this trick didn't do the ostrich much good,' she spat out at him. 'In a few minutes I'm going to run out of these woods with my dress all ripped and I'm góing to cry my story out to everybody I see, of how you raped and ravished me here on your own coat.'

His eyelids sprang open and he stared in horrified disbelief at her. 'Ah, ha! that's made you think hasn't it,' she said triumphantly, 'and it won't be any good you denying it because remember John Flynn saw us coming in here together. Well?'

His mouth opened and his hands flopped heavily to his lap. The expression of fear and terror on his face compelled Mary to stop and gloat at the effect her ranting had had on him. She stood up and stared triumphantly down at him, then bending slowly so that her face was inches away from his, she said quietly, 'And when I've finished screaming out there, I bet a few people will rush in here and a fine state they'll find you in, won't they?'

As she spoke she gripped the bottom of her dress with both hands and pulled with all her strength until the thin linen rasped apart in protest. She stepped back from him, a wily smirk on her face.

'Then think how my dear mother will feel in a few weeks when some of the fuss and bother has died down and her dear daughter who had suffered so terribly at the hands of the sex raving O'Neil tells her that she is pregnant. Why I'll be nursed with more care than all my younger brothers and sisters put together. I'll have the sympathy and love of every living soul in Kilenmore.'

She stood in front of him, legs apart, her dress gaping and torn but her body erect, savouring the triumph to come. The rustling of the crisp needles induced her to look at him again. He was shuffling towards her on his bent knees.

'Don't think of doing things like that, Mary,' he pleaded pathetically. 'Our God is a kind forgiving God. Come, kneel with me please, we'll pray together, here, now.'

Her long hair splayed out as she threw her head back and laughed.

'Please don't laugh, Mary,' he begged, gripping the backs of her knees with his hands, 'you'll see, it will be all right. Have faith please.'

'Oh get up off your knees, you make me sick,' she mocked.

'Please, Mary, listen to me,' he said earnestly, 'I'll come home with you, now, this very minute and I'll speak to your mother for you. I'll see that no harm comes to you I promise!'

As he spoke he moved his fingers up to hold the back of her warm thighs. But Mary, excited with her triumph only laughed louder at each of his wailings.

'Stop laughing, Mary, please listen to me I mean every word,' he said gazing beseechingly upwards at her. But she continued to laugh, setting her round breasts quivering spasmodically with the effort. But the dark protruding tips failed completely to stimulate him as they danced on their trembling mounds.

'Mary, stop it,' he screeched up at her suddenly. 'Stop laughing, Mary, I can't stand it do you hear Mary? Stop.'

He tightened his grip on her legs and pulled them hard towards him. The unexpected force upset her balance and she toppled with a shrieking giggle backwards, but even this failed to stem the peals of laughter. If anything it seemed to him to increase the volume.

He was now beginning to panic at the possibility of some-one being attracted by the noise, coming to investigate and finding him and Mary in this state. He crawled clumsily between her splayed legs and leaned over her. 'Shut up, Mary. Stop it, Mary, for God's sake,' he screamed at her face, a fine spray of spittle peppering her bare throat. 'Stop, stop, Mary.' But nothing he said seemed to have any effect on the bared teeth and vibrating tongue. His right hand was wedged on something hard and cold. Still trying to drown her gurgling with his shrieking voice he swung his right hand across her face.

Immediately her erratic peals of laughter changed to the single higher note of a scream. He crashed his hand against her face yet again. A gush of bright red blood spurted free as the mashed remains of her left eye slopped on to her cheek. It hung there suspended by a few twisted red strings while the flooded socket pumped a steady scarlet flow around it. He thought the pitch of her scream was going to shatter his eardrums any minute. Her long nails clawed desperately into his shirt as her body squirmed beneath him. He pounded again and again until the red stone was too slippery for him to hold any longer. Exhausted, he dropped the stone and rolled slowly off her. The screaming had stopped at last although the mouth was still open. The split lips hung in shreds into the toothless bleeding gums. Pieces of splintered teeth lay embedded in the oozing redness that had once been a tongue. He put on his coat to hide the blood splashes and slipped the slimy stone into his pocket. If he was lucky enough to get home without being seen he would be able to destroy the evidence. There was nothing for it he would have to get a new suit now. He took a last glance at the ivory white body with its mound of undulating red pulp surmounted by long strands of matted hair. Then he dashed off for home struggling to control his chilled stomach from being violently sick until he got there.

A week after the tragedy Father O'Neil was kneeling in prayer in his confession cubicle. In the last week he had spent so much time on his knees that already his new black trousers was beginning to show the strain. He was interrupted from his appeals for mercy and forgiveness by the familiar clatter of the door in the next cubicle. He sat in his place and forced himself to clear his mind as best he could to listen to the confession.

'Hello, Father O'Neil. It's me John Flynn.' The familiar voice was accompanied by the familiar stench. 'I have a confession, Father. Last Saturday I followed yourself and the poor Miss Mary into the wood and I committed the terrible sin of being a peeping-tom.'

Father O'Neil sat rigid in his box without uttering a single word. 'Now I thought to myself, Father,' the voice continued, 'how terrible it would be for the Church and yourself Father if I told the police about what I'd done and what I'd seen. So I decided if you were nice to me Father and let me come and stay with you then I'd never have to tell them about it, would I, Father? Hello, Father O'Neil. Are you still there?' But Father O'Neil made no answer, he was down on his knees praying as he had never prayed before.

A COMEDY OF TERRORS

John Burke

THE STORY conference had been in progress for three hours – if you could call it progress. The casting director, who had hoped to be in his girl friend's bed by eight o'clock at the latest, realized that the evening was likely to be a long one and that he would be lucky even to get home to his wife before midnight. This made him vindictive. He said something rude about the screenwriter; but the writer had already heard three of his best ideas turned down flat and was sulking anyway. One more insult made little difference.

Erwin Hodek said: 'The same rules we've always followed, right? No monsters. No gloomy castles, no mummies, no vampires. Right?'

'Right,' said the assistant producer loyally.

'Something psychological. Something creepy happening to the girl. And I want the girl from that picture we ran this morning.'

The casting director took dour pleasure in saying: 'Sorry, Erwin. I checked. She's tied up for six months on Clarion's thing about the bubonic plague.'

Erwin sighed. 'So we wait six months. The way we're going right now, it'll take that long to get the story line straightened out.'

The casting director lit another cigarette. His eyes were smarting from the smoke haze in the room, but he had to do something to stop the frustration tightening into a hard knot inside him.

Robbie, the designer, sat back and thought, with self-indulgent detachment, of the best way of showing a boa-constrictor crushing the life out of a man. Or perhaps a child would make the audience gasp a bit more. Or a kitten. He would have to do some research to see whether the eyes popped. Might get a nice effect that way.

Not that it fitted the current story, insofar as there was a story.

Erwin was staring straight at him. 'Any ideas, Robbie?'

Erwin Hodek had made his reputation – and worked wonders for his bank balance – as *the* creative force in contemporary horror films. At a time when cinema attendances were declining, Erwin had found a way of pulling people in. He showed them things they wouldn't see on television; things they could never have imagined in their wildest dreams – or wildest nightmares.

Statistics showed that over half the cinema-going audience today was made up of people under twenty-five years of age. And most of those were probably under twenty. Mainly they were kids wanting to get out of the house, wanting to get their girls away from watchful mothers and sniggering younger brothers; he wanting an excuse to put his arm round her, she wanting an excuse for him to put his arm round her. What better than a horror picture to lure them into the semi-darkness? 'Give me a scream every two minutes,' as Erwin put it, 'and we can't lose.'

He was breaking away from the crude shocker. Lumbering creatures from the deep or from outer space were dead, box-office-wise. Erwin's pictures blended sex and creeping fear, jarred by sudden psychological shocks – a touch of nausea, something to provoke an instinctive 'Ugh' and then a shiver of near-orgasmic ecstasy. Not that Erwin would have put it in quite such words; but intuitively he knew the ingredients of the most profitable shivers.

Erwin had worked in California and then come to Europe in search of cheaper facilities and wonderful backgrounds. He found both. He made a clutch of B pictures in Rome and two Gothic thrillers in Vienna. Then he discovered England. England, he announced, was spooky. England was really way out. All those crazy old traditions, and those crazy places, and those kooky people! The most celebrated and most gruesome murders had all been committed in England: any connoisseur of crime knew that. There was something sinister in the air. He liked it. He settled down and did some real work.

The last few years had been triumphant. And the triumphs, the real successes, dated from the day he engaged Robbie Sennidge as designer.

After their first picture together, Erwin put Robbie under contract. It became known through the trade, in the way these things do get known, that Robbie was not just a set and costume designer, and not just a special effects man of genius: he thought his every thought in film terms, he saw the whole thing in his mind; from Robbie's ideas came all that was most characteristic in a Hodek production. A reviewer on one of the Sundays once said that Robbie Sennidge thought with his eyes.

It was never the basic story that counted. Writers were hired merely to string together the grotesqueries which Robbie dreamed up. Robbie produced new *frissons*, and the writer had simply to devise a surface logic and linking dialogue for the whole sequence.

The current writer sank deeper into his chair. He wasn't even trying any more.

'Robbie?' Erwin prompted.

'I'm thinking,' said Robbie.

Erwin said: 'Something to do with the mind. Telepathy or brainwashing or something. There's a lot of talk about it these days.'

'It's not visual.'

'I'm just talking off the top of my head, of course,' said Erwin. 'But I've got a *feeling*. The mind. Folk are scared of what goes on in their own minds.'

'Don't blame them,' said the casting director.

Erwin swung his swivel chair from left to right, right to left. He gazed up at the ceiling. He said:

'What really frightens people? What gets right under their skin?'

'Snakes,' said the assistant producer. 'Most people are scared stiff of snakes.'

'We've used them.'

And beetles, thought Robbie. And spiders we've used too. He smiled at the memory. There had been nothing corny in their spider picture. It had been cumulative, suggestive, quiet ... and chilling. At the end it was as terrifying as only a whisper can be. There was never any bombastic uproar in a Hodek production. 'Any time I hear the music or the effects on the soundtrack getting loud,' Erwin had once proclaimed, 'I know somebody's trying to cover over something.'

And moths, thought Robbie. The lighting and camera work in the moth picture had been out of this world. Sound, too. Restrained sound blending perfectly with the visual tension – the flapping, the whirring, the insistence ... Yes, out of this world. A woman in Llandudno had had a heart attack and died in the cinema. Her husband had tried to sue the company, but had stood no chance against Erwin's lawyers. The publicity had been great.

'We've used so many things,' said Robbie. 'We're running short.'

They all laughed because they knew this was absurd.

But they had certainly devised terror in an awful, awful lot of ways.

Claustrophobia ... with Ronnie's concept of long, slanted walls, closing in at the wrong, dizzying angles; and the muffled drumbeats like heartbeats, and the shadows that rushed out suffocatingly into the very audience.

Hypodermics ... funny how people gagged at the sight of the needle entering flesh. And the drawing of blood samples, the blood rising ...

Mice and rats. Vertigo. Fear of slimy things ... the texture of a human brain oozing out through a hole in the skull ... the implication of something sticky and amorphous just off the edge of the screen.

Light, darkness, and shadow. Obscene shadows.

They had exploited every possibility. They had built up an incomparable skill in distorting the commonplace and making it hideous.

But there must be more. There were as many fears as there were human beings in the world. Out of night sounds and daytime silences there were still a thousand terrors to be conjured up.

Robbie half closed his eyes and mused . . . mutely addressed a vast unseen audience. I'll find a fear for all of you. For each of you. A special one for you . . . and you . . . and *you*. Your secret nightmares – I'll get round to them all in time. And for those who think they don't have nightmares . . . Oh, just wait till I've finished with you.

Unexpectedly Erwin said: 'I don't know about you guys, but I'm pooped.' He spread his arms wide and yawned. 'Let's break it up. Sleep on it – and be back here at ten tomorrow with something real, huh?'

They got up slowly. It was never good policy to seem in a hurry to leave Erwin's office. The casting director stood with his hands in his pockets and stared at the floor as though he might, at this late stage, come up with one sudden splendid notion. Then he braced himself and went almost reluctantly to the door. 'See you, Erwin. 'Night.'

He might just manage half an hour.

Robbie adopted a more leisurely pace. Robbie had no need to rush through his pleasures. He was not married and he had all the time in the world for whatever it pleased him to do.

When he got home he would ask Doreen what her own special horror was.

The idea of ever having to work for her living, probably.

Robbie lived in a mews in Kensington. His home was neither a cottage nor a house. It was a conglomeration – a solid old stable converted into a garage and now into his workroom, linked with a small house, a studio, and a small paved garden which ran up against a tall, thick wall dividing the whole group from small gardens beyond. Next door was a garage from which proceeded, at times, a great deal of hammering and the revving up of engines. Robbie had often been asked if he didn't find the noise distracting; but in fact he liked to experiment with sound, with things to set the teeth on edge, with grating juxtapositions.

Besides, the row was often useful in drowning out some of the noises which he himself was producing.

This evening he let himself in and strolled into the sitting room. The lights were on, and he expected to find Doreen sprawled on the couch as usual, fingering through magazines as usual and drinking yet another bottle of coke or another gin and tonic and abstractedly stroking her left thigh as usual.

The room was empty. A book lay open, face down, on the couch. Doreen had been reading about flagellation and flaying. She liked to pretend that his work for Hodek gave her the creeps, but her tremors were as ambivalent as those of any writhing girl in a cinema audience; in such moods she was very responsive and he was glad to have her around.

Not that he wanted her around all that much longer. Custom had staled her far from infinite variety.

But tonight, thinking of her, he was prepared to enjoy her. As he went towards the black and green bedroom he conjured up a picture of her – thinking with his eyes, seeing her as vividly and immediately as though she were only a few feet away. Her bright blue eyes, pale in a strong light. Her fair skin with its delicate surface – misleading, because she was tough enough and strong enough. She had led a despairing young cameraman a dance for a couple of years, had been cited in his divorce case, and then had risen in the world to become Robbie Sennidge's mistress.

He saw her so clearly that it came as a surprise to find that she was not there in the bedroom, waiting for him.

He heard the swift rustle of feet. She was coming along the passage from his workroom, trying to look airy and unconcerned.

'Robbie, darling, you're so late.'

He said: 'Where have you been?'

'Oh, just wandering about. I was getting so impatient, sweetie. I just couldn't sit still.'

'You've been in my workroom.'

'Sweetie, let's have a drink.'

She tried to brush past him. He seized her wrist and forced it round until her clenched fingers opened. She had been clutching a key.

He said: 'I told you never to go in there.'

'I was just drifting about. I didn't do any harm. I didn't touch anything.'

'You were snooping.'

'You left the key in the door, so—'

'I never leave the key in the door. That's the spare one – you got it out of my dressing-table.'

'Well, what if I did?' When she was utterly in the wrong, Doreen always grew venomous and aggressive. 'It's high time I saw what you've got hidden away in there. I'm not surprised you keep the door locked. Some of those things . . . Robbie, you do have a kinky mind, don't you?'

He dropped the key into his pocket and half dragged her towards the sitting room.

'Never heard of Bluebeard's Castle?' he said. 'And what happened to the silly, snooping girl who couldn't leave well alone?'

'You're hurting me.' Doreen shook herself free and collapsed petulantly on the couch. 'Some of those things,' she said again. 'Those hooks . . . and that awful thing with spikes in the corner . . .' She put both hands on the couch to prop herself up, and knocked the book away. 'And that book! All that stuff about blood from wounds, and beating men to death. And hanging, drawing and quartering them – spilling them out all over the place. Ugh . . . I mean, honestly. Can you *imagine*?'

'Yes,' said Robbie.

He could not merely imagine. He knew. Knew the sight, sound and smell of it. Every detail.

'And flaying a woman alive,' Doreen persisted. 'I suppose you know all about that too?'

'No,' said Robbie thoughtfully. 'No, that's something I've never tried.'

'Anyway' – she thrust her plump, moist lower lip out at him – 'what about *you*?'

'What about me?'

'What about you and your own fears. You're so good at frightening other people with all this stuff you swot up. But what about the thing that scares *you*? Shall I tell you what I know about it?'

'You don't know a thing.'

'You talk in your sleep.' She laughed derisively, unsteadily. 'That's a nasty dream you keep having, Robbie. Do you ever tell your Mr Hodek about that one?'

'Be quiet.'

She looked insufferably pleased. He could have shaken her; wanted to get his hands on her and . . .

His imagination stopped there.

For the moment.

Doreen's anger drained away into smugness. She got up and walked towards the bedroom, waiting for him to follow. He went slowly after her and watched her as she undressed. She swayed and pirouetted in front of him, silently boasting about her body and about her hold on him.

When she was naked, he took the workroom key from his pocket and tossed it a few times in the air.

'I'll just go and make sure nothing's been disturbed.'

'Robbie, don't be such a fusspot. I swear I didn't touch anything.'

'All the same,' he said.

He went along the passage and let himself into the converted garage and switched on the light.

The anatomical diagrams along the walls formed a backdrop to his collection of wooden and iron racks, pincers and various screws. The butchers' hooks swayed gently from the ceiling as he crossed the floor. Immediately under the centre light stood the stake with its looped chains and steel manacles.

He opened the manacles in readiness and put a leather gag on the nearby bench, where he could reach it quickly.

Then he called: 'Doreen.'

'What is it?'

'Come here a minute.'

'I'm not getting out of bed.'

'I thought you told me you hadn't touched anything?'

That fetched her. She came indignantly along the passage, tugging a dressing-gown over her shoulders.

As soon as she was in the workroom he closed the door and tore the dressing-gown from her. She began to laugh as he put his arms round her, thinking this was something new, something attractively perverse he had thought of. It was not until the manacles clamped on her naked flesh that she tried to scream; and then it was cut short as he crammed the gag between her soft red lips and hard white teeth.

He set to work.

It was a long process. He was a perfectionist, and he wanted to be absolutely sure of what he was doing. After twenty minutes he began to wonder if the supposed experts of the past had been any good at their job. Without the sharpest implements it would surely have been impossible to work to the required degree of accuracy. One needed the finest scalpel edge and the steadiest hand to remove the top layer of skin without slicing too deep. To get the best effect it was essential to lay bare a redness which bubbled without smearing too messily.

As the garage was not working at this time of night, there was no hammering or revving of engines to drown the noise that Doreen might make, so reluctantly he had to keep her gagged. Not that he really needed the sound of her voice. It wouldn't do for the sound-track of a Hodek film: too crude, too raucous and naive. As he drew the blade delicately down, flaying her with loving care, he thought of Couperin. That was it. Some of Couperin's harpsichord music – steely cobwebs of austere beauty on the sound-track.

When he had finished, it was dawn. In the final stages he had taken what he recognized as a childish pride in the rhythmic continuity of the operation – the sort of absurd pleasure one gets from taking the peel off an apple in one regular, unbroken curl.

For another hour he took colour pictures of his handiwork. When he was quite sure that his mind and his camera had recorded all the essential reference material, he went out and ate a hearty breakfast.

Before leaving for Erwin Hodek's office in Wardour Street he gave Doreen a drink. She was just conscious enough to accept it, but unable to make any sound other than a long, retching groan.

In spite of his lack of sleep and the intensity of his concentration during the night, he was in a good mood when the story conference started up again.

'Flaying alive,' he said chirpily, within a few seconds of Erwin settling into his chair and demanding coffee.

'Maybe you've got something there,' said Erwin, not because he quite grasped what Robbie had in mind but because he had learned to trust Robbie's hunches.

'A girl,' said Robbie. 'Flayed alive and in agony. Like Hans Andersen's mermaid – every step, every breath is agony. Every breath of wind . . . she can't bear to be touched . . . can't bear to wear clothes.'

'Nice,' agreed Erwin.

'Hypersensitive. And then there needs to be some particular menace—'

'Piranhas,' said the casting director. He, too, was bright and brisk and cheerful this morning. 'She falls into a river – and you know what those deadly little fish are like at the smell of blood.'

'Too quick,' said Erwin. 'No suspense. All over too damn fast.'

'Maggots,' said the writer gloomily, sure that nobody would pay the slightest attention.

Ronnie nodded. 'She's buried alive.' It had just come to him. Beyond Erwin's shoulder, through the window and through another window on the far side of the street, he saw a girl in a crisp white blouse at a typewriter, laughing and talking to someone else in the room. Such a fresh, eager look about her; such a fresh feel about the whole day. 'Buried alive,' he said, 'and the earth is pressing against her exposed body. Earth . . . roots . . . maggots.' The idea flourished, sprouted, put forth beautiful buds. 'What goes on in her mind? Perhaps there's a medium – someone psychically in touch with the girl, reporting on every sensation. She starts living it out, living through it all, here above the ground, before our very eyes. She becomes *possessed* by the terror of the girl below the ground – and we know the girl is dead when we see the medium slowly starting to decay although she's still alive. Or something on those lines.'

'Not before she's carried out a revenge on the girl's killer,' contributed Erwin.

The writer shifted in his chair and looked sceptical. But the others reacted with a growing delight that one could almost feel.

'Playing on people's nerve endings,' said Robbie. And he added: 'We could call it *Creep Flesh, Creep*.'

'I like that,' said Erwin. 'Yes, I'll buy that. Now, look, I think we've got something here. The way I see it . . .'

They listened for ten minutes to the way Erwin saw it, and then they all began to contribute. And now it began to work; it made sense.

That evening Robbie went home late and jubilant. He hummed to himself as he went into the mews. In a minor key, of course – it was more appropriate.

He was fascinated to observe how Doreen's texture had changed and how the colouring had staled and darkened. She was still alive; but, he estimated, only just.

After a drink and a light supper he set about disposing of what might, he thought wryly, be referred to as his raw material.

He wrapped Doreen in some old sacking and loaded her into his car. The texture of the sacking might rasp on her, but the sensation could not last for very long.

The road was a familiar one. He had driven along it in darkness several times before. He headed out beyond Slough and down a long, gentle slope to the vast dump under the trees. For years now there had been a growing chaos of discarded cars here. It amounted now to three or four acres of rusted metal, rotten seats and cushions, old tyres, shattered glass, crumpled boxes and cartons. Every now and then someone complained to the local authorities and asked when something was going to be done about this eyesore. It had grown so large and intractable that the authorities seemed unlikely ever to tackle it now.

Robbie carried what was left of Doreen into the sombre heart of the metal graveyard. He buried her and pulled some ragged strips of rusted corrugated iron over the newly-turned earth. Then he drove home, relaxed and fulfilled, planning new possibilities to suggest to Erwin the next day.

His ideas were so successful that at one stage the writer went out of the room to be sick. Robbie had watched writers like this come and go. They all wanted to be paid for doing something they wanted to do instead of working on what they had been commissioned to do. This youngster really longed to write pessimistic sociological scripts about the doomed passions of young lovers in a materialistic, stagnating world; but he had to force himself to make money out of any kind of writing job he could get in order to support the wife he had acquired and the two children they had produced in some of his less doom-laden moments.

While waiting for him to return, Robbie said to the casting director, 'As a matter of interest, what do you find most frightening?'

'Dealing with agents.'

'And what about you, Robbie?' asked Erwin jovially.

'Mm?'

'Come on, boy – give. What about your own custom-built nightmare?'

Robbie ought to have expected this at some time or other, but was caught off balance. He glared. Erwin Hodek or no Erwin Hodek, he glared.

Erwin gulped and forced a grin. 'Okay,' he said. 'Sorry I asked.'

The writer came back, they all laughed like hell at his ashen face, and the discussion went on.

Things shaped up well. The writer was sent home to get it all down on paper. Robbie set to work on some roughs. It was all so lucid in his head that he resented the time that would now have to be spent on detailed work, on wrangles with technicians, on the whole protracted business of getting the picture moving. Robbie thought with his eyes, and so far as he was concerned the thinking was finished. The picture existed in his mind – complete and perfect. All the rest was at best routine and at worst drudgery.

In the middle of the third week after Erwin had given the thumbs-up sign, Robbie had a visitor.

He was lying on the couch with a book of engravings from an old manual of mediaeval tortures, contentedly sipping a glass of brandy, when the buzzer sounded. It was unusual for anyone to call on him in the late evening unless specially invited. He went grudgingly to the door.

Under the light stood a young man with shaggy hair, a blunt chin, broad shoulders and a grubby raincoat.

With no hint of a potential welcome, Robbie said, 'Yes?'

The young man said: 'I'm Doreen's brother.'

'Oh?' Robbie had not thought of Doreen for more than a week and did not even have to feign indifference. 'I didn't know she had a brother.'

'What have you done with her?'

Robbie's neighbours had never disturbed him and he had no wish to disturb them in the slightest degree. Quietness, seclusion and near-anonymity had suited him very well. He stood aside and waved the young man in.

In the confidently individual style of Robbie's sitting room, the visitor looked a trifle less sure of himself. He wouldn't sit down and he wouldn't have a drink. He shifted his weight from one foot to another. Weighty but not dangerous, thought Robbie.

'Where's Doreen?'

'I'm afraid I have no idea.'

'She's been living with you.'

'Until a few weeks ago. Then she went away.'

'Where to?'

'I've told you. I simply do not know.'

The young man growled, 'She didn't tell me she was thinking of leaving.'

'Perhaps she wasn't in the habit of confiding in you.'

'She told me everything.'

'Everything? Rather indiscreet of her – and somewhat distasteful.'

'I want to know where she is. She wouldn't have disappeared without saying a word to me.'

'But that's precisely what she has done.'

The young man shook his head doggedly. He was vague but

stubborn. But still, Robbie was sure, not dangerous. He knew nothing and could prove nothing.

'We met once a week. Always. Never missed.'

'She didn't tell me.' Robbie kept it light. 'She was obviously a girl of many secrets.' He gave this time to sink in, then moved a hint of a pace towards the door.

Automatically the baffled young man turned, and then it was easy for Robbie to shepherd him to the front door.

Outside, in the mews, there was a final protest. 'I don't like it. There's something fishy about it.'

'It was never what you'd call a permanent arrangement, you know. If she told you everything, as you claim,' said Robbie with what he conceived to be the right flicker of disdain, 'you must be well aware that the relationship was for . . . ah . . . our mutual convenience. And now she has gone.'

'If ever I find out . . .'

But there was no way of finishing the sentence. Doreen's brother hadn't even a glimmering of what there might be to find out. He wavered for a moment, then stamped away over the cobbles.

He wouldn't go to the police. He wouldn't do anything, because there was nothing to do.

The picture gathered momentum. The girl whom Erwin had fancied for the lead was free at the right time after all; the production manager set up locations in the spring, and the weather was good; shooting started, and the writer was paid off on the first day of shooting and went home to write a bleak novel about corruption in the movie world.

The rushes looked good. The first rough cut showed up a few holes, which Robbie plugged with some spontaneous, grisly sequences. The next cut sent Erwin into ecstasies.

'Fabulous. This is the greatest. After this, the distribution deal I can set up for the next one . . .'

Already there was a next one. They were talking about it, tossing gimmicks to and fro, when a local authority some thirty miles from London decided to clear an old car dump and encourage development of the reclaimed land.

Robbie, like most people in the business, read nothing but

trade papers, the Sunday critics, and material directly related to the job in hand. He therefore knew nothing of this
clearance scheme until the doorman at the office mentioned it
to Erwin's chauffeur, who told Erwin, who brought it up with
relish at a story conference.

'Now, there's a fantastic idea. It's made for us. All we have
to do is figure out a motive. It's all there – by God, I'll say it's
all there. A whole cache of bodies – or what's left of 'em –
under a great heap of clapped-out automobiles. How did they
get there? One guy or several? And some of the things that
happened to those corpses . . . *man!*'

Erwin raised his arms in gratitude to the gods for such a
gift.

The find had indeed been a spectacular one. There were the
remains of a male body which had, according to the pathologist's findings, been hanged, drawn and quartered. There was
another similar one where the subject appeared to have committed hara-kiri . . . or to have had a similar disembowelling
forced upon him. A flayed, decomposing corpse of a young
woman had been dumped on top of several dead dogs
and cats, killed in various ways. There were other
limbs and fragments marked in ways which the pathologist
could not identify or, possibly, was at this stage unwilling to
publish.

Robbie could have explained them all.

There was one they didn't mention. He wondered if they
had found it yet – the man on whom he had experimented for
the sake of that Viking film Erwin had made. The spread-
eagle of Danish savagery . . . the chest ripped open and the
rib-cage forced open and outwards. Set against the sinister
background of the Suffolk coast, that had been quite a taut
little thriller.

'Can you imagine the kind of guy who'd do that kind of
thing?' raved Erwin exultantly.

The casting director looked at Robbie and went pale. It
looked as though he could, at a pinch, imagine the kind of guy.
But Robbie doubted that he would ever come out and say
anything about it.

On the way home that evening he didn't hum and he wasn't altogether happy; but neither was he unduly worried. There was nothing to lead the police or anyone else to him. Just that if some little thing went wrong, some fidgety little rumour started, it could be annoying for a while.

He put his key in the front door and walked in. And a bulky shadow launched itself abruptly from the far side of the mews, charged against him, and hurled him along the passage.

'What the hell . . .?'

Doreen's brother manhandled him on into the sitting room with one large, meaty hand. In the other hand he swung a small black bag.

Robbie tried still to keep it light, as ever. He had nothing to fear. Nobody could prove a thing. He said, 'You look like a plumber. Or a doctor with his little black bag.'

'A doctor,' said the young man.

'I didn't know.'

'You're always telling me a lot of things you don't know,' said the young man. 'And actually' – his hand was clamped on Robbie's arm – 'there are plenty of things I don't know. Even as a doctor. Haven't finished my training yet. I've got a lot to learn.'

'Haven't we all? A real professional never stops learning.'

'Experiment helps. Isn't that so? Experiment,' said Doreen's brother furiously. And his arm went back and swung forward, and knocked Robbie into a corner.

Robbie whimpered. Before he could scramble to his feet, the young man had whipped a length of rope round him and fastened his wrists painfully behind his back.

'You can't . . .'

A grubby cloth was stuffed into his mouth.

Robbie lay on the floor, struggling impotently, while the young man prowled through the house. His footsteps receded, came back, went away again. Robbie heard him trying various doors; heard him rattle at the workroom door.

He came back and probed into Robbie's pockets. When he had found the keys he set off again. Robbie heard the work-room door open.

There was a long pause. Then the young man came back again.

He stood over Robbie and looked down at him. 'I think I can guess now what you did to Doreen.'

Robbie tried to mumble through his gag, but the young man had no intention of listening.

'Yes, it's pretty clear.' He hauled Robbie to his feet and shook him slowly, incredulously. 'You've got a diseased mind. You know that? A diseased mind. And your eyes . . . they're not so healthy.'

He began to propel Robbie, stumbling, along the passage. The workroom door was open. The light was on. They lurched into the room. Robbie heard the door slam behind them, and then his legs were kicked away from under him and he was swung dexterously up on to the bench.

'There's no way of bringing Doreen back. But I'm an old-fashioned type. An eye for an eye . . .' The young man laughed harshly. 'That's so appropriate.'

Robbie began to sweat. It couldn't be true. It was coincidence, this young fool couldn't possibly know, couldn't mean what those words might just possibly, hideously have meant.

'She told me everything,' said Doreen's brother. 'Told me you talked in your sleep. Mr Sennidge – that's a nasty nightmare you keep having.'

There was the click of a catch. Robbie knew that he was opening his bag.

And still he wasn't going to believe. He wasn't. The nightmare couldn't come true. On film, in the mind, yes . . . all things were possible. But not really; not here and now.

'I'm going to give you a local anaesthetic. Not to save you pain – you can have the pain later, and welcome to it. But without an anaesthetic you might pass out, and that would never do: I want you to be conscious of exactly what's happening.'

No, said Robbie inside his head. No, he screamed without a sound coming out.

He closed his eyes. But the young man's hard fingers forced them open; and there was the jab of a hypodermic; and something cold and metallic was forced into place, and he couldn't close his eyes. A slow numbness crept over them.

The young man leaned forward. There was a flash of steel under the light.

'Before your very eyes,' said Doreen's brother.

Not true, not true, not true. It *had* to be just another nightmare, like all the others. Soon he would lash out with one foot and kick the blankets away and he would be sweating in his own bed, not stretched out on this bench with the cold moisture running down his forehead and over his nose.

'So proud of your eyes,' said the steady, ugly voice. A voice so like Doreen's. 'So acute. So sensitive. I'm told you have the reputation of thinking with your eyes. Doreen told me how you worried about them. That dream . . . King Lear, Oedipus, the lot. And the pain. But this won't hurt. Not right away.'

Robbie tried to kick out with one foot.

'If you wriggle,' said the young man, 'I shall make a real mess of it, I'm afraid.' He bent closer, and the blade shone again in the light. 'You know, I haven't finished my training. I'm going to be awfully clumsy as it is. But there's one consolation . . .' The blade was less than half an inch from Robbie's left eye, quite obscuring his vision now. 'When they find you,' said Doreen's brother, 'think of the really fabulous idea it'll give your Mr Hodek for his next picture.'

The blade descended.

THE BOY WHO NEGLECTED HIS GRASS SNAKE

Tim Stout

PLEASE DON'T misunderstand me. I'm very fond of snakes. Fond of all reptiles, in fact. There are usually several of one sort or another in the glass tanks in my house and there's not one I would exchange for a dog or cat. You can keep Rover and Tibbles – I'd pick something with scales every time.

Which is why telling this story makes me feel a little guilty. Not that anyone with any sense would attach any blame for what happened to the snake concerned, because I think it is clear enough who was at fault. No, the reason I feel apprehensive is that most people are funny about snakes. They get ideas about slimy skins and being stung to death; mention a snake in a story and at once it's cast as a menace. Nobody stops to wonder if it could be anything else. Now I can't deny that the one I'm going to tell you about seems to have been responsible for some decidedly foul play. At first glance, that is. All I ask is that you should be fair-minded about the whole business and I think you will see that far from being the villain of the piece the snake was the victim of inexcusable neglect and that it did no more than take a well justified revenge.

But to my story. I suppose that I myself am as good a starting point as any. Certainly it is no use pretending I was not indirectly responsible for what happened. My name is Rodney Drummond and, as I said, I go in for reptiles. Not professionally – I'm in insurance, and there is little room for snakes in that line of country. No, I'm an amateur herpetologist, and if you care to consult a Greek dictionary you'll be able to work out exactly how that comes to mean 'a student of crawling things'. Lizards, toads, crocodiles, tortoises – things like that. Snakes, too, of course.

And naturally, since I'm interested in these animals, there are some in captivity in my home. An unused bedroom on the ground floor makes an admirable place in which to house the tanks and cages acquired over the years and several additional points have been installed to provide adequate heating and lighting for their inmates. The tanks line the walls of the room and apart from a desk and a swivel chair the place is otherwise bare.

I had been keeping reptiles for some years when I first met Bill Cater. This is not the place to describe the stag party we attended together nor the post-closing time chase in which we finally got away from a pursuing police car. It is enough to say that we got to know each other well and in more mature years often went round to each other's house to spend evenings together.

When he married his young French teacher and my own affaire broke up I expected to see less of him but things didn't work out that way. For some time our meetings were less frequent and then, after his son passed out of the nappy stage, he started to come round again. Our friendship picked up from where we had let it lapse.

It is Bill's son Trevor that I particularly want to talk about. He was the most irritating, smug little boy I have ever come across and regardless of the way he went I could not be more pleased that I will not be called upon to see him again. Bill doted on him. I suppose that was the trouble. And when the boy was old enough he began to bring Trevor with him on his visits. Perhaps an account of our first encounter will show what a little wretch he was.

It was early one Friday evening and I had just returned from London with a new acquisition, a South American caiman. I'll explain – a caiman is a member of the order Loricata, and is very similar to an alligator. There are some differences, but for practical purposes the two animals are the same. This is especially true of young individuals, and the specimen I had purchased was a little under a foot long.

In the reptile room I had set up a long, water-tight tank with an inch of water and a retreat-cum-island made out of small slabs of sandstone. This was heated by an overhead two hundred watt bulb, which I hoped would push the water temperature up to seventy-eight degrees.

I sat at the desk, eating some fish and chips bought on my way home and hunting through the reference books beside my plate. The point I was trying to establish was whether the caiman should be fed every day or every two days. In its tank by the wall it lay motionless under the light, not caring twopence about being fed and only interested in building up its body heat after the long, cold journey from Camden Town.

The bell rang, and I went to open the front door. Two visitors stood there. Bill I had been half-expecting but not the boy with him. Tight grey trousers gripped his burgeoning paunch, and his pullover spread comfortably across his pillow-sized tummy. Puffy pink cheeks and a generous portion of double chin surrounded his supercilious little eyes, which slid over me and then looked away.

Bill placed his hands on the boy's well-upholstered shoulders.

'This is Trevor,' he said, and I could see he thought his son was the eighth wonder of the world. 'Say hello to Uncle Rodney, Trevor.'

'Hello, Uncle Rodney,' said Trevor with all the boredom and indifference he could muster.

'Glad to meet you, Trevor,' I said, thinking otherwise. 'Hang up your coats, Bill, and come on through.'

As I went into the reptile room I heard Trevor's piercing whisper 'Daddy, when can we go?'

In a few moments we were together again. Bill looked about with interest, searching for any new arrivals. Trevor gazed silently at the tank-lined walls, and I noticed with pleasure that his heavy features were losing some of their previous glumness. I took them over to the caiman's tank. It was still lying directly beneath the powerful bulb, immobile but alert.

'What is it?' Trevor asked baldly.

I didn't think it worthwhile to go into the biological differences that made it what it was just for the benefit of a rude little boy.

'It's a baby alligator,' I replied. 'I only got it today and it's feeling a bit uneasy in this new tank so be careful not to talk loudly or disturb it.'

'Where did you get it?' Bill asked with interest.

'The dealer in Camden Town,' I told him. 'Near London Zoo, where I bought the sun-gazer lizards.'

He knew where I meant since he had several times accompanied me on visits to the shop and he listened while I gave him an idea of the rest of the stock that I had seen. In enumerating the other animals I forgot Trevor until he spoke again.

'It's not an alligator, it's a caiman,' he said flatly. 'Why did you say it was an alligator? Did you think it was? Well, it isn't.'

He was standing beside the desk and I realized with chagrin that he had been looking at my books. One of them had been open at a colour plate that clearly showed the difference between the two reptiles. He must have been astute enough to have gathered from the illustration that I had misled him.

'I knew very well what it was,' I said abruptly. 'I didn't want to go into the rather technical reasons why a caiman is not an alligator.'

He said nothing. In the face of his reproving silence I felt a fool and proceeded to act like one.

'The skull of a caiman,' I began pompously, 'differs from that of an alligator—'

'Oh, I know now,' he interrupted. 'I've just read it here.'

Bill saw that his son was doing a very good job of rubbing me up the wrong way and halted the conversation by leading Trevor over to another tank. He finally settled down with a set of old colour prints I had taken in Africa years ago, and Bill and I talked of this and that. Time passed as it does until I gradually became aware of a splashing from the caiman's tank on the other side of the room. I swung round in my seat. The little blighter had his hand inside and was teasing the animal, which was throwing itself up from the water in an attempt to bite the pudgy, pestering fingers.

'Stop that!' I called out sharply.

He jerked up and his arm caught the light housing suspended

over the tank. The bulb fell in, struck one of the rocks and exploded.

I ran to the tank and peered in. The caiman had hurtled out of sight into the artificial cave.

'That was a stupid thing to do,' I said furiously. 'I told you not to disturb it, didn't I?'

Bill, I was pleased to see, was almost as angry as I was. While he went for him as only a father can I left the room to fetch a bucket and syphon in order to remove the broken glass from the tank's gravel bottom. When I returned they were putting on their coats.

'I'm awfully sorry, Rod,' said Bill. 'It'll be all right, won't it?'

My friend wasn't to blame for his son's stupidity.

'Don't worry,' I reassured him. 'It may stay off its food for a day or two but there's no real harm done. At least I know now that it's healthy and active – did you see the way it went for his fingers?'

A moment later they were on their way out of the front garden. The next morning, the caiman had recovered sufficiently to gulp down a dead mouse and, later, draw blood from my own hand when I tried to pick it up.

I've related this incident in some detail in order to show what a cruel, insufferable youngster he was, the kind that was bound to come to a sticky end. If I had remembered this later perhaps he would not have come to a sticky end – at least, not so soon. I don't think I need say very much more about him . . . I remember accompanying him and his parents to the zoo, where he tried to press all manner of indigestible rubbish on the caged animals and infuriated me by thumping the showcases in the reptile house to make the occupants move. There was another time when he swung a kitten by the tail . . . And all the while – unaccountably, since I am afraid he must have seen how I disliked the boy – Bill kept bringing Trevor along on his visits.

The events I want to talk about began, I suppose, the day I acquired a grass snake. A tame follow-up to a caiman, you may think, but the fact is that I had not kept any kind of snake for some months. It was not a purchase but a gift from a local farmer and according to him it had had a tangle with a hedgehog. I could see for myself that it was pretty badly cut about. Naturally I did what I could to clean the wounds and afterwards quiet, warmth and food were all I could offer the snake. Anticipating a visit from Bill and his confounded progeny I placed the tank in the kitchen where no one would disturb it.

They paid me several calls during the snake's convalescence but I neither mentioned nor produced the patient. The first they knew about it was four or five weeks later, when I judged it well enough to be transferred into one of the reptile room tanks.

Trevor spotted the new item straightaway.

'What's in there, Daddy?' he asked Bill. Since our first meeting he had never addressed me if he could help it.

I told him. As I have already said, there had been no snakes in my collection lately and I doubt if the boy had ever seen one outside the Zoo's Reptile House.

'Can I see it, Daddy, please?' he wheedled.

Since it had healed well and could be handled without mishap I took it out of the tank. It slipped quickly through my fingers, and the head and neck swung out from my hand like a slender twig swaying in the breeze. The dark, yellow-rimmed eyes were bright and clear and the delicate tip of the tail slid daintily over the palm of my hand.

Trevor gazed studiously at it. I squatted down beside him, pleased to find someone with such admirable first reactions towards a snake.

'Can I hold it?' he asked.

'You mustn't make any sudden movements,' I warned him, and placing our hands together I let the snake transfer itself from my fingers to his.

He was certainly very interested. I showed him how to turn his hands in a continuous platform and he quickly found the knack of supporting the ever-moving reptile. Then he began to ask me questions.

I told him about the snake's tongue, the wonderful organ that appears to do the work of both smelling and tasting, and

T—E

the twin Jacobson's organs into which the tips of the tongue transmit their sensory reports. I pointed out the distinctive yellow collar by which the cautious can tell the harmless grass snake from the poisonous adder, and I showed him the big belly scales which help the snake move along. He wanted to know about the specimen's recent injuries so I indicated the uneven scale formations where the lacerations had been.

Then, anxious that he should not become sentimental about one of Nature's most efficient killer mechanisms, I got him to look at the unfeeling, remorseless eyes and to gauge the power of the restless length of muscle forming the body. I described how a snake lies absolutely motionless in wait for its prey, and showed him with my own twitching hand the deficiencies of human muscular control. He asked about a snake's methods of feeding, and I talked about the vast meals swallowed whole, the ensuing period of digestion, the onslaught of returning hunger and finally the cold, slithery hunt in search of further prey.

I put the snake back in the tank, but his interest did not abate. We looked at pictures of a snake's skull and he saw that the sharp, recurved teeth ruled out the possibility of escape for anything caught behind them. At last, after a moment's consideration, I brought out some horrendous colour photographs of the ingestion of a captured frog by a large grass snake.

'Look at it,' I said, pointing to the frog's large blank eyes. 'It is resigned to its fate. It is very unusual for a snake's victim to offer much resistance.'

He listened with surprising attentiveness to all I had to say and it was with decidedly more cordial feelings that I said goodbye to him and Bill when the time came for them to leave. Surely, I said to myself as I turned down the reptile room lighting and heating for the night, good sense such as he had shown in the matter of snakes outweighed a lot that might be said against Trevor.

A few days passed and I saw Bill again, on his own. It soon developed that he wanted my help about his present for Trevor's forthcoming birthday. Apparently, since I had shown him the grass snake, he had done nothing but plead with his father for one for himself. Could I get one for him, Bill wanted to know. He and his wife would certainly have no objection to their son having such a pet provided I gave instructions on how to look after it.

I was pleased, naturally; as I have said, such enthusiasm as Trevor's is rare. But in my readiness to help my friend I forgot other things I had heard Bill mention before – the now neglected train set, outcome of a fortnight's persistent grizzling; the scale model yacht that Trevor had stuffed away in the loft after it had barely wet its hull; and the puppy that had to be put to sleep to save it from further cruelty at the hands of its irritable 'owner'. I did not, as I say, remember these things at the time. I told Bill I would get him a snake for his son's birthday.

I didn't anticipate any difficulty in keeping my promise. One warm, sunny Saturday I drove out to some fishing grounds, a series of three small lakes five or six miles out of town, where the fish and frog population was a powerful attraction for all the grass snakes in the vicinity. After fifteen minutes of strolling by the water's edge I spotted a fair-sized specimen basking on the gunwales of a derelict punt. It led me a bit of a chase for a minute or two and then fell victim to the curiosity of its kind and I was able to bag it. It was easily two feet long, a thick, squirming beauty. I took it home and two days later went with Bill to the local pet shop where we chose a tank for it. We arranged the tank together and I gave him a small supply of baby frogs that would be ample food supply for some weeks, until Trevor had arranged to obtain food himself. And that, so far as I was concerned, was that.

Bill came round the day after the birthday. He told me how it had gone and it seemed that Trevor had said and done everything suitable to the occasion and had intoned the appropriate responses of gratitude. The snake was doing fine and had eaten one of the frogs.

'That's a good sign,' I told Bill, and relaxed. 'If it's eating there's nothing to worry about.'

And I didn't worry. For a fortnight after that I found myself kept very busy by my job, since the firm had been asked by the Press to prepare detailed lists giving comparisons between the different classes of policyholders. I didn't see anything of Bill or Trevor which was just as well since I got home tired and sleepy most evenings. I assumed that the snake was doing well in captivity but to be honest I didn't waste much thought on it.

In fact I don't believe I wondered about the snake at all until the day I met Bill in the High Street. He was pleased to see me; apparently he had tried to look me up several times but on each occasion I had still been in London. I told him how things had been. Then he said the snake was not as lively as it had been – could I come round some time and have a look at it? Trevor was worried and couldn't think what to do. You mean you're worried and Trevor can't be bothered to do anything, I surmised, reading between the lines. I agreed to go round the following day, when Bill said he thought his son might be at home.

Anticipating what the trouble was likely to be, I stopped at a hardware shop on the way to Bill's house and there bought a hundred watt bulb. There are very few snake problems that cannot be solved by extra heat and light. Trevor was out when I arrived, I didn't ask why.

Bill took me into the boy's room, where the tank had been placed, and as soon as I saw it I regretted ever having consented to furnish Trevor with a pet. The water bowl had not been cleaned out or refilled, the gravel and peat floor was fouled with the snake's droppings and the sides of the tank were almost opaque with dirt. Much more serious was the absence of a light in the canopy; the thermometer I had stuck on the side was registering fifty-five degrees Fahrenheit, a temperature that would make any snake sluggish. It was fairly obvious that what I had mistaken for genuine enthusiasm on Trevor's part had been no more than a passing craze that had quickly burned itself out.

I found the snake itself coiled up behind the water bowl, thin and dispirited.

'Do you know when he last gave it anything to eat? I asked Bill.

'No,' he answered. 'I suppose he's been feeding it on the frogs you gave us. I haven't seen him put one in, though. Marie might know.'

He went off to ask his wife while I inserted the bulb I had brought with me and placed the snake back in the tank. With any luck, I thought, the heat might restore its appetite – though that would be little good if there was nothing on hand to appease it.

Bill came back holding the tin in which I had put the frogs. The perforated lid was missing.

'It seems that a lot of them got away,' he said awkwardly. 'The top wasn't put back on properly after he took out the first one.'

I took it from him and rummaged around amongst the clumps of moss inside. The tin was empty.

'You say he only gave it one of them?' I said. 'Bill, a snake this size can't last long on one tiny frog. It's been a matter of weeks now.'

I spoke with some feeling. Bill should have had more control over Trevor's irresponsibility.

'I didn't know they had all gone,' he said, and I saw that he felt he was to blame.

'Bill,' I went on, 'this is sheer callousness on Trevor's part, I'm afraid. A snake is rather different from us, you know. It can't forget hunger by reading or going out for a walk. A snake is a predatory machine that exists to find and eat food. Having to do without for this long will have caused it serious discomfort. You really must make Trevor understand that, you know, if you expect the snake to stay alive.'

I said rather more – afterwards I felt guilty at having let fly at Bill when it was Trevor who was to blame – and left Bill's house soon afterwards, after giving him the name of a shop where small newts and frogs were usually on sale. Certainly I had no intention of procuring a second supply. Trevor could obtain and pay for it himself this time.

What happened next is quickly told. About a week later,

not having seen or heard from Bill, I called round one evening to find out how the snake was doing. As I walked up the garden path the windows of Trevor's room faced me and I noticed there was no light in the tank. Once again, Trevor was out and Bill was in.

This time I didn't go and look in the tank. There was no point. From Bill I learned that Trevor had never troubled to go to the shop I had suggested, the inevitable result had taken place and the limp body had been thrown into the dustbin. I didn't spare Bill this time; I told him just what I thought of his son. He took it for a while without saying very much but was finally stung to retort and we did not part on good terms.

The conclusion of the story is something I cannot explain. Indeed, since it took place, I have tried not to think about it and I am currently making plans to move away from the district. A rational explanation could be, I suppose, and probably has been fashioned by officials concerned. Luckily I have not been caught up in anything of that sort, so I cannot say for sure how plausible it sounded. Doubtless something reasonable was concocted which everyone accepted without question.

I'll never be able to do that: I'll never be able to forget the discovery that suggested the truth of the matter to me, and as far as I know nobody shares my knowledge.

I cannot prove the theory I put forward. You may think, as I do, that the final indication is sufficient corroboration. Or you may not. Maybe some will decide that I have an exceptionally macabre imagination and so dismiss what I say. So be it; I can hardly blame them and perhaps after all it would be for the best. I like snakes and would wish others to feel the same. But I must not let that deter me from describing, as far as I can, what really happened to the boy Trevor after his pet snake starved to death.

It died, or at any rate was found dead, on the morning of the day on which I went to see Bill. Like a length of slim, olive-green rope it lay on the gravel beside the water bowl, probably having expired on a last, desperate search for something to eat. Marie, Bill's wife, saw it there when she went into Trevor's room to make his bed. When he returned to the house for dinner she told him about it and, as might have been expected, the boy showed little interest or guilt. During the meal Bill asked him to bury it in the garden and he made some noncommittal reply. Later he repeated his request several times, with no result, until the bad-tempered little boy flung the dead snake into the dustbin and flounced out of the house. He came back late in the evening and settled himself in front of the television. Bill tried to make some reproving remarks but was drowned out by the blaring programme. The family stayed before the screen for three hours until eleven o'clock when Trevor, having seen all he wanted, allowed his parents to send him to bed.

From then on I cannot be sure of the sequence of events. I can do no more than draw on my specialized knowledge to make deductions and intelligent guesses but I am fairly certain that what I describe or something very much like it actually took place within Trevor's bedroom after the shadows had lengthened and everyone had settled down for the night. It must have been horrible beyond endurance, but I am afraid that it is the truth.

Trevor, I should imagine from his appearance, was a heavy sleeper. He drowsed off quite soon after turning in, untroubled by any thoughts about the death of the snake. Short but fat he lay in the bed in his striped pyjamas, his plump, unruffled face protruding from between the sheets.

It is impossible to say what time it began. The fact that Bill and Marie were not disturbed suggests it was after midnight, but perhaps they could not have heard anything in any case. The disturbance may have been of such a nature that it could be experienced by Trevor alone. Clearly it was an unearthly, unnatural thing that happened within the room that night.

I think I can guess what roused Trevor. It was not the sudden crash of the dustbin lid, heaved up off the bin until it toppled sideways and fell onto the ground. If he had understood the significance of that sound he would have leaped from his bed, quit the house and run for his life. But he didn't

– he may have dimly heard the clatter, stirred and turned over, but he went back to sleep again. He had two or three minutes' grace before he was disturbed again.

I believe I have said already that I was once in Trevor's room. On that occasion I observed that all the windows faced the same way. Above the large panes were two ventilators that were always kept open on the first notch, leaving a gap of a few inches between ventilator and frame. What woke Trevor was the noise of something trying to widen the gap so that it could come through and get in the room with him.

Like the constant miaowing of a cat that wants to be let in from the windowsill, the sounds went on and on relentlessly. It was this that eventually made him open his eyes and sleepily lever himself up on the pillow to find out the cause.

Did he see it rightaway, I wonder? Or did he lie paralysed with fear until the catch was nudged away, the window pushed up and the visitor's head appeared, a huge, wedge-shaped shadow that filled the ventilator frame?

I see it all – the head came farther into the room, firmly supported by the muscular, olive-green coils steadily following behind. It was looking for another base of support and it moved onto the top of the tall bookcase at the foot of the bed.

Perhaps Trevor screamed, but I doubt it. I think he stayed where he was, sweating with terror, without making a sound. Perhaps he huddled silently up, hoping to shield himself in the warm, safe darkness under the bed clothes.

The body kept coming in through the ventilator, sliding over the sill like a sinister, flexible cable. The head slid slowly round the side of the room, sounding out the unfamiliar objects with a glistening, yard-long tongue.

When its whole length had heaved through the window and dropped onto the floor it gathered itself in a corner and coiled up to take in the contents of the room. Its sense, sharpened by enforced fast, told it plainly that prey was at hand, lurking within the bed.

I visualize the dark, yellow-rimmed eyes, big as a man's

fist, filled with terrible hunger, unquenchable in this world. I picture the great head beginning to slide forward from the stacked coils and nearing the bed.

A hunting snake normally studies its victim for some seconds before its sudden, savage strike. But this spectral devil-snake had been waiting a long time and, caught between the sheets, the boy was unable to escape. I see it poised over his pillow like a mother about to kiss her child good night. Trevor makes one panic-stricken movement, and then I try not to think any more.

A lot of fanciful nonsense, you think? Perhaps I should relate my ideas to a psychiatrist? I have made no mention of what I feel until now.

And no one save me knows that inside the dustbin in which they found Trevor are the distended remnants of his pet snake – strewn round the boy's body as though the two-foot reptile had once contained it.

JOLLY UNCLE

Lindsay Stewart

WHEN GRANDMOTHER Mason died, it was with a sigh of relief. Since her son Ralph and his wife Chloe had drowned in Jamaica a year ago, she had been burdened with the upbringing of their nasty child, her grandson, Mason. What a silly woman Chloe had been, despite all her money, and fancy giving a child a name like Mason! Mason Mason, how ridiculous. But now she was free from the vicious little terror who had strangled her Pekinese, Chubby, plucked her budgie, Chirp, and broken her vase, Ming. And now it was all up to Clive, her eldest and dearest son, Mason's uncle. Clive, that angel in human raiment, had taken it upon himself to care for the child. Not that he was doing it for peanuts. Grandmother Mason had allowed Clive ten pounds a week for Mason. Mason would receive the rest of Ralph and Chloe's money when he was twenty-one. Of course, the money would go to Clive, should the child die. Granny's eyes twinkled. Dear Clive, how he loved children! And, with that thought she turned her face to the wall.

When Grandmother Mason had been buried under a gross marble monument in Brompton Cemetery, Uncle Clive and Mason moved into a tall terraced house near Regent's Park, which had been bought from a distant cousin who had emigrated. Mason, who hated animals, loathed being so near to the Zoo, for at night he could hear the raucous screaming of the birds and the roar of tigers, which frightened him. Uncle Clive thoughtfully moved Mason's bedroom up to the attic, farther away from the night noises. Despite this consideration, Mason disliked the attic even more than his second floor room. The attic had night noises of its own. There were many dark shadows there, many rattling and creaking noises. Uncle

Clive said Mason was too old to have a night light, so the latter went to bed quivering every night.

Uncle Clive was a fat, jolly man with plump rosy cheeks, who always wore clothes too small for him. He was sixty-five years old and had spent most of his life making and losing vast fortunes in the Persian Gulf. When he returned from abroad three years ago he brought with him a captain's chest full of mysterious African symbols, of trinkets, medicines and magic. There had been a rumour that there was even a shrunken head which could blink its eyes. But there was no money. Uncle Clive existed on his old-age pension, the odd win at the race track, and Mason's allowance, all of which he spent in five minutes flat. Most of the time Clive and Mason Mason lived on Mason's school dinners, which the child could sometimes manage to smuggle home in brown paper bags. And every other day, Uncle Clive would write a begging letter to the distant cousin who had gone to Greenland after his wife had committed suicide in a mental hospital; as a result a postal order for six pounds three and fourpence would arrive once every two months.

Clive was the only person that Mason thought he had ever loved. He had looked upon his father and mother with contempt, so much so that it had been hinted at the inquest upon their death that he had deliberately omitted to tell his parents of the radio warning of an approaching hurricane. Mr and Mrs Mason went as usual for their afternoon canoe trip around the island, and were never seen again. (A shark had been found later with human remains in its stomach, but they were too well-digested for any identification.)

Clive at sixty-five years of age and Mason at six were an odd couple. Both of them were deeply fascinated by crime and detective stories, so every week Uncle Clive would take Mason on a tour of the more unsavoury parts of London where the most brutal of murders had been committed. They would stand at the scene of some ghastly crime while Uncle Clive would describe in detail how each murder was committed, and give lecturettes upon the latest fashions in body disposal. Owing to this, Mason Mason developed a stupendous imagination. In his attic room at night he would lie in his bed and conjure up the most horrible but delicious visions of tortures and murders. He would play this game for hours until it went back on him: black wooden rafters began to squirm and wriggle like pythons. Rats appeared round each bend in the oddly-shaped room, and every night he would lie awake until the small hours of the morning, trembling at the sound of things that went Bump in the night. His fantasies were endless, following him from the night into the day. One afternoon he was sent home from school wih a note from his headmaster telling Uncle Clive that his nephew might profitably visit a psychiatrist. Uncle Clive took no notice of this advice, but, strangely enough, appeared only to encourage the child in his dreaming. He did, however, take Mason Mason to a doctor for a medical check-up. 'How kind of Uncle,' thought Mason, 'to take such trouble over my health!' The doctor, whose bedside manner was known in that district to be somewhat lacking except when applied to young ladies, shook his head in consternation and said, 'Hum.'

'Is there something wrong with the boy?' asked Uncle Clive eagerly.

Mason overheard the stage-whispered conversation: suddenly he felt quite ill. 'In my opinion this child will not live very long unless he takes extremely good care of himself. There is a defect in his heart. He must take part in no athletics, and above all, you must take great care to see that emotional stress of any kind is avoided. Here are some pills which may help. The directions are on the bottle. I'll send you my bill.'

The child and his uncle gave each other a long, long look. 'Poor little lad,' said Uncle Clive loudly, patting Mason on the head. Uncle Clive pocketed the pills, and that was the last Mason saw of them.

Mason Mason might have been a disagreeable boy but he was not a stupid one. The vanishing of his heart pills made him realize that something odd was going on: with every day that passed he began to regard Uncle Clive with increased suspicion. Before Grandmother Mason had died, she had informed her grandson of the thousands of pounds that would be his upon his coming of age. Mason Mason also realized that as his next of kin, Uncle Clive would receive the lot should Mason die. But how could he possibly think so unkindly of dear Uncle? He was always being taken for exciting walks; last week they had visited the waxworks, not to mention the Chamber of Horrors. The memory of these sent Mason's pulse racing. And next week they were going to a film called *Dracula's Curse on the Virgins*. Last month they had seen *Psycho*, which Mason had adored, except for the part where the thing had stabbed the girl behind the shower curtain. Then Mason had screamed. The local cinema wasn't too fussy about letting children into 'X' films. *Kinky Darlings* was on next month; Mason wanted to see this, but Uncle had said 'No' quite firmly. 'I suppose he doesn't want me to see those sex films,' thought Mason Mason. 'They're not good for you,' Uncle had said, 'I have to consider your moral welfare.'

Mason Mason never quite recovered from *Dracula's Curse on the Virgins*. He had screamed when the tall dark monster had thrust his gleaming white teeth into the fair white neck of the maiden; he had screamed when the coffin lid had opened slowly to reveal the bloody corpse of a victim; he had screamed when the eyeballs had bounced down the stairs, plopping on each other. And then, when the stake had been hammered through the bloated body of Dracula and a torrential spout of blood had blotted out the ceiling, Mason Mason passed out altogether. Uncle Clive waited until the end of the film before taking him home – after all, he had paid good money for it.

In the taxi afterwards, he fanned Mason's face with a handkerchief. Mason screamed again when he opened his eyes and saw it: the handkerchief was spotted with blood.

'I had a nosebleed,' said Uncle Clive.

'Dear Uncle, you do frighten me sometimes,' said the child, sobbing.

'But you must learn to be a big boy now,' said Uncle. 'And I've got to teach you not to be afraid of the dark, haven't I? When we get home you must sit in the cupboard in the cellar for a while; I know it's dark there, but at least you'll never be afraid again!'

'No, no, Uncle,' cried Mason.

'It's the right thing to do, I'm sure of that,' Uncle replied firmly. Mason opened his eyes and looked at him questioningly. He was a reasonable boy.

'If you really think that it will teach me to overcome all fear, then I'll do it,' he said. The taxi lurched to a stop outside their house.

'There's a good little lad,' said Uncle.

The cupboard in the cellar was large and dark. Mason sat in a corner, shivering with cold and fright. He fumbled in front of him and thought he touched something soft. He withdrew his hand violently, then thought he heard something moving in the far corner. It was a scrabbling sound and seemed to be coming towards him. Mason screamed his head off, but to no avail. 'Uncle Clive may be a monster,' he thought, 'but there's no one else in the world who cares so much for my welfare as he. Now, is there?'

Meanwhile, in the centre of the dank stone room that was the cellar, Uncle Clive stood poring over his box of magic that he had brought home with him from Africa. The leather-topped captain's chest was six feet long and two feet wide. It seemed bottomless. From out of the rubble within it Uncle Clive took a large sack and began to fill it to the brim full of old rags and pieces of coke from the floor. When this was completed, he carefully sewed the top of the sack to close it. From the very bottom of the chest Uncle Clive pulled out a large green hat box. Whether it was green because it was supposed to be green, or whether it was green from mould, it was hard to tell. Uncle giggled and licked his lips as he removed the top, and drew out the rumoured shrunken head. He held it by the lank hair and gazed into its face. It was the size of a large grapefruit. The skin was wrinkled and prune-coloured. The yellow eyes were half open, as was the mouth, which was puffy and moist with a thick red tongue. From a bottle in his pocket, Uncle took two large pearly white shark's teeth, and thrust them into the upper gums of the mummified head. The effect of this was so pleasing that he cackled with pleasure. The monstrous head was then secured tightly to the sack, and a large black cloak thrown over the shoulders. A black cravat was tied around the neck to hide the sacking. Uncle Clive then gently laid the dummy to rest in the chest until such time as he should need it, which would be soon, and closed the lid. 'This should do it,' he thought.

He opened the cupboard door after an hour or so. The child lay silent on the stone floor. Fainted again. He was carried up to the attic and laid on his bed. He opened his eyes. Gazing into the darkness, he saw his uncle bending over him. 'Poor little cuss, we mustn't overdo it, must we? We have your heart to think about.'

Mason moaned, 'What are you doing to me, Uncle?' Then he buried his head under the pillow, the tears running down his cheeks. Uncle Clive left, locking the door behind him, removing the candle. Mason was alone in the dark, with only the pallid moonlight for comfort.

Uncle went downstairs again, opened the chest and dragged the dummy out, making sure the head didn't fall off. It seemed a little heavier than before, and was surprisingly warm compared with the dripping dankness of the cellar. 'We'll really finish him off this time, won't we, Drac, old boy?' said Uncle, laughing merrily. The pearly teeth gleamed white in the darkness, and for a moment Uncle imagined he saw the eyelids blink in reply to him. Uncle Clive put the dummy on his back and began to reclimb the steps to the attic.

He was halfway up the staircase when it sank its teeth into his neck. Mason's uncle, with a yell of terror, fell backwards down the long staircase on to the landing below. He lay there motionless, his neck twisted sideways, whilst the dummy clung to him, sucking from him what little life there remained.

When the police arrived, attracted by the cries of a child from an attic window in North London, they found Uncle Clive dead on the landing. His face was as white as milk. Next to him lay the sack full of coke and rags. That was all. The cause of death was said to be a broken back, due to a heavy fall. The police surgeon failed to notice the two small red punctures beneath his left ear; anyway, by the time the autopsy was made, they had entirely disappeared.

MRS ANSTEY'S SCARECROW

W. H. Carr

KILLING ANSTEY by the remote, impersonal impact of a
bullet, he saw, would never be satisfaction enough.

A club, now, was hand-filling, satisfying.

The heft of it!

The blow of it, to the hand of the wielder pleasantly tingling! In his imagination, he could already feel the impact of
it on Anstey's skull.

'Aa'!'

So.

It was not that Lawson decided to kill Anstey, and then
went looking for a club. Rather, he found the club growing
and its purpose was immediately plain to him. It transfixed
him. He stood and looked at it in a kind of vacuum of time,
letting the realization of it, and the fierce joy of it, seep
through every cell and molecule of him.

A hawthorn club, with which to kill Clive Anstey; growing
here, in this hedge; awaiting *his* hand – how many years?

He saw that the thing was fated, fore-ordained, inescapable.

He and Anstey had gone to the tiny village school to-
gether. Both had won scholarships and gone on to Grammar
School, and that was the start of it; for no matter how
Lawson tried, Anstey always outstripped him. Unfairly,
Lawson thought; secretly, he regarded Anstey as no better
than himself. Only sharper, glibber, glossier, more lucky.

Clive Anstey went from Grammar School to Agricultural
College, but Lawson had no such luck. He had to take up the
burden of the few rods of market garden owned by his father,
on account of the latter's failing health. Two years and six

months later, his father died, and his mother shortly afterwards, leaving Lawson living alone in the bungalow, half-
heartedly working only enough to grub a bare living from the
soil.

He felt cheated. Doubly so, whenever Anstey came home
on long holidays from College. Lawson saw him as mealy-
mouthed and cocky. Anstey always greeted him cheerfully,
asked how he was, and how was the market-garden business;
and Lawson considered this to be condescension and mock-
ery, and his schooldays resentment of Anstey became more
bitter.

He was bitterest of all about Lorna, from the neighbouring
village.

Lawson had had his eye on her from Grammar School days.
Lorna wasn't like the other girls. She didn't giggle or
shriek. She was dark and intelligent, and, somehow – strong.
She was attractive, as a deep and mysterious pool can be. Not
that she was gloomy; she could sparkle and gleam.

But, not for Lawson.

He'd tried to date her home from local dances, but she always had the excuse of being accompanied by a girl friend.
One night the friend had found a date of her own, and Lawson, waiting, had literally forced his company upon Lorna,
insisting on accompanying her home.

Before they reached the village, he tried to kiss her. She
pulled away, he tried to be masterful, and she slapped him.
He'd been slapped before, being a mite over-brash about the
girls, and hadn't minded; but Lorna's blow held a quality of
bitterness and contempt that seared his spirit to the inmost.

'Come, now, you can't blame a fellow for trying,' he
muttered

'You should make sure you're welcome, first,' she told him,
in cold anger.

He seized her arms. 'What's so special about you, then?'

She didn't struggle, merely stood as rigid as marble.

'For one thing, I don't like being roughed.'

He released her, finally, with an oath.

'There's others that's not so particular,' he sneered.

'They're welcome.'

'What's wrong with me, then?' he snarled.

She thought, 'Somewhere inside, you're warped, twisted, evil—' Aloud, she said, '—If you don't know, I can't tell you.'

Still, he was consoled by the fact that at least she didn't particularly favour anyone else.

So it was doubly galling that Anstey should be the one. He came on summer leave from College, and Lawson saw him and Lorna out-and-about the countryside together, obviously in love.

One day he came upon them unexpectedly in a lane, embracing. It ground him up, inside. He closed his eyes, and thought that he should fall; after a while, he made his escape, unobserved. He couldn't have borne for them to have seen him, then.

'Why is everything so easy for *him*?' raged Lawson.

Why should *he* so casually pluck the fruit to which Lawson aspired in vain?

They became engaged. Clive Anstey left College, and stepped straight into the stewardship of the best and largest farm-estate in the neighbourhood, without ever having to grub, or soil his hands.

It made Lawson sick.

He didn't attend Anstey's and Lorna's wedding, although they held open house to practically the whole shire.

Afterwards, he'd see them sometimes in their smart new estate car, the like of which Lawson could never afford. They never failed to salute him, nor indeed any of the local people; but Lawson interpreted this as lordly complacency, and sly affront, and was filled with bitter fury.

'Swine! ... Bitch!' he spat after them. 'Think you own the bloody earth, don't you? But I'll get even with the pair of you. . . .'

Nights, he would brood about them, in the solitude of his kitchen. He became obsessed with the idea that, but for Anstey, Lorna might have been his. He neglected his work, visited the local pub each night, and after drinking morosely and alone, returned home to brood. On his way he passed the Big Farm, set some way back from the road, and he'd stop and glare, picturing Anstey and Lorna inside, behind the cheerfully lighted windows, secretly laughing together ...

He'd growl deep in his throat, and grind his teeth.

He took to mooching about the hedges ...

A hawthorn club ...

One of those freak growths, tall and straight, but with a twist to the dark green sinews of it which spoke of corded strength.

Hawthorn seasoned hard, he knew. Its knots sandpapered to an iron smoothness of tactile pleasure; and afterwards, it would be disposable, utterly, by fire.

There'd be no murder weapon for the police to discover.

Just about the right thickness, too; for he might have to carry it about his person, truncheon-fashion, for many days, awaiting his chance.

He went back and sawed it in darkness, and put it in a dry, dark cupboard to season, after sealing the cut ends of it with candle-wax, so that it would not dry too quickly and split.

From the cupboard he would take it out, nights, and appraise it, hefting and visualizing. So ... he would drill the core of the root end, and tap into it a long rod of lead, snugly weighting. The hole he would stem with a plug made with the offcut of the upper growth, smearing it with impact glue, and tapping irremovably home. He pleasured in the doing of it. The finished club was a joy to feel and heft and swing.

'*Like this*,' he said. 'Aa' ...! Aa' ... Aa' ...!'

He killed Anstey's dog first, for the two were inseparable when Anstey was afoot, and he'd never have stood a chance against man and dog together.

The dog was a sheep Collie which never worked with anyone but Anstey; and on the days when he took his wife in the smart grey estate car to the market town five miles away, the beast invariably went foraging on its own about the estate, as though to assure itself that all was well in his master's absence.

Lawson had noted this, and down by the wooded river he dropped the animal with a single shot. Knowing what ballistic experts can do, he dug out his bullet just in case, securely wired a large flat stone to the body, and tipped the dead dog into a deep and brooding pool.

From the river, the woods ran up almost to the back door of Lawson's bungalow, and he made his way there unseen.

So much for the dog.

Now for the master!

He had not foreseen how soon the killing of the dog would give him his opportunity.

The very next day, he saw Anstey coming along the weed-grown path to the bungalow, and was at the door before Anstey knocked.

' 'Morning?' said Lawson.

Anstey looked at him with a distaste which he strove to hide. Taking in Lawson's unkempt, neglected appearance, he sensed a concealed mirth, a sly malice, about the man. He fancied he intercepted from Lawson's eye a shaft of covert triumph, quickly hooded.

' 'Morning,' he said shortly. 'You haven't seen my dog around, have you?'

Lawson pretended to consider.

'Gyp? Not this morning . . . He missing?'

'Since yesterday. He generally meets the car. Yesterday, he didn't. I whistled around for him, last thing. I was afraid something had happened to him. When he didn't show up this morning, I was sure of it. I've been asking around. Someone heard a shot yesterday, down by the river. None of my men owns to firing it.'

'That'd be me. Shot a rabbit,' said Lawson quickly.

'I see.' Anstey knew that Lawson augmented his income from shooting rights on the estate. 'Did you see anything of Gyp down there?'

Lawson quickly made up his mind. The situation seemed to be ideal. It was known that Anstey was out searching for the dog, afoot. If he didn't return for lunch, or even tea, it would be assumed that he was beating the countryside, and had gone far afield. No immediate hue-and-cry would ensue. There'd be plenty of time; it seemed that Fate had played into his hands.

'As a matter of fact, I did see Gyp down there,' he said slowly.

'You did? Whereabouts?'

'Right where I shot my rabbit. I flushed two, got one, and Gyp shot past me after the other one. I had to hold my fire. I don't know where he came from. Didn't see him before that.'

'Which way did he go?'

'Upstream. I soon lost sight of him among the trees. I came home then. I only wanted one, for the pot.'

'Show me,' said Anstey. 'He may have broken a leg or something.'

'Sure. I'll get my jacket.'

As he accompanied Anstey into the woods, the slim hawthorn club with its weighted head swung down his right trouser-leg. In his jacket pocket was a long polythene bag.

It was easy, for Anstey did not suspect.

They came down upon the bottom woods by the river. Lawson showed Anstey where he had purported to have shot the rabbit, and pointed upstream in the direction supposed to have been taken by the dog. Anstey moved off that way through the trees, and Lawson followed close behind, loosening the cord loop by which the club depended from his trouser band. He slipped his wrist through the loop.

Anstey stopped and put two fingers in his mouth as if to whistle for the dog, and Lawson raised his club in a smooth motion and struck hard the back of Anstey's skull.

Anstey pitched forward like a felled ox, without a cry.

Lawson did not finish him there and then, but stayed his hand. He wanted Anstey to be fully aware of his fate – and the dealer of it – before he died.

He stood over him, at the ready; and presently the felled man groaned, and stirred.

Lawson waited.

Anstey turned his head and looked up at him, sideways; at first in bewilderment, then recognition; and, finally, seeing with a widening of his eyes the club in Lawson's hand, a comprehension of how he came to be lying there. With the realization, he instantly tried to surge to his feet and grapple with his assailant; and on that instant, Lawson struck again.

He hit Anstey repeatedly, again and again, on the back of the skull; not in a flurry of blows, but with slow, deliberate, calculated viciousness – thud – thud – thud – until the bone cracked; then shifting the blows from the centre, and spreading them until the back of Anstey's head was soft and unresisting, the crisp resistant thudding changing into mushy squashes.

'– Aa' . . . ! Aa' . . . ! Aa' . . . !'

– Until Anstey was dead beyond any possible doubt . . . Dead . . . dead . . . dead . . .

Lawson gazed down upon him long moments in hatred and in satisfaction. Then from his pocket he drew the long polythene bag, and carefully lowered the scarlet head of the hawthorn club into it, laid it on the grass, and securely tied the neck of the bag about the club, before slipping it once more to its hiding place. He shuddered a little as it came in contact with his bare thigh.

But at least there'd be no bloodstains on his clothing.

He made his stealthy way home through the woods unobserved, and put the polythene-encased club on his fire. There'd be no murder weapon.

Leaving it safely burning, and locking the door of the bungalow behind him, he immediately went out and busied himself about the market-garden, where he would be seen by any passer-by.

Lorna Anstey slept little that night. The night before, the dog was missing; and now her husband, seeking it, had failed to return. Phone calls established that he had not called at any of the larger farms, nor on any of their friends in town, nor even in the town's one small hotel, which she rang as a last resort, knowing that he would have called her if he had intended spending the night there.

The following morning she organized the men of the estate into a search-party, advising them to ask all householders of the sparsely-populated countryside if they had seen Anstey, and thus, perhaps, pinpoint the spot where last seen. Then she called the police.

When approached, Lawson played the innocent man to perfection, readily admitted Anstey had called the previous day, inquiring after the dog, and that he, Lawson, had directed him to the river-woods, having seen the dog there the day before while shooting; whereupon Anstey had stated his intention of searching that locality. Lawson himself professed concern on 'learning' that Anstey had not returned, and accompanied the party to the river-woods.

But he allowed someone else to discover Anstey's body.

The affair was a nine-day wonder. Lawson, as the last person who admitted seeing Anstey alive, came in for perhaps more police questioning than anyone else; but they could not shake his statement that Anstey had departed alone for the riverside, and that that was the last he had seen of him.

No one could prove to the contrary. No murder weapon was ever discovered. Lawson's clothing proved innocent of human blood. Several people testified to having seen Lawson about his work as usual on the morning in question. No motive for the killing could be unearthed.

A verdict of murder against person or persons unknown was recorded.

Several weeks went by. It seemed to Lawson that he was safe from retribution.

With the cessation of her husband's stewardship, Lorna had to leave the Big Farm to make way for his successor, a man with a family; but the gentleman who owned the land, anxious to do the right thing for the bereaved young widow, installed her as manager of one of the smaller farms of the estate; which she undertook with the assistance of a capable man and several land-girls who already knew the run of the place.

The new steward regarded her with a kindly eye, and saw to it that she never lacked good advice or assistance, and she soon settled in.

Lorna Anstey's new home adjoined Lawson's tract of market garden, and lay on his road to the local. A week or two after Lorna's installation, the darkness of the country road was cut by the swathe of light from a car overtaking him, and he stepped aside to make way for it. It pulled up beside him; the headlights dimmed. Through the open window, in the subdued glow from the dashboard he recognized Lorna Anstey. She was alone.

Oddly enough, Lawson had begun to *miss* Anstey.

His very first reaction after the murder was that he had been mad to kill Anstey, that somehow the crime would be brought home to him; but after the verdict of the inquiry, this feeling was gradually replaced by one of complacency and even secret jubilation. He was a clever fellow; he had committed the perfect murder; he had fooled everyone; and, above all, he had finally got the better of Anstey.

Then, he began to find life lacking in motivation. When he realized he'd lost Lorna, his desire for her had been replaced by his hatred of Clive Anstey, who had won her; his hope of somehow besting him, and finally by his obsessive wish to kill him. Living alone as Lawson did, his hatred had given, after a fashion, a fullness and meaning to his life.

Now Anstey was dead, and with him, the hatred; and he, Lawson, was left with nothing.

Once more, his thoughts turned to Lorna.

With her husband out of the way, he decided, he might, after a decent interval, try a discreet approach, and again essay an attempt at friendship with her. Which, in the fullness of time—

'Lorna Lawson,' he said to himself. The name had a fine and proper ring to it.

So Lorna became an obsession with him, replacing his obsession with Anstey; but for a different reason.

He was in this frame of mind when Lorna's car drew up beside him, and he encountered her for the first time, on a person-to-person basis, after the death of her husband.

As with so many women, after marriage Lorna's girlhood promise had quickly been fulfilled. From an attractively slim, rather naïve and leggy girl, she had swiftly burgeoned into womanhood, the 'married' look – slightly rounder of hip and breast, and with that indefinable bloom and assurance of the woman who has fully realized her femaleness, in ideal conditions of love and trust. She was infinitely more desirable, thought Lawson, than on the night he had clumsily tried to force a kiss from her. She seemed to him to exude a lure more animal, more full-bloodedly female.

Above her shapely knees Lawson could see a froth of filmy white nylon which she didn't bother to conceal. He wondered at this; was it unawareness, or coquetry? In his previous experience of her, she had been instinctively modest, the kind who was careful of her clothing.

Lawson experienced something he hadn't felt since the day he had murdered Anstey – the surge of male hunger in his loins and belly.

'I've been meaning to tell you, Lorna – Mrs Anstey, that

This sudden encounter with her, his feelings for her, the dark thing in the secret but immanent part of his mind, flung him into a flounder of speculation and indecision.

'I've been meaning to tell you, Lorna – Mrs Anstey, that is—' he groped – 'I'm sorry about – about—'

'Save your sorrow for yourself,' she said, in a voice edged like a chilled razor. '*I know you killed him!*'

The words smote about his ears like thunder, and he staggered.

'I – I—'

'I . . . *know*,' said Lorna Anstey. 'It's plain to me. He was struck down by a coward's blow, from behind. No-one could have crept up on him to do that, unawares. He was with some-one he knew and trusted. . . .'

'I – I—'

'. . . You,' she said flatly, as though he hadn't spoken. 'And I know the motive, though it was one that wouldn't have been considered, if I'd mentioned it at the inquiry.'

She gave Lawson a level and penetrating look.

'Jealousy. You were jealous of him. He was a better man than you. He bested you – at everything, didn't he? And he had me. You couldn't bear it, could you? You're warped, twisted, evil. I've always known it.'

Lawson, in shock, gaped at her, his slack mouth working soundlessly. Lorna pressed home her advantage.

'You killed the dog first, then *him*. Don't deny it.'

Lawson was in no state of mind to deny it. He was un-manned. This encounter, her onslaught, had been so unex-pected that his tongue felt paralysed, swollen and frozen in his mouth.

'You think you've got away with it,' she pressed on inexor-ably, '*But you haven't got away from me!* Now, remember this, Andra Lawson, because I'm speaking to you with my soul:

'There's a legend of witchcraft in my family. Always, one daughter in each generation has the Power. You can't ignore it, it's been so for hundreds of years. This time, I'm the one, and I've known it since I was a small girl. I knew it by instinct, and my grandmother recognized it, and taught me. And I've studied. There are books . . .

'And I'm dedicated. I'm dedicated to your destruction! '*Watch out for the crucified man!*'

She slipped-in the clutch and the gear-lever, and went blaz-ing into the night, leaving him in a drench of fear and specula-tion.

Lawson sat long into the night speculating on his encounter with Lorna. Time was, when he could have dismissed what she had told him about being a witch, as a farrago of the purest nonsense, in spite of allusions in the press to witch-cults, covens, and black-magic ritual killings. The idea of Lorna, whom he had known since childhood, being a witch, would have struck him as utterly fantastic.

But now he was in no state to laugh the thing away. He had committed murder, and thought to have got away with it; then the wife of the murdered man had told him that she was a witch, after taxing him with the crime. Too, she was the woman he desired, who had become an obsession with him, a fever. When she had spoken to him this night, the effect was as though some terrible power had gripped his very soul and shaken it almost loose from his body. The words she had said were burned into his brain, like a brand on a beast. '. . . I'm speaking to you with my soul . . . one daughter . . . has the power . . . I'm the one . . . dedicated . . . to your destruction . . . look out for the crucified man—!' – Ah, but those words had encased his heart in ice!

What terrible allusion, what symbolism, was this – and what did it terribly portend?

The following night, as in the deepening dusk he made his way homeward alone from the local country pub, the first terror fell on Lawson.

The vagrant, fluttering movement plucked at the corner of his restless vision, and when he turned the thing smote him fully, like a blow between the eyes; and the black icy waters from the nethermost well of fear surged shocking and rocking and seething up through the labyrinths of his brain, well-nigh submerging him, and almost he fell; for, framed in the gate-gap in the tall hawthorn hedge that brinked the narrow road to the right of him, Clive Anstey was resurrected tall and terrible, and darkly striding upon him.

Then, as Lawson's knees crumpled, and in the moment before the black waters would have entirely closed over him, the man in the field wavered, and, like one magic-lantern slide replaced by another, in a flick became a scarecrow instead of a man; with one leg pole-stiff, and the other a mere empty flapping.

But although Lawson's stopped heart leaped to life again, and the blood began to course once more through his frozen veins, the toad-cold hand of fear still grasped his throat; for with every hair on his head stiffening, he saw that the scarecrow wore the clothes of Clive Anstey – the ones he had worn when Lawson killed him.

Tall it was, to fit the clothing of the dead man, and broad in the shoulder yet gaunt. Beneath the brim of the tweed trilby, the face was a shadowed hollow of menace; and in that setting, and that attire, it seemed to Andra Lawson that he sensed the ghost-features of Clive Anstey. And, silhouetted with arms outspread against the ghost-light of the horizon, the imagery was that of a man crucified.

This, then, must be the thing of which Lorna Anstey had spoken.

Portending . . . what?

And what manner of woman would make such a thing of her murdered husband's clothes?

'Only a witch-kind,' he answered his own unspoken question; telling it to his shrinking soul, in the chill breeze that clammied his sweat.

He plucked his lip as he scurried homeward, not daring to look behind; only aside and aside, in the piling darkness.

From the moment that Lawson saw the scarecrow, his life became a nightmare. This terrible reproach, this worse-than-ghost – for a ghost does not stand, by night and day, for all people to see – was always in his inner vision. What peace of mind could he ever have, knowing that *there*, in *that* direction, over *that* hedge, stood the likeness of his victim, brooding in the very clothes of him, with the wind giving them the simulation of ghastly life?

What could he do? Attack it? He quailed at the thought. Burn it? No; he was afraid; it might be a trap – he might be seen. Even if not, such a burning would be sure to cause renewed police investigation; because who would set fire to it? Only the guilty . . .

He did not believe that Lorna Anstey would go to the police

with what were, after all, unproven suspicions; in any case, he was convinced that what she had in mind was something more terrible, and the more dreadful because of its uncertainty.

He dared not break the habit of years, for fear of causing comment, by staying away from the local pub. He wondered if the other habitués had noted the gruesome fact of the scarecrow's garb . . . whether they would comment on it.

They had, and did.

'A rum do,' said one.

'Doesn't seem natural, to me,' opined another.

' '*Tain't* natural!' foreboded an ancient.

'Oh?' From his tone, the others scented something.

'What do you think, then, Tom?'

'It's *super*-natural,' said the old man.

Nobody smiled.

'What do you mean by that, then?'

'It's a *haunt*. That's what it is. She dressed up that scarecrow in her dead husband's clo'es – the very ones, mark you, that he was murdered in – to haunt his murderer. Aye, and to hunt him down!'

A chill silence fell on the listeners.

'Do you really think so, Tom?' someone broke it, at last.

'Mark my words! That thing was put there to scare more than crows . . . I shouldn't like to be him as done it, that's all!'

'God, no . . .' said an awed voice.

That night, it seemed to Lawson that the scarecrow was a little nearer the gate. He hurried past with fearfully averted eyes, reaching his own front door in a perfect welter of trembling terror.

After a sleepless and horror-drenched night, he was impelled, against his shuddering will, to go down to the gateway to look at the scarecrow, to convince himself that it had not changed its position. When he reached the gate, he found a small, weathered board tacked to it. On it, crudely lettered in white paint, were the words, 'I WAS MURDERED.'

The scarecrow was nearer the gate . . .

The chain was unfastened, and swinging.

Lawson convulsively looped the chain about the gatepost, fastened it, and fled.

He stopped going to the pub. Let the locals think what they would, he could not face passing that gateway, and that *thing*, in the darkness of night; but he could not help creeping, against his crawling will, each day to the gate.

Always, it would be unfastened, the chain idly swinging. Each day, the scarecrow drew almost imperceptibly nearer. Lawson became aware that, however still the day, the scarecrow's clothing would fret and pluck, as if in moving air; and equally without apparent cause, the chain would be swinging, swinging. The very air about that gateway felt alien and chill, as though emanating from a place that was dark and dank.

It became a compulsion with him to go each day and fasten the chain. It was much worse than the compulsion which makes people avoid stepping on the cracks between paving stones, or causes them to worry if they miss touching a single lamp post in passing. All *they* had to contend with was a feeling of vague anxiety; what Lawson contended with was a foreboding and clammy dread, a guilty ague, a bowel-melting terror.

It was almost a week after Lawson had stopped going to the pub, and a Sunday morning. From behind the drawn curtains he had peered out at people going to church in cars or afoot, while he had envied them so carefree, and wished that he could join them, though he had never been a church-going man.

The sky became overcast, the day dark and forbidding; but that inner compulsion about the gate kept gnawing and gnawing at his vitals, and he knew that he'd have to go there, and fasten the chain, before he could attain any measure of peace. He knew that, once fastened, it would stay that way until nightfall, at least. Whoever – or whatever – unfastened it, did so only at night.

The people would be in church now, and no one was likely

to be about; he could have done, before they started trickling homeward. He put on his hat and coat, and crept forth on his miserable errand.

Once near the gateway, he kept his eyes aground. It was his habit to fasten the chain, then steal a quick glance at the scarecrow before quitting the accursed place. This gloomy Sunday, the very grass about the gateway looked forlorn and rank, and a shadow darker than the rest of the day seemed to crouch about that part of the road. He had just finished fastening the chain when a HAND fell on his shoulder.

He leaped, turning, and came to ground a yard away, crouched, his mind a shocked blank, to face. . . .

. . . Lorna Anstey.

Her eyes were full of the power she held over him, and about her lips played the smile of the tiger.

He was filled suddenly with a blind rage, and would have—

'Don't do it,' she said softly, with meaning.

He waited to hear the meaning.

'It came to me,' she said in the same soft tone, 'that you might think to do me a mischief, cornered rat that you are . . . Don't . . . I've taken steps to protect myself. There's a letter in the bank vault, to be opened in the event of my death. It says that if I die by violence, *you* will have been the cause of it. It says you've been threatening me . . . It also voices my suspicions about you being the killer of—' she nodded in the direction of the scarecrow, and he shuddered.

'Such a statement,' she went on, '– coming from a murdered woman, would start something that could only end in your hanging.'

'What if I get beyond caring what happens to me?' he said, with the false courage of desperation.

'It won't be long now,' she said, smiling in tender ferocity. '*He's* getting quite close . . .'

The blankness descended on his mind, so that he knew only a dim half-light, and in it the appalling scarecrow looming over him. When he collected himself, she had gone; and he never remembered the journey home.

The following day he did not go to the gate; and that night his formless terrors coalesced into a dream .

It was night. Darker against the darkness, the scarecrow stood unmoving to one side by the gatepost, just within the field. The chain hung still, and there was a silence. The gate swung inward, and the terrible scarecrow, wearing the clothing of murdered Anstey, gathered itself and hopped; and hopped again.

The gate closed.

The scarecrow hopped to the middle of the road, and paused; then it hopped three times in the middle of the road, turning a little each time it hopped – hop – hop – hop – and when it stopped, it was facing in the direction of Lawson's place. Then, purposefully, frightfully, it began to hop yard-long hops down the road towards Lawson's bungalow. Terribly flapping and bobbing, hop ... hop ... hop ... hop ... through the darkness.

Lawson awoke screaming horribly, sitting bolt-upright in his tangled bed, the cold sweat streaming, his eyes glaring; the bedclothes twisted into ropes, and he half-strangled in them. He tore them from about his neck and body, flung on his dressing-gown, and staggered from his bedroom and the Judas, Sleep.

In his kitchen-cum-living-room he drank a stiff whisky, built a fire, and sat in front of it in a big chair, shivering, to await the dawn.

And slept.

And dreamed again; this time of Lorna.

Her farmhouse kitchen, by candle light. She was seated at the table, and she was doing something peculiar.

On the table lay a blackboard; on each corner of the blackboard stood a shallow brass bowl, and in each bowl a small pyramid of something – herbs, incense – smouldered. On the board was chalked a careful map of the immediate vicinity – the fields, the woods and river, the farmhouse in which, by some necromancy, he stood – the road, and Lawson's own bungalow. Over it all, the smoke from the smouldering incense wreathed and roiled, and through it the chalked lines seemed to waver into a semblance of reality.

Lorna herself was changed. She looked gaunt, sexless, witchlike; her eyes glittered strangely in the candle-light, and about her was an aura of implacable intentness and menace. From a thread, held between the thumb and forefinger of her right hand, dangled a tiny effigy; a manikin in the likeness of a scarecrow; and Lawson saw that it was suspended over a square on the map, representing the field in which the real scarecrow actually stood.

As he watched in mounting horror, she began bob, bobbing the dangling manikin in the direction of the road, and he saw that a spent match was placed across the gap in the chalked hedge, to represent the gate. Lorna manipulated the manikin until it stood just inside the gate, the position in which Lawson had seen it in his dream, which he could perfectly remember in this one. Then she carefully swung open the matchstick gate, paused, and bobbed the scarecrow through it and into the road, closing the gate behind it.

Now the incense smoke seemed to thicken, converging on Lawson's bungalow; and the manikin began to hop, hop, hop, along the road in the same direction . . . .

Lawson awoke, cold, to grey ashes in the grate, and a grey dawn light. He awoke in fear, to fearful questionings. Had he dreamed, or had his astral self, his *doppelganger*, witnessed horrendous Truth?

Like most people, he had read his share of hauntings and hexes, of wax images for pin-sticking and slow melting, with dire results for the people in whose likeness the images were made. He had heard of voodoo death pointing, and could visualize how potent an effect this must have on ignorant and superstitious savages; but the idea of people or events being influenced by the manipulation of puppets was a new form of witchcraft, at least to him.

So now he was faced with two propositions. Either Lorna Anstey, by means of her accursed scarecrow and her claim to be a witch, was fighting him with auto-suggestion, aided by such ruses as moving the 'crow and persistently unfastening the gate-chain, or   – she was really manipulating the scarecrow and the gate chain by means of Black Art.

He realized that his position, as her husband's murderer, would render him particularly vulnerable to suggestion. He knew, and knew that she knew, that he was distraught, unstable, because of his guilt and her confronting him with it. His only possible recourse, he saw, would have been to do away with her, silence her forever; but she had foreseen this, and foiled him by placing the letter in the bank vault, and telling him of it.

... There was, of course, one way of ascertaining if she was, indeed, herself lifting and shifting the scarecrow by physical means, herself unloosening the chain – the chain! – he could k--p w-tch by n-ght – no-no, he couldn't! – his mind daren't even properly formulate the words.

What if, by Black Art, she *were* imbuing the scarecrow with a fearful travesty of life – Anstey's life, conjured from beyond the grave?

What if the 'crucified man' actually came hopping towards him from out of the darkness, clad in clothes of horror?

His whole being recoiled from the thought, 'Because I am guilty, guilty, guilty ... Dear Father God in Heaven Above – why did you let me why didn't you stop me – guilty ...'

'And what will happen when IT reaches me, for that must be the aim of her conjurations, no, no, no, no, that way lies madness – I must sleep this day in order that I may keep vigil tonight because I no longer dare sleep in the night—'

But try as he might, sleep eluded him, and gathering dusk found him wandering from room to room in the bungalow, distraught, haggard, with redly smarting eyes, his hands wringing and plucking each at the other.

'—A prey to horror, the grinning skull of my own sin ... blow, stroke, burden, load, bitter draught, cancer, scourge ... Lacerate, gnaw, corrode, horrify, appal. Hideous, grinding my mind in the mills of envenomed, agonizing— Cowering, terrorized, beset in my own home—'

Before darkness fell, he ran about preparing himself as for a siege. He laid in sufficient fuel for the night; he locked all doors, even the one leading to his bedroom, lest it creep on him unawares. The windows were shutterless – shutterless! – but that couldn't be helped.

Finally, he stood his gun to hand by the side of the fireplace, and settled himself in the big chair to vigil away the long, the dark, the hellish night.

And slept, and dreamed.

Again, he stood in Lorna Anstey's farmhouse. All was as before, only this time her face was alight with the certainty of success, and it seemed that she looked up, her eyes great like glittering silver coins, and he mirrored in them, trapped.

'Ha!' she said, smiling terribly. 'You see what I'm about, then. Go, now, and stand by the gate, and watch the scarecrow! There's hair from *his* corpse on its head, and fingerparings from his corpse in its pocket; and if you know anything at all, you'll know what that means . . .

'I'LL BRING HIM ALIVE!'

He fled like a soundless shriek from her presence, faster than sound like smoke between the rushing hedges, and stopped by the gate like a hapless pin caught in flight by a cruel magnet.

It was too dark to see, but he could hear . . .

Then he was home in his own kitchen watching himself in the chair, sleeping.

'Wake up, wake up, you fool! Don't you know *it's* coming? You fool, you fool, HE's coming, sent by that besom – how can you sleep, you log of wood, poor fellow, when it comes thump, thump, thump through the darkness? I've heard it—'

Then he was in his own body and awake with a leap to a scrabbling and a scarecrow at the window.

'—I am crushed, paralysed, now my heart has actually stopped beating – it must start, or I die now, the light dimmer – Aa'! Aa'! It leaps, I pant, it hurts . . . throbbing heart, icy sweat, the light brightens again . . .'

It had reached him at last. Only the window-pane kept it from him. The blank, sacking, seeking face was more terrible than features; a blind, ravening voracity of which Lawson knew himself to be the one coveted lure, a helpless maggot impaled on the hooked thorn of potent terror.

'My soul, hapless, loosening from the fibres of my body, racked and wrenched, ah, like a tooth in its socket for the drawing . . . *Wait, wait – wait, you fool!*'

He clutched the mane of his madness and checked it in mid-gallop, and for the first time in days pulled the unreal, distorted shapes of his dissociated world into some semblance of logic and rationality.

'Steady, just in time . . . Are you a child, a savage, to be imposed upon by a charlatan? Where's your logic? *That* is no conjuration! *That* is not Anstey! It is not even a scarecrow. It *must* be a person, for Anstey is dead . . . *Lorna* Anstey! Who else – Lorna Anstey, who seized upon my vulnerability, and sought to plant in me the seeds of madness . . . Autosuggestion . . . The whole thing's a manipulation – a grisly, ghastly, monstrous jest. Ha, she's tried to drive me mad! . . . Ha! She's tried to stop my heart – she's laughing – how cruel, how inhuman! Nothing is an excuse for cruelty like that – nothing, nothing could excuse it!

'Wait a bit, steady now, wait a bit . . . Though I refuse to be terrorized any longer, she must not see – *she has left the window, what now?* – I will no longer skulk, ha-ha! a prisoner in my own house – *Ha!* – *she tries the door* – your crucified man has crumbled into sticks and straw, a bundle, a scarecrow, nothing – *she rattles the door* – and *you* are nothing, a scarlet pounding and thunder inside me, a thunder of torrents, torrents of red in dark labyrinths surging upwards, I will open the door, I will let you in, I will grapple you and kill you with my hands . . .'

He leaped to the door to open it fast and astonish her, but no sooner had his raging fingers shot back the bolt than the door burst wide-in upon him, and it seemed that the outraged universe stopped, aghast at the immensity of the thing that stood framed in the doorway and the darkness on no foot, only a pole, and the other leg emptily swinging . . .

Then he was shouting and shouting with his voice against the impossibility of it, and beating and beating with his arms in denial as the darkness and the cold pressed ravening about his racked and draining spirit.

Mad, they said, he must have gone mad. Else why had he scattered straw all over his kitchen?

'Must have been a seizure,' said the doctor. 'His muscles contracted so terrifically that they snapped his own bones. They can, you know. Never expected to see it, though.'

Of course, Mrs Anstey took down the empty scarecrow after that, and burned it.

With a special ceremony . . .

NOT ENOUGH POISON

Alex Hamilton

SHE COULD take nothing more off. The last four or five ounces of nylon were the irreducible minimum, the White Woman's Burden. Not earthquake nor a Fahrenheit reading of 110° could excuse Sarah Hart in her own eyes for lightening it. Discovered in her slip she could still be indignant – discovered naked she would be down to 'their' level.

She had never seen one of 'them' naked, but she had heard about it and she could imagine it. 'They' were naturally a nude sort of people, but with clothes on. Any sort of dress on them looked to Sarah like fancy dress. Notwithstanding this idea of the people of Juanmarco she had lodged an instant complaint when from her kitchen window she caught sight of a young man undressing for the sea. The youth had been jailed for a time: the national laws relating to public decency were stringent. Just how stringent was shown when, on the day following the bathing boy's conviction, her husband Trevor was taken off a tram for being improperly dressed. With his white cricket trousers, spotless white shirt and white canvas shoes she had slaved over, and his hair all faultlessly combed back, he had yet been arrested because the law said that all men must wear jackets on the public transport. Meanwhile in swimsuits and pyjama jackets the locals had looked on grinning. The fine turned out to be minimal, but the humiliation had been extreme!

Sarah sat back in a cane lounging chair, with her bare feet planted flat on either side of it, so that the cool tiles should have a chance to draw off some of her exasperation with the people and the climate. She sipped at her drink with increasing speed, watching the rapid dissolution of the ice in it with dismay. When she had finished it she knew she would have to haul herself out of the chair and trail into the kitchen, to make herself another one, but she could not envisage herself ever moving again.

The heat was like a great, fat, unpleasant wrestler who had put an unbreakable hold on her and yet was unwilling to relinquish her, but kept her powerless while teasing her with small, vexing discomforts for the amusement of himself and the crowd. With perspiration starting in every crease of her skin, whenever she bent a limb sufficiently to fold two surfaces against one another, she had moments when she felt she must be an only slightly less fat wrestler herself.

Evening would bring back the true picture of herself a slender woman with wide, calm eyes like waveless inland seas, and sharp autocractic features, and short blonde hair set like a wave struggling still to come to its peak. Thin-hipped like a model, only the slight overdevelopment of her calf muscles in any way matched the foul image of the wrestler. But exaggeration was the natural expression of her mind, and while it presented itself to her she loathed herself and the people of Juanmarco and her European acquaintances with them.

It was mid afternoon, and at any time soon, she was sure, something must burst into flames.

On her knee lay an old novel, inverted. The silverfish were getting through it faster than she was. They seemed to thrive on Victorian prose, as a staple, but for a real à la carte silverfish order, a prewar thriller like this one was their favourite. The gum in the binding perhaps. When she got back to England, if she ever did, she'd make a suggestion to the publishers that they incorporate a poison in the binding gum. And what was left over they could feed to some of their authors, judging by what she had read recently. She shoved the book off her knee and swished it across the tiles under the divan. Later on Trevor would pick it up for her, she thought. When he had finished picking her out of this chair. She put her head back for the last of the drink, and then rolled the empty glass over her chest above her breasts.

Long after this had ceased to give her any pleasure she was

still doing it as she watched smoke coming out of the ground in her garden.

'My God, a volcano!' she said aloud, as she noticed it for the first time. 'I'm watching one born,' she thought, 'like that stupid idiot of a farmer in Mexico.'

Then she remembered from the account of the farmer in Mexico that he had felt it hot underfoot for three days before the earth crust blew up, and that furthermore Juanmarco was at least a thousand miles from any volcano belt. The smoke came out of the stoniest, most arid part of a generally arid garden. It hung around the stones for a while before seeping upwards into the casuarina tree. Sarah's dog staggered to his feet from the house steps and wandered over without any urgency to examine the phenomenon.

'Pete, you're a cretin,' she told the dog, through the open window.

The dog turned his head and wagged his tail a little, in an absent-minded way, before resuming his study of the broken patch of ground from which the smoke was escaping. Once the animal backed suddenly, with a little startled jump, and gave anxious attention to a forepaw. Then he went in close again. His snout continued to point at the mystery, while his hindquarters started an independent sideways march.

The smoke held together, dense and viscid, clinging to the underside of the leaves of the tree, and smearing stickily all along the branches until it looked like the disturbed dressing of a Christmas tree. The idea occurred to Sarah when she took her dark glasses off.

At the same moment she saw, through the branches of the tree, the two men working with the smoke pump. They were perhaps two hundred yards away, on a mound in the Fallon compound, and silhouetted against a scalded sky, but she recognized them for two of the *peones* the Fallons had trained, virtually from the ground up.

'Reaching about knee level,' commented Sarah viciously, and put her glasses back on. She noticed with a vague irritation that the *peones* had set up their machine under a palm, no doubt with the idea of having some shade as they worked, though in fact the tree was so tall that the patch afforded must have been exiguous.

Sarah made the effort of moving her chair, scraping it round on the tiles inch by inch until she could watch them without discomfort. It struck her as stupid, but *typical*, to pump the smoke into the ground at one of the highest points in the whole Fallon compound. It stood to reason that it would be harder work.

'That's *their* funeral,' she murmured, hoping mischievously that they would see her, stretched out and desirable, before they dropped from exhaustion. She pulled her slip down a little to cover the eternal snowline, and crossed her legs at the ankles. The men could hardly be expected to know the difference, but as a matter of personal integrity she would not forgive herself if a display of desirability degenerated into a vulgar peepshow. Her notion of herself as a defeated wrestler had been completely scattered by the sudden gust of excitement.

But the two on the mound were not yet seeing her either as wrestler or siren. One cranked the handle, in a mindless sort of way, imparting to his body the beginnings of a rhythm like those of a man who stands on the fringes of a dance wishing he could join in. The other, taller and apparently younger, skipped to and fro, alternately feeding the machine and banging about on the ground with the flat of his shovel. Once he leapt off the mound and reappeared more slowly, dragging a sack of what Sarah guessed to be the powdered formicide. Both looked away and shielded their eyes as he stabbed the sack to open it, and the fine powder burst out.

She could see now other columns of smoke rising, within the Fallon compound. The younger *peon* dashed from one to the other as his older companion directed him, digging up hasty shovelfuls of earth and then tamping down the openings to the ants' warren, so that they should be imprisoned and the fumes from the burning powder annihilate them wherever they might run in their enormous underground caverns.

Sarah saw that she ought to get herself out of her chair and tamp down the hole in her garden. But she could hardly go out undressed as she was. And it seemed to her that the *peones* might eventually notice her column of smoke, and Sarah with it. Perhaps one of them might come down to attend to it. That would be an interesting piece of impudence!

And a better reason than any for letting the smoke continue to issue from the ground under her window was that the Fallons might see it. Her column of smoke was proving conclusively that she had been right to complain to the Fallons. She had been playing host to the Fallons' ants. The Fallons' ants had wandered *ad lib* in the Harts' garden, and this activity with the formicide had been delayed quite long enough. She was only sorry that Trevor was not home to see it all, because while agreeing that ants' nests ramified to an astonishing distance, he had been ever so slightly cool to her when he heard that she had complained to the Fallons.

'It's not,' Trevor had said, 'as if either we or the Fallons are in the least interested in gardening. Live and let live — there's room for the Fallons and us *and* the ants with all this land unused.'

'The antidote is poison,' she had replied brightly and as so often her caustic humour deflected his critical intention.

A squall of annoyance from her dog diverted her attention from the two men back into her own garden. She laughed as she perceived that Pete had quite evidently been bitten on the snout by an ant. He was sneezing and snuffling and shaking his head. 'Serve you right for being so nosy!' she called to him as he slunk back under the steps and looked out from behind them at the calm ooze of smoke which had responded to his inquiries with such an unexpectedly combative stroke. 'Just 'cause you're bigger doesn't mean anything,' said Sarah gaily, and tossed a bottle-cap at him. He watched it reproachfully, all the way, as it ran past him over the hard earth and smacked against the wall as if it too might suddenly turn and nip him.

When Sarah lost interest in Pete's predicament and looked up again she realized that the two *peones* had in the meantime noticed her. They were standing on either side of the machine, gazing down with open interest. The younger one had his hands on his hips, and the elder had his in his pockets in that detestable personal fashion that she saw and loathed wherever she looked at men looking at her in South America.

Both immediately moved into action then, as if her glance were a charge of life. The younger one leapt almost deliriously from bolt hole to bolt hole, though he had perfectly well sealed them before, and beat them in a perfect frenzy of self-consciousness. The elder more slowly took his hands from his pockets and shuffled to the machine. As he cranked he snatched occasional glimpses of her, over his shoulder, until the rhythm of his effort took over and his head sank low on his chest. Only sporadic bursts of intenser smoke erupting from the fissure in the garden remained as evidence of his internal agitation.

'The young one's too embarrassed to come down,' was her disappointed thought as he returned to the mound without risking another look at her. 'And the old one's on his high horse.' She smiled ironically at the grumpier pufflets of smoke issuing irregularly from the ants' backdoor. She could see that the old one was bullying the younger, commanding him from one spot to another in an unnecessarily jerky and impatient fashion. She disliked him for that and made up her mind that if the young one looked down the hill at her once more she would give him a clear and patent signal that she wanted the ant outlet blocked. If she once got him out of the Fallon compound and into the Harts', the old boy could put his hands in his pockets till he bust himself.

Unfortunately the whole of the emotional and physical energy of the pair of them seemed to be burning up with the poison, pumping away madly down into the earth, to be wasted on the death and destruction of a hundred million ants. A million million! Whatever the quantity there must by now be enough poison in their rustling, secret galleries to have glutted them all. Idly Sarah considered phoning the Fallons to suggest that if the poisoning were being done at her instigation, perhaps she had the right to call a halt?

'And you two dumbbells would then just pack up all your kit and go home,' she murmured, withdrawing her hand from

the phone on the tiles beside her. These half-focused specula-
tions were creeping as murkily through the corridors of her
mind as the smoke in the ant colony. She lay prone and only
half hopeful. She did not, she decided, really care that much.
The complaint about the ants had worked, but no complaint
about stifling heat could be addressed to anybody. The heat
came out on top in every encounter. She was seeing the
wrestlers again, sliding back into their suffocating embrace,
when a curious high screech from the garden called her back
to the world outside, and the smoke, and the ants and the
rhythmic, sensual labouring *peones* of Juanmarco.

All the images resolved at once into one terrified, writhing
creature. The Harts' monkey, tethered by a chain to an old
and seedy palmtree, which had only been left standing out of
courtesy to him as his ancestral home, had run down the bole
and was now, at the extremity of the chain, wrenching at the
collar and fighting the chain to be free. He was in imminent
danger of strangling himself as he leaped again and again into
the void and was plucked back to earth as the chain reached its
limit.

Sarah sat up. She tore off her glasses and disregarded them
where they fell and broke on the tiles. With them off she could
see that the monkey was crawling with ants. And the inside
wall of the Harts' compound was almost unrecognizable as
newly whitewashed. A shimmering copper red, it was vibrant
with a senseless but spreading pattern of ants. Like a great
crowd, criss-crossing one another's paths, grouping and
breaking up again, turning back on their tracks, taking any
direction but a straight one, they nevertheless filled out to the
ends of the wall, and in their many thousands climbed to the
top, which was soon covered in patrolling insects.

Rigid at the edge of her chair, Sarah watched the monkey
agonize. She knew she should run out and release it, but its
rolling eyes, its grimaces, its desperate, pointless bounds in the
air and the uncontrolled snapping of ochrish teeth at its own
fur, filled her with disgust. At any time, at its most tranquil,
she had never been able to bring herself to approach the
monkey. It was Trevor's responsibility. He fed it, blandished it

and paid out conscience money when it bit anybody. The tradesmen all knew the length of its chain and detoured to stay outside its radius.

They had taken over the monkey with the house: it had been a pet of the Caryesfort children and when Sarah had heard that it had even bitten one of them and that the child had had a nasty forearm for three months from the poison of the bite she had wanted the beast destroyed. But Trevor had said that Caryesfort himself had agreed that in a sense the child had got its deserts for teasing it, and that a frightened animal always turned savage.

And savage it certainly was now. Tearing at the ants it had gashed itself. Horrified she watched flecks of blood spinning off it into the dust as it wrenched round and round in its grotesque struggle.

She thought of Trevor's gun. Suddenly she ran. She hit his writing desk so hard that for a moment she could not pull the drawer open. In a panic she decided it was locked and yanked at the handle so violently that the drawer came clear out of the desk, spilling its contents all over the tiles. Among them was the gun, and she snatched it up and ran to the window.

The monkey had vanished. She stared for a moment bewildered. Then she saw that it had run up the tree. She sighted it with difficulty and pulled the trigger. Nothing happened. The gun had misfired. She pulled the trigger again, and again, without any result. The chamber was empty. She looked despairingly at the articles littered about the floor, and saw no bullets. Trevor with a gun would never go beyond bluff. In a rage she flung the gun through the window at the swelling mass of ants. Its heavy sheen flickered for a moment as it pitched among them, and then was extinguished by the dark and rising tide of insects.

And at that moment, with a shrill scream, the monkey jumped out of the tree. In mid air its impetus was suddenly checked as the chain pulled taut. A second later it was hanging down the trunk of the palm, apparently lifeless. Sarah supposed it could only have broken its neck with that last frantic leap.

She would not look at it again – she fixed herself in the window in such a way that she could not. While all the time, busy in the silliest way up there on the mound, those idiotic, impenetrable *peones* continued to pump their inadequate smoke into the ground. And now like some great burst water main, the fissure in her garden heaved with a thick outpour of ants.

Could they not see what was happening? Almost she blamed them for not hearing the shot she had been unable to fire.

As the ants – unbelievable that the quiet, still earth should erupt with so many ferocious millions – spilled, somersaulting across the garden, she thought again of Pete.

'Pete!' she called sharply. 'Come here this minute!'

But there was no response from the dog.

She leaned far out of the window, trying to see under the steps, but he had moved from there. She called again, angrily. And saw him suddenly, over by the gate, walking stiff-legged across a rocky lacuna still more or less bare of ants. His tail was between his legs and he was sidling obsequiously towards the gate, already sinking his belly to the ground to wriggle under it, as he always did.

'Pete!' she wailed, as the dog moved hock-deep through the ant-shallows. Then the dog was hurling himself madly at the aperture under the gate, and wriggling and yelping as he tried to squeeze his way through. The gate shook and rattled with his efforts, and battalions of the hideous army tumbled off it on to his back.

Then he was through and gone. Briefly she saw him racing through the brush which surrounded the Harts' compound, stop in a clearing where the sand was as fine and white as bone-meal, and roll on his back, to move about as if he were only playing. Then he was on his feet and running again, and Sarah lost sight of him, though she could hear crying as he continued his battle, in a diminuendo as he moved farther and farther away.

'This is absolutely ridiculous!' announced Sarah loudly. As loudly and angrily as she could, to keep the fear from lapping at the edges of her mind. The fear had the shape of the ant army now, and was darkening and thickening with it, all round her. 'Those bloody Fallons!' exclaimed Sarah, picking up the phone and poking her fingers into the slots to dial as if each one were a Fallon body.

She hoped it might be the boy, Edwin, who would come to the phone. He was the only one of the Fallons she was likely to get any sense out of, a big boy who spent most of his time sailing in the bay, but who was already beginning to have a bit of an eye for the girls. When she heard Jane Fallon's voice she had an eerie sense of her isolation being increased instead of done away with. Jane was utterly unpredictable, the kind of woman who right out in the wilds would insist that all the women ride sidesaddle. And get her way.

'Listen Jane,' said Sarah, 'I haven't rung up to pass the time of day. This is urgent. Your bloody ants are all over my garden!'

'Oh, that's all right,' replied Jane, in that voice that men always said sounded as if it were bubbling through a gin and tonic, 'I've got a couple of my boys smoking them out. Don't you remember, you complained?'

'I know I complained,' said Sarah, 'and I was right to complain. They *are* your bloody ants . . .'

'Oh, I wouldn't say *ours*. They come and go much as they please, you know. But Collie wanted to please you so we're *smoking* them out . . .'

'But you've got absolute idiots on the job!'

'Oh no, my dear. Cipriano's *very* good. Did I tell you about the trap he set for a *gambá* which was having our chickens? Most ingenious.'

'Jane, please listen. From where I stand at this minute I can see all my chickens going down under an onslaught of ants. The monkey killed itself, driven mad by ant bites and now . . .'

'That dreadful monkey, Sally! Why ever did you keep it? It had the most abominable record. Malicious, obscene and dangerous, I really can't say that I'm sorry – it was a wretched creature.'

'Let me talk to Edwin, Jane? May I, please, as a favour to me?'

'I can't think why you should want to talk to Edwin.'

'I'd like him, as a favour to me, to block up these antnests.'

'Oh, Sally, darling! You would be wasting your time. Edwin doesn't know an antnest from a hole in the ground! All he ever does is think about sailing. And actually that's where he is now, with the boat Collie had shipped in for him. From Port of Spain, lovely place, we were there once on a contract.'

Sarah took a deep breath and wiped the sweat from her palm on her slip before speaking again.

'Jane!'

'Sally! Nice to hear from you. You must both of you climb the hill and dine. Such fun to hear from Trevor about all his new improvements. Have you your diary handy? He might fix a firm date.'

'I'd love that. But for a moment, please listen. Will you listen, Jane? Without interrupting.'

'I'm listening. My but it's hot. Do you know sometimes I just feel like pulling most of my clothes off and sitting about in my slip. Too many people running around the house, that's *my* bugbear.'

'Well, I'm alone,' said Sarah, 'and unless you do something to help me I'm going to be killed by ants. Do your hear me? They're right round the house now, Jane.'

'Oh, dear, what an exaggerator you are, Sally! Don't worry, they're all up to the gills with poison. Like our husbands after a club dance. They'll walk a few yards and make terrifying gestures and just keel over. I've seen it dozens of times.'

'I don't think they're using enough poison!'

'Don't you believe it. Cipriano's got enough poison out there to kill off all the ants in South America. And if there are any stragglers he can always wipe them out with that foul cheroot of his.'

'There's one running up my leg now. They're in the house!'

'I must admit it's amazing how they get about. Oh well, flick it off and I'll see what can be done. I'll see if I can put out a signal to them and call it off for today. Nice to hear from you, Sally. Thank you for calling, dear.'

'No, they're not using enough poison,' screamed Sarah. 'Tell them to go on, but use *more poison!*'

But the phone had clicked in her ear. She ran to the window and retreated again, as the ants advanced over the sill.

Up on the mound the *peones* had stopped working. They were huddling together and looking into the cupped hands of the elder. Playing about with a lottery coupon, or a beetle or any simple-minded trivial thing, blast them! No, evidently they were lighting cigarettes, because they drew apart, and the younger put his head back as if to clear his eyes of smoke. The elder drew a forearm over his brow, reached out for the shovel and set it under his shoulder and, leaning on it stared straight down the haft into the ground.

The younger turned full on to look at Sarah. She lifted an arm, gesticulated wildly around at the ants, advance columns of which were probing in all directions, eager as fire. The young *peon* puffed solemnly at his cigarette, and once snatched a glance at his companion and straightaway looked back at Sarah again.

Sarah pulled her slip over her head and slung it casually away across the tiles. Even as it slid along the ants were mounting it, burrowing in the lace, slashing it, killing it, conquering it. Shuddering, she looked back at the mound. Languidly she removed the last of her underclothes.

The young peon rubbed his jaw and moved forward uneasily. She waved to him. He was about to leap down from the mound when the arm of the elder peon caught him and pulled him round. He was pointing in the other direction. Sarah guessed that the older one had caught sight of Jane's signal from the Fallon house, invisible on the far side of the mound.

The younger waved his hand at Sarah. The elder made an impatient gesture and then pointed at the machine. The younger looked again at Sarah and shrugged. Together then they pulled the nozzle of the pump out of the ground and filled in the hole. The young one waved at Sarah and was angrily told off. Looking backward over his shoulder he helped the elder slowly bear away the machine towards the Fallon house and moments later they were disappearing from view on the far side of the mound.

If she ran, as she wished she had done when the *peones* had first shown up on the skyline she would have to go the way the dog had gone. And he had gone when the going was still more or less good. She tried to build up a rage inside her, to help for the moment when she opened the door and ran.

'You'll all take formicide,' she swore, 'and there'll be enough for everybody.'

But she was naked, and afraid. Being angry was not helping. She looked for something to wear, but the ants swarmed in the bedroom and the curtains were sibilant with their hurrying feet. She gave up the idea of finding anything. She ran to the door and opened it.

Like a small wave breaking high up on the beach, the ants which had piled up against the door swirled around her ankles as she opened it.

Even as she started to run it flashed through her mind that she was right and that Jane Fallon was wrong. These ants would *never* keel over. Like masters, like servants, and they'd botched the job.

Then she forgot about the Fallons, and their servants. There was nothing, anywhere in the world, but ants.

OLD FEET

Martin Waddell

RICHARD HELD the foot before him at arm's length, his thumb and first finger gripping the top of the grey sock, so that the foot below swung slowly round.

It was undoubtedly a foot, although in an advanced state of decomposition, so that the fluids it secreted had stained and soiled the ordinary grey sock it was in. Richard held it up with a good deal of care, fearful that the fabric of the sock might give way; then he lowered it on to the table before him, there to consider it in all its aspects.

He sniffed it, then he prodded it with his thumb, then he sniffed his thumb before wiping his hand carefully with his handkerchief.

It might look like a grey sock full of ... of ... Have you ever cleaned out a blocked drain? ... that's what it looked like, soft and oozy, yet with a certain substance to it, a shape where the flesh had rotted into the wool ... or had the wool rotted into the flesh? It might look like a sock full of oozing mud and bone but he felt reasonably sure that it was, in fact, a foot.

Whose foot?

It's a reasonable question, but Richard didn't know the answer. Apart from the tab on the sock, numbered in purple ink Tankard /53/9J there was nothing to distinguish it from any other decaying foot you might find around the place. Was it a foot of distinction, the foot of a gentleman? Or the foot of a roadmender, a chorus girl ... it did not look like a girl's foot, it was a big foot. I say was, but I mean had been, for it wasn't big any longer, but the sock was a big one and presumably the foot inside had originally fitted it before ... but there's no need to go into unpleasant details, is there? It was a mystery, an enigma, and Richard sat with the decaying foot in a soup plate in front of him as he ate his supper, now and then absently prodding it with his fork, to see how sound it was.

His meal finished, he made himself a nice cup of tea, read a chapter of Proust ... he had a Plan for Proust, and was working his way through a set amount each day ... cleaned up his things, and returned to the foot. It had dripped a little over the edge of the soup plate and made an unpleasant looking stain on the table-cloth, but that couldn't be helped; a soft squelchy foot is a difficult thing to fit into a soup plate, try it sometime. He carried the soup plate across to the telephone table, settled down on his new blue sofa beside it, and rang up his friend Emma.

'Hullo Em,' he said. 'Guess what?'

'What?' she said. You may as well know at this point that Richard had a very low opinion of Emma, not entirely based on fact. Emma, in his opinion, was not bright. Richard, in his opinion, was. He had met her at the Hammersmith Palais one St Patrick's night and noted the distinction at once, with the result that he thought he'd been exploiting Emma ever since. Some of the things Emma did her mother wouldn't have believed in, let alone approved of, but she got along quite nicely thank you, with the aid of several suitors, one of whom was Richard. Emma's mother certainly wouldn't have thought him suitable, for he was known all over Acton for not doing the sort of things Emma's mother thought Emma should do only Emma didn't, if you see what I mean. What I'm getting at is that knowing Richard was no skin off Emma's nose, and her mother did very nicely out of it too, though she thought Emma worked in a banana factory.

'I got something for you Em,' Richard said, idly squeezing the foot.

'Ohoooo!' gurgled Emma in delight.

'A surprise,' said Richard. 'You'll never guess.'

Actually Emma was never much concerned with guessing; it was valuing that took up her time. The important thing about a gift, to Emma's mind, was what she could get for it.

It was her proud boast that she could get *something* for *anything*.

'It'll put our relationship on a new footing,' said Richard . . . he *was* a lad, was Richard.

'Oh Rich,' said Emma. 'You shouldn't have .'

Now although Emma didn't know it, this was basically very realistic of her. Richard *shouldn't* have brought the foot home. He should have left it where he found it in the tea-urn, or else he should have taken it to the management and complained. 'This tea tastes of old feet!' Goodness knows he'd said that often enough, but right up until the moment he actually found the foot he'd never imagined that there really was one in there, slowly decaying among the tea-leaves. With any normal good fortune the foot would have been thrown out one day when the urn was cleaned, and no one would have known the difference, but the old grey sock had somehow become entangled round the heat regulator and there the foot had hung, for all the world like a tea bag, adding its own distinctive flavour to each cup.

'You coming over then?' Richard inquired seductively.

'I can hardly wait,' said Emma, and she couldn't either, because her mother had been drinking the grocery money again. She rushed to the bathroom, took out her teeth and cleaned them, gurgled at herself . . . she was a funny girl, she liked gurgling . . . put her teeth back in, hitched up her tights . . . she wore those green ones with the silver bell decorations . . . tugged on her snakeskin boots and fairly bounced down the stairs to the front door and out through it to the bus stop, where she had to wait half an hour for a 31.

As for Richard at the other end of the line, he wasn't in a good mood at all, which was a pity, because when he'd put down the phone after calling Em up he'd been feeling quite full of himself. 'Put our relationship on a new footing,' he said to himself, smugly smiling into the sitting-room mirror and thinking what a catch old Em had got herself. But his happiness didn't last. He was standing by the mirror combing his hair into flounces . . . he liked flounces, they went with his image . . . when his elbow caught the soup plate, and over it went, foot and all, making a great big slimy ooze stain all down the side of his trousers. I don't know if you've ever tried sponging decayed foot and tea-leaves off your cavalry twills while your lady friend is on the way over ... he wasn't to know about the 31 ... but you can take it from me that decayed foot doesn't sponge off all that easily. It's like grease, only worse ... more like cat food left to fester in a tin, then mixed briskly with cob-web, only not quite like that either. If you're very particular about it and want to know for yourself you can always ask your friends if they've got a foot they can spare or you might even find one rotting somewhere one day, as Richard did ... though admittedly a tea-urn isn't the most logical place in the world to look for one. A tea-urn not being a logical place to look for a foot ... even though the tea in Richard's did taste as though a foot had been dripping into it ... well, oozing into it ... a tea-urn not being the place you'd normally expect to find a foot is probably the reason why it got left there. Probably the person who put it there had every intention of coming back for it, but forgot where it was hidden and simply couldn't find it again. It may even have been put in there for a joke ... you give some people a foot and they'll take a mile ... or someone may have put it there out of malice thinking the manageress would shout out 'Hey, there's a foot in my tea!' and the lady with the trolley would get the sack ... not that she didn't deserve the sack, she should have cleaned her urn more thoroughly, right up inside, instead of just taking out the little tea-leaves tray at the bottom ... but on the whole I think it more likely that somebody was quite innocently taking the foot home ... maybe it was a souvenir of his operation ... and absentmindedly put it inside the urn pro-tem to keep it cool, or hot, depending on the season, and we don't know the season for the simple reason that Richard had no way of telling how long the foot had been in there before he found it, though he might have been able to work out how long the tea had tasted of rotting foot, but he didn't bother. What we do know for certain is that Richard found the foot which had somehow got into the urn and was flavouring the tea. Instead of doing the proper thing with it, complaining, or putting it back in the urn and keeping his mouth shut, he put it inside his cardigan and walked stiffly back to his office where he slopped it into his briefcase, because he thought it would make a splendid and unusual present for Em.

This was one of the recurring problems about Emma. Because she was making a living out of it, she encouraged people to give her presents, but as she sold them all, she always needed more. Her boy friends naturally thought she had everything, and had to go to a great deal of trouble to come up with something new and original which expressed their personalities. The foot seemed the perfect answer and Richard congratulated himself on his shrewdness as he came home on the District Line that night. What if it had smeared his shirt, if it was even now slopping around in his briefcase, slithering around his library book? It was unusual. It would show her what a lad he was. No one else could possibly have given her a foot. It was bound to come in handy . . . in *handy*, the very phrase he used, which shows you again how bright Richard was, footloose and fancy . . . but, that's unpardonable! It would be a surprise, a novelty, wouldn't it? A necklace of teeth, yes; a hair piece, yes; maybe even a purse made out of an ear . . . they have 'em, it's for sophisticates living up in Canonbury, but they do . . . but has anyone ever given you a *foot*? It's not a practical gift . . . what can you do with it? A-foot-in-the-door, I suppose, or you could make it into a lamp, or wire it up as a telephone receiver . . . but that's while your foot is firm, and Richard's foot wasn't firm. Richard's foot had been in the tea-urn goodness knows how long, and it showed.

'Hullo Em,' Richard said, when he opened the door.

'Hullo Rich,' she said. 'What's afoot then?'

He could have said, 'It's a wet slimy thing in a grey sock that gets right into the fabric of your carpet,' but he didn't. He caught her in a passionate embrace and there wasn't any sensible dialogue that bears reporting for a long time.

'I got you a present Em,' he said, when they were having their cups of cocoa . . . despite being a bit of a lad and a personality, Richard was basically conservative, cocoa was good enough for his dad, so it was good enough for him. It builds you up, cocoa.

'You shouldn't have,' said Emma, unconvincingly. She should have thought up something new to say, but she hadn't bothered. You're better to stick to the things you know. She was basically conservative, too, which is probably why she got on so well with Richard.

'Close your eyes, Em,' he said.

'Oh no I couldn't,' she said, blushing prettily, though it was a bit late for that really.

'Go on Em,' Richard said.

'All right then Rich,' she said, 'I will.'

Emma closed her eyes and sat there hopefully, and something cold and soft was placed in her lap.

'You can open your eyes, Em,' said Richard.

'What is it, Rich?' she said, looking at the gaily wrapped parcel on her lap. 'You really shouldn't have you know.'

'Open it, Em,' said Richard proudly.

Emma untied the pretty blue ribbon with fluttering fingers, tore back the paper and looked at the foot, most of which Richard had got back inside the sock after he'd scraped it off the carpet.

'It's lovely, Rich,' she said, mechanically.

'It's a foot,' he said, expectantly.

'Ohooooo!' said Emma. 'A foot! You shouldn't have.'

'I did though, didn't I?'

'A foot,' said Emma, thoughtfully. 'I don't think I've ever had a foot before.'

'Don't be silly Em,' said Richard. 'You've got two already.'

'I know,' she said. 'But this one's special, isn't it?'

'Course,' he said. 'I wouldn't have given it to you else, would I, Em?'

They both sat and looked at the foot which, freed of its protective wrapping, was beginning to ooze out of the sock again.

'Rich,' said Em. 'What does it do?'

'It doesn't do anything, Em,' said Richard. 'It's a foot.'

'What do you do with a foot, Rich?' she said.

'Walk on it,' said Richard, a little impatiently.

Emma looked at it for a moment. 'I don't think I'd like to do that Rich,' she said. 'It would get all over my shoes.'

'You could put it up before the fire,' said Richard, warming to his subject.

'Could you?' said Emma.

'Or put it in a slipper,' he said. 'You could get it a whole range of shoes to show it off. It's unique Em. You're the only girl in London with three feet, think of that.'

'I am,' said Em, perhaps a little bitterly. She didn't even know where you went to sell a foot, let alone what you were supposed to get for it. The ordinary presents people gave her, jewellery, furs, pretty little things from the Portobello Road; she could dispose of them without so much as a moment's thought ... but a foot, and a pretty dodgy looking foot too, she thought to herself, now what do you do with a foot? A butcher ... no. A taxidermist ... even if it could be stuffed, then what? And stuffing costs money. A hospital ... for students to study ... that seemed a good idea.

'Thank you ever so Rich,' said Emma, rewrapping the foot, a puzzled frown on her brow.

Emma didn't show the foot to her mother when she got home. Her mother might have wanted her to keep it, like the golden brooch or the silver fox fur, and Emma didn't really fancy the foot. She agreed with Richard that it was an unusual gift which expressed his personality, but she still didn't want it lying round the house gathering dust. Basically, it was an old smelly foot, and she wanted rid of it.

Right, you may say, put it in the bin, or burn it. She couldn't burn it, her house in Acton had oil-fired central heating, but she could have put it in the bin. You might even say she *should* have put it in the bin, just as Richard should have left it in the tea-urn, but she didn't. She was a hard working girl and she had a living to earn, just like anybody else, and the way she earned her living was by getting a price for anything, *anything*, no matter what.

She had one left foot in a grey sock, so she was going to

sell it. Somebody somewhere wanted a left foot, of that she was sure.

'How much will you give me?' she said, plumping it down on Mr Blackburn's counter. It made a horrid little sucky noise, but luckily he didn't seem to notice.

'What for?' he said.

'That,' she said, prodding the foot.

'It's not a bad sock,' he said. 'How many more have you got dear?'

'There's only one,' she said.

'One pair of socks?' he said. 'You can't come pestering me with that. If I went round buying single pairs of socks like that I'd soon be out of business.'

'It's not a pair,' she said. 'Just the left one.'

'One sock,' he said, shaking his head in disbelief.

'Not one *sock*,' Emma said, 'one. . . .'

But it was no use. Mr Blackburn had gone to his little room at the back, where he was counting army surplus vests. Sadly, Emma picked up her foot and left.

Somebody, somewhere must want a left foot.

She didn't like to go in through the main gate of the hospital, so she went round the side and bumped into ever-such-a-nice-young-man, who was pushing a wicker basket.

'I wonder if you could direct me?' Emma began.

'Any time,' he said, saucily.

They went for coffee in a little-place-he-knew down the road. Emma knew it too but she didn't say so. She was trying to work her way round to introducing the foot, which lay all damp and clammy inside her shopping bag.

'Rex,' she said . . . the young man's name was Rex. . . . 'Do they buy, you know . . . bits of people, up at the hospital?'

'How do you mean?' he said cautiously.

'Well,' Emma said. 'Supposing a person had a bit of a person to sell . . . would they buy it?'

'All depends,' Rex said.

'A left foot?' said Emma hopefully.

'I don't know about that,' Rex said. 'Feet aren't much in my line. I'm more a body man myself.' He said it with a sort of a leer, but luckily Emma wasn't taking any notice, she was too concerned about the foot getting on to the butter in her bag.

'Do you think you could find out for me?' she said.

'Come around to my place and I'll look it up,' he said. So they went back to Rex's and, a long time later, he actually did look it up, or at least poor Emma thought he was looking it up, but actually the little grey book he thumbed through was Caesar's Gallic Wars III.

'What's it say, Rexie?' she said, hitching up her tights ... they were always getting bunched round her middle those tights, which came of having short legs and a big behind she called her Disaster, but that's by the by. Emma never could get a pair of green tights to fit her.

'You really want to sell your feet?' said Rexie ... it was Rexie now, not Rex ... who was really quite an ordinary hospital porter, and found the whole thing a little difficult to grasp.

'Not my feet,' she said. 'Just my foot.'

'Ha ha,' said Rex, thinking what a funny little thing she was. 'I should hang on to it if I were you. Wait'll you get a pair.'

'I got one too many,' said Emma, ungrammatically, but not without a certain charm.

'You look a bit of all right to me,' Rexie said, wittily. 'And your feet do too,' he added, as an afterthought. So far as he could see there was nothing at all the matter with Emma's feet, of which she had only two, despite her protestations to the contrary.

'If only I had a pair,' she said, sadly.

'Hullo Em,' said Richard, when called to the office phone that afternoon. 'How's tricks?'

'Listen Rich,' she said. 'You know my foot?'

'Yes Em?' he said.

'You know *feet* Rich ... they come in pairs don't they? Two of them.'

'Not always Em,' said Richard, guessing the way the conversation was going.

'Oh Rich,' she said, heavy breathing and pause, 'I would so love to have the other one.'

'Well Em . . .'

'You'll get it for me, won't you Rich . . . promise?'

'Well Em . . .'

'I do fancy you Rich, honest I do.'

'Well Em . . .'

'And I *love* my foot, Rich.'

'You see Em . . .'

'Please Rich?'

'I'd like to get you the right one too Em, honest I would, but . . .'

'Ohooooho Rich, you are a love,' said Emma, and quickly put down the receiver.

What a dilemma! (Dil-Emma thought Rich . . . he was a lad, remember?) He sat at his desk, his fingers pensively flipping through his invoices, his mind elsewhere. Em wasn't really being unreasonable, feet do come in pairs. One left foot was no use to anybody. But where was the other one? So greatly perturbed was he that he had almost finished his tea before he realized that it tasted of . . . old feet!

It was the work of a moment to walk to the door, stroll down the corridor, peer furtively round the door of the kitchen, step inside, remove the top of the urn and reach down inside it where his groping fingers found the second rotting sock, complete with foot. This one, he noted with interest, still had toenails, though they had been discoloured by the tannin.

A happy ending? That's what Richard thought. He sent the foot round to Emma special delivery, and she put it in the shopping bag with the first one and carried them both to a man she knew in an antique shop.

'Do you buy feet?' she said.

'If the price is right,' he said, mechanically.

She put her two feet on the counter.

'Eeuugggh!' he exclaimed, quite naturally. 'Take them away.'

She looked hurt, and Emma could look very pretty when she was hurt.

'Apart from anything else,' he said, to soften the blow, 'You'll agree that they're in very bad condition and ...' he peered closer, 'and, they're not even a pair!'

'Of course they're a pair,' Emma said, but they weren't. She had two left feet. Or rather three left feet and one right one, but the pair were her own.

'Hullo Em,' said Richard, when called to the office phone the following morning. 'How's tricks?'

Meanwhile, in the tea urn, two right feet were brewing very nicely, thank you!

DON'T AVOID THE RUSH HOUR

Peter Richey ·

THE TRAINS had stopped running. Paul knew this the moment he awoke on a bench on the platform of Leicester Square tube station. The place was in total darkness. He was alone. There was silence. Only the mixed odour of tobacco smoke and vomit had lingered to remind him of his whereabouts.

He looked at his watch. It was 3.30 AM. His mind became confused. Could it be 3.30 PM? An afternoon power-cut perhaps? But no; he began to remember. He had been drinking on the previous evening. He had spent some hours in a Wardour Street pub, and had tasted his first vodka. He recalled feeling pleasantly old for seventeen. He had felt like a man in that pub. By the time he came to leave he had smelt like one too.

That was at 10.30. What then? Strip clubs – that was it. He'd walked past some strip clubs.

'Lovely girls! Ten bob only to you sir. All naked!' But he hadn't gone inside. The breasts on the photographs had looked revoltingly large, shaped like the domes they have in Russia. Besides, he'd read somewhere that strip clubs were for men who couldn't find girls. The thought of joining the ranks of London's dirty old men hurt his pride. So what had he done next? Nothing very exciting, or surely he wouldn't have forgotten about it so soon. He was presumably still a virgin.

Then he realized, with disappointment, that he had done nothing at all. He'd come into the station. He'd bought his ticket for Kennington. He'd wandered down to the platform. He'd sat down. And here he was still, nearly five hours later.

How odd that they should have closed the station down for the night without waking him. What time had he promised to be in by? Midnight? There would be a row when he got home.

When . . .? With sudden shock he realized that it was more a question of if he got home. Like a man dozing in the bath who notices that the water's run out, Paul began to feel uncomfortable. He became frightened. And cold — it was like being shut in a deep freeze vault. He had to escape.

He stood up, swayed a little, then began to grope his way along the platform, keeping a hand on the wall to guide himself. His fingers slid across grubby advertisements, normally so bright and demonstrative, now impotently invisible. A change for the better, Paul thought with inappropriate flippancy; he was still slightly drunk. He remembered that somewhere along the wall was an exit to the moving staircases. If only he could creep his way to the surface he might find an open window or something.

But when his fingers felt cold steel, he knew he was trapped. A massive iron door was blocking the way to the staircases. London Transport's security service. Paul banged his fists on the door. The noise echoed like a gong down the platform and into the tunnel. It frightened him further, and made his hands ache.

He tried shouting — 'Help! Let me out!' — but he felt silly uttering such things. 'Help!' was an exclamation used on television and charity appeal posters or in foreign lands; not in the Underground. 'All Change!' was the only thing people shouted in the Underground. And anyway he knew in advance that nobody would hear his cries. The streets were hundreds of feet above him.

It was 3.45 now. Paul resigned himself to spending the rest of the night on the bench. He wandered back towards it.

'London Transport wishes Paul Lancer a very good night and trusts he will find the accommodation to his liking' Paul half sang, as if to persuade himself that it was all rather fun, another manly adventure. But this false gaiety drained from him instantly. His heart palpitated. He was almost certain he'd heard a muffled 'what?' being spoken somewhere in the darkness. He stopped and listened intently. Not a sound. Too much vodka, he gladly and rather proudly concluded.

He reached the bench and slumped down on it. Much too

much vodka – the bench was soft and warm like a sofa. Then it wriggled. Paul gasped in horror and jumped to his feet again. There were no sofas at Leicester Square however much you'd had to drink. He had sat on another person.

Paul was halfway down the platform before he fully believed in the new situation. He hadn't noticed anyone earlier. He thought he could hear his own footsteps echoing behind him as he ran, but when he stopped to check the sound continued, click, click, click. He was being followed. He remembered something he'd once seen in a comic about commandos; he removed his shoes and ran on silently in his socks. Now he could move this way and that undetected. The pursuer would have no means of knowing where he was.

Yet the footsteps continued, click, click, click, click, like a man late for work who doesn't wish to lose dignity by running. There was something appallingly methodical about the footsteps; they seemed to exist on their own, without a brain to control them, like an escaped robot working its wicked will in the absence of its master. The sock plan was not working. Comics were a load of lies; rubbish for children. Paul was seventeen; he drank vodka in Soho. Comics were rubbish.

Paul crashed into a litter bin on the wall at the end of the platform. It buckled before the force of his stomach, and winded him severely. The footsteps came closer and closer. There was only one way out of this. He stuffed his shoes into his jacket pockets, jumped down on to the lines and ran into the curving tunnel; the current was off, so he could tread on the conductor rail without danger. He stumbled on for about a hundred yards, then paused to listen for the footsteps. They had stopped.

Just as Paul was congratulating himself on his cunning he heard the distant sound of someone jumping down on to the track shingle. Then the menacing steps resumed, running now, crunch, crunch on the stones, into the tunnel. Paul ran on, but the crunches were catching him up with alarming rapidity.

By chance Paul remembered that tube tunnels have little recesses built into their walls for the maintenance staff to stand in when trains go by. If he could find one of these, and enter it quietly enough perhaps this unseen threat would crunch on past. Paul held his hand out to the wall just as he had done earlier on the platform. At last he felt a hollow. He crept into the recess and pressed himself against its back wall. The space was only three feet deep, and not much higher or wider. But it was better than nothing. Strange draughts kept descending from the blackness and blowing against him as he crouched. He tried to breathe as quietly as his over-worked lungs would allow. His feet began to ache, and with his fingers he could feel great holes in his socks. He'd only had them for a week, and there was something about long life printed on them. That was a joke. Not that Paul laughed. He took one of the shoes from his pocket and ran his hand across the steel-capped heel.

The footsteps were almost upon him now. 'Go past!' Paul pleaded silently. 'For God's sake go . . .' He caught his breath. He had repeated the plea out loud. The game was up. He had given himself away. He tightened his grip on the shoe.

The crunches, of course, stopped abruptly just level with the recess. The person coughed in the dark, and shuffled his feet on the shingle, wondering, no doubt, where the words had come from. Paul's lungs were almost bursting with restrained air, and he was certain his heart beats must be audible enough for the stranger to locate his hiding-place. But there's no way of hushing up heart beats; the quieter you want them, the louder they go.

Neither Paul nor the stranger moved. There seemed to be a kind of stale-mate between them. If this were a film, Paul thought, now would be the time for the ice cream intermission. He longed to hear that stupid voice – 'There will now be a short . . .' – but the silence continued. There would be no drinks-on-sticks down here. He toyed with the idea of springing out from the recess and striking blindly with the shoe. Anything seemed preferable to the strain of this awful cramped tension. But somehow he couldn't bring himself to move. It was as if his limbs had detached themselves from his consciousness, as if they were no longer subject to the dictates of his brain. He regarded them as a commander might regard troops who have mutinied just before the battle, half angered by the disobedience and half relieved that the prospect of death or mutilation had been postponed.

It was 4.30. Paul's legs had gone numb with cold and cramp. And his mind had become oddly removed from the danger he was in. Fear paralyses portions of one's awareness. Nature's safety catch, perhaps, provided to prevent insanity developing in moments of crisis.

Now the man took to walking up and down with slow, deliberate paces, as if looking for something he'd dropped. Ten paces one way, ten paces back, then off again. He seemed in no hurry. Perhaps for him the pleasure lay in anticipating rather than carrying out his foul plan. If so, he was certainly making his fun go a long way. He didn't seem to be making any real effort to find Paul. He was like some glutton wandering round a feast table, sniffing the flavours and contemplating the joys to come.

His steps lulled Paul's mind into a state of semi-trance. He began to engage in luxuriously remote speculation as to what the man looked like. Was he tall or short, young or old? Had he a beard? A tramp perhaps? Yet the paces had been too fast and sure for a down-and-out. He must be young then, or at the most, middle-aged. And vicious. Maybe even mad. Paul was hardly aware that any of it concerned him at all. The safety catch was down. The ticking of Paul's watch mingled with the beats of his heart and with the crunches on the line, a sinister orchestra with too much emphasis on percussion.

But at 4.45 a hopeful thought dragged Paul's mind from its stupor. It was nearly daybreak. Soon the early staff would be down. But above all, the trains would start running. If only he could hold on for another half-hour or so, there was a good chance that the man would be reduced to a bloody, squashed hulk. This prospect both thrilled and horrified Paul. It would be most unpleasant. But on the other hand, what alternative was there? If you stand on a railway line you can't expect to be granted right of way.

Slowly the luminous hands of Paul's watch crept round

the dial. 4.50, 4.55, 5 o'clock. 5.10, 5.13 . . . at exactly 5.15
Paul heard a sound like the sizzling of sausages. There followed a short, pained gasp. Simultaneously, the tunnel lights
went on. Standing on the lines was a skinny man of about forty,
dressed in a shabby suit that was several sizes too large for
him. The eyes beneath his battered bowler hat were staring
intently at the wall above Paul. His face wore a startled expression, with the mouth slightly open. He looked very pale
and ill under the dim illumination. At his feet lay an open
brief case, and sticking out of this was the gleaming blade of a
sharp knife.

Quite suddenly the man swung round on his heels and fell,
rigid as a tree, to the ground. The sizzling noise began again,
and Paul noticed a smell of burning. A small flame appeared
under the man's stomach. Within seconds the body was en-
gulfed in fire. Orange and yellow streamers leaped and stabbed
up at the vaulted roof. Paul crouched, immobile, in the recess,
nearly choking from the fumes and wanting to be sick. The
man began to twist and turn and twitch. He sat up inside the
flames, fell back again, arched his back, kicked his legs frantically. Paul caught a brief glimpse of his face. The eyes were
staring with blind madness now, and seemed on the point of
melting. And the jaws were opening and shutting, as if chewing
a tough piece of meat. The skin was charred and peeling from
the skull inside. The body collapsed and lay still again. There
was a popping sound, followed by a foul stench as the stomach
bag burst. Intestines flowed out and were consumed in the
flames. The clothes were all gone, and ribs were poking from
the trunk like teeth on a giant comb.

Paul could stand no more. He slipped his shoes on, pulled
himself from the recess and ran off down the line towards the
station. As he rounded a bend in the tunnel, he looked back
over his shoulder. All he could see was a cosy, homely glow, of
the sort that goes well with Christmas carols. But the smell
wasn't turkey.

The station came into view, all lit up now. As Paul emerged
from the tunnel, an alarmed sweeper waved a broom at him.
Not 'sposed to be down there. 'Spose a train come along, stupid

young fool. Right mess you'd be in and don't ask me to sweep it up.'

Paul climbed up on to the platform. The sweeper came closer. He was old and bald. He squinted at Paul, obviously determined to make the most of his small authority. 'Just a minute. Shoes undone. Hair like a haystack. What's going on? What you been up to down there? You ain't one of these drug people are you? One of these hipsters? Eh?'

It was useless trying to explain to this man. 'I dropped a coin on the line. I went to pick it up.' Paul mumbled flatly; this was no time for polished acting, and the sweeper was not convinced.

'Dropped a bloody coin! At 'alf past five in the morning? What was it? A gold sovereign?'

Paul pushed past the old man and ran through the exit that had been blocked by the steel door.

'Come back, you young hooligan! You bloody hipster. I ain't done with you yet . . .'

Paul went up the moving staircase. He must find a sensible station official or the whole place would go up in smoke. It had all happened so fast, like in a nightmare. He could hardly believe in his own experience. And the rest of the station seemed so normal. Was it really possible that a body lay burning less than a mile from these slick underwear advertisements?

But by the time he reached the top of the staircase, Paul had changed his mind. He would tell nobody, disclaim having had any part in the affair. The station people would discover the body soon enough, and it was unlikely that anyone would listen to the sweeper's story about the 'hipster'. Nobody would ever find out that he had been anywhere near Leicester Square that night.

Paul slipped out of the station by a side door unnoticed. It was half light and very chilly in the streets. He began walking rapidly in the direction of Kennington, across Charing Cross Road, round Trafalgar Square and into Whitehall. He heard a violent ringing noise. A fire engine sped past, followed by five more. Then a solitary ambulance went by. Paul started to laugh uncontrolledly. 'Ash trays,' he bellowed. 'He needs an ash tray, not an ambulance.' Imperceptibly his laughter changed to tears. He cried and cried. A few early walkers pretended not to notice. Some drunken idiot, they judged, absolving themselves from further involvement. Nothing to do with us.

It was only when he reached Lambeth Bridge that Paul began to realize what must have happened in the tunnel. The sizzling noise must have been caused by the man being electrocuted when the current was switched on. The gasp had been a dying one, and the pale, inquisitive expression had been that of sudden death. But by some freak of balance the body had remained on its feet for a few seconds before falling. Paul was on the verge of taking pity on the man when he remembered the knife in the brief case. There could be no sympathy for a man with a knife like that, for a man who had attempted murder.

Paul arrived home just after his father had left for work. His mother came to the door.

'Had your Dad and me worried to death, you did. Had no sleep all night. Lucky you missed him. If you'd seen his face . . . and don't you look awful?'

'Thanks.'

'Come in and wash your face. It's covered in black. Can't think what you've been doing. Don't much like to either. I shan't ask where you've been. I know a thing or two about what boys do at night. I didn't marry your Dad for nothing. But I mind my own business. Don't go poking my nose where it's not wanted . . .' Her words droned on, a stream of well-meant triviality. They meant as much to Paul as would the sound of rain on a window pane.

After breakfast he went to bed and fell into a troubled sleep. He kept seeing an image of the burning man's contortions. Over and over again he saw that agonized face with the jaws opening and shutting. And the knife blade was there, all wound up with the central theme of death.

He awoke in time for tea. As he went downstairs he caught sight of the evening paper lying on the kitchen table. 'MAN BURNED TO DEATH IN TUBE' was the headline. Paul went over and picked up the paper.

'Mr Wardale, 42,' it went on 'whose burnt remains were found early today in the south bound tunnel of the Northern Line between Leicester Square and Strand stations, was un-employed and lived at 17 Kempley Street, S.E.13. It is thought that the fire was started by the electric current igniting the contents of a cigarette lighter discovered among the bones. Said fifty year old Mrs Crawford, his landlady.

' "I asked him to get me a new knife that's just come out. It's specially for cutlets. He was a lonely man, and he'd been all depressed lately, due I suppose to his being jobless. When he got like this he used to go all funny and absent-minded. He hardly knew where he was half the time. And he would follow strangers through the streets for hours on end. He wanted com-pany. I can't believe he's gone yet. He was a perfect gentleman for all his strange ways. The last thing he said before he went out to get my knife yesterday afternoon was how he'd once seen some beautiful girl at Leicester Square station who'd smiled at him. He said he'd find her again even if he had to wait there all night. I don't suppose there was any girl there, and if there was she was most likely laughing at him, not smiling. He did look funny in his flappy old suit. He though he was keeping up appearances. As I say, he was funny like that. But he was only trying to be friendly." '

THE WHISPERING HORROR

Eddy C. Bertin

I HAD known Harvey Denver, since we were both four years old. We went together to the kindergarten, and thereafter to the same small-village school. We shared the same friends, the same enemies and a dislike for the same teacher. We enjoyed the same games and hobbies, almost as two brothers.

To his memory, I will now write the real facts, as much as I know them or WANT TO KNOW THEM, about that summer day, many years back now, when I ran screaming from the graveyard where Harvey was buried. Maybe you'll think them part of a boy's nightmare, something which doesn't or *can't* happen in this nice, safe little world of ours, where there is no place for the unknown, the impossible. I know otherwise, and I don't care if you believe me or not. There is no proof, not any more. The only proof is in my brain, where it has been haunting me ever since, always returning in horrible nightmares, in a fear for dark places. But maybe this is the way to whip it all out of my mind, where every detail is engraved, our walks together, the ruins . . . and the whispering . . .

It started the summer when we were both nine years old. We were born the same year, Harvey in April and I in June, which made him the natural leader for our two-man expeditions, the more as he was bigger and stronger than myself. After schooltime, we enjoyed taking long walks so that we could play in the forest which was about a kilometre from our village.

The wood was nothing exceptional, a bunch of trees and bushes, thrown together by playful nature, but to us it was paradise. Usually, we didn't go deep into the wood; we had felt once (on our bottoms) the troubles which arose when we had stayed out too late. Also, the forest soon became much thicker and darker, and we still feared we would get lost someday. We no longer believed in witches and gnomes, but we were still afraid of the dark, even if we would never confess it. Still, on a free afternoon, with time to spare, we penetrated much deeper than usual.

It was then that we found the house, or what was still left of it. That wasn't much, just the entrance to a cellar, a mass of stones and part of one crumbling side-wall, miraculously still standing, like a lonely sentinel. It must have been a very small house, most of which was built of timber, that later on had been used for other purposes. Only the cellar seemed to be intact. Curious, we went and looked into the black hole, waiting each for the other to go in first. It would have to be Harvey, of course. But he didn't seem very anxious to lead the way. He descended two steps, bent and looked once again.

'Can't see a thing,' he whispered.

'Of course not, how could you?' I answered, whispering too. 'There isn't a single window anywhere. Must be dark like hell, down there.'

I don't know why we whispered. Maybe it was the loneliness of the ruins of the house, the dampness which welled up out of the dark cave in gulps of foul air. I shivered, although it wasn't cold, but somehow the warmth couldn't quite reach me.

'Could there be anyone there?' Harvey asked. His voice, soft as he spoke, seemed to bounce back against the spider-webbed cellar walls and return to us in a hollow whispering, like some lost voice, drifting off on far-away winds.

'Are you crazy?' I hushed him. 'Who could live in a hole like this? There's nothing there. Come on, let's go and play somewhere else.'

Our voices answered out of the dark entrance. The lonely, crumbling wall, bitten through by time, the damp steps, leading down into the abyss of shadows, almost seemed to radiate a feeling of . . . there's no right word for it. Something old, unholy, something evil. Evil, especially to us, intruders in its domain.

'Come on, Harvey,' I whispered. 'I don't like this at all. Let's get out of here.'

But he didn't hear me. His head bent, he was listening very sharply. Suddenly he looked up at me.

'Did you hear that?' he asked.

'I didn't hear anything,' I answered. I tried to laugh, but it sounded so strange and out of place, that I stopped immediately. The only thing I heard, was the echo of my own voice.

'I thought . . . I thought I heard someone breathing,' he whispered.

My ears had received no sound, and I didn't like it at all. Whatever could breathe in a dark cave like this? But then, it couldn't, he must have heard wrong. There was nothing down there. There couldn't be.

I took Harvey's arm. 'Come on, let's get away.'

'No, wait.' He shook himself free and listened intently, holding his breath, spying the darkness with his ears, almost eager to capture a sound.

'It sounds . . . like a dog panting . . .'

'A dog?' I said. 'Why should a dog be down there? Could be anything, even a wild animal.'

'Maybe he fell,' Harvey said. 'Maybe he slipped on the stairs and broke a leg. Maybe his owner got tired of him and just chained him in there to let him die of starvation. Some people would just do a thing like that.'

He had stopped whispering. 'You wouldn't let a dog die down there, all alone in the darkness, hurt and wanting company, would you?'

I didn't answer.

'Listen,' he said, 'it's almost like moaning. Now I'm sure, there's something down there, something alive and hurt. I'm going to see what it is.'

Suddenly, I was deadly afraid to be left alone. I grasped Harvey. 'No, please, don't go down. It is bad, I feel it.'

'Now don't start acting like a sissie,' he snapped. 'The poor thing's probably just hungry. You stay here if you're scared.'

Slowly, taking care not to slip on the stone steps, covered with lichens and dirt, he descended. It smelled dusty and damp. Small creatures hurried away over the steps. Of course, I couldn't stay behind now, which would have proved me a coward. So I followed him, the fear throbbing in my throat. Down there, into the absolute darkness, filled the first seconds with coloured lights and stripes and circles, dancing on my irises. Then, after a while, I made out the dark shapes of old furniture, the walls of the cave, and ... something dark, in a corner of the cellar, something slowly moving. It seemed almost to flow, an indefinable black form, laying flat on the floor.

'There is the poor animal,' Harvey said. With a courage I would never have believed him capable of – or maybe it now seems recklessness – he stretched his hand to touch it.

And then ... the thing WHISPERED. Not a moan or a groan, not a recognizable sound, but a thick, slimy whisper, which seemed to go on and on between the slippery walls. The whisper of something old and feeble, something slimy and swollen, which seemed dead and yet alive, as if it had just awakened from a long sleep. Something petrified and time-less, suddenly coming to itself.

I turned and ran, my only thoughts for free air and light. I slipped on the stairs and hurt my knee, but then I was out of the darkness and away from the horrible whispering.

Outside I got my breath and courage back, but not enough of the last to go back inside. I cursed my own cowardliness, but I didn't return. I just sat down and waited, then got up and started to walk around the ruins. Twice I called, but got no response of any kind. Not a sound came from the cellar. Harvey was alone down there, with the whispering thing. I waited. There was nothing else to do. Then, after a quarter of an hour, Harvey came out of the infernal darkness. He was pale, and so I knew that he too had been scared, even if he was laughing now.

'Coward,' he teased, 'whatever did you run away from? There's nothing horrible down there, just a poor sick old dog, feeling lonesome.'

I didn't say anything. I knew Harvey had lied to me. What-ever had whispered down there in the slimy darkness, hadn't been a dog or any other animal I knew.

We went home and got our second spanking for being late for supper. The next days and weeks, I saw less and less of

Harvey. He almost seemed to evade me. Whenever he spoke to me, he was short and unfriendly, not at all his usual self. Sometimes, on free days, I saw him leave the village, as soon as he could get away, to go to the cellar in the forest. Twice I accompanied him, but I didn't follow him down into the darkness, although he asked me to. He told me the dog was better now, and wanted to play with me also. It was a very old and friendly dog, Harvey said, he was so long and thin. Harvey nicknamed him 'Stake' for that.

Sometimes he told Harvey stories, and that's how I cornered Harvey. Outside a circus, I had never heard a dog speak, and everyone knew in a circus it was just a trick. So Harvey had to admit, it wasn't a dog that whispered to him. Stake was a man, he said at last, a friend. He was old, very old. More than two hundred years, he had told Harvey, and he had come a long way. He had been very sick, and he had been so long in the dark, that the sun hurt his eyes. He never came out, even not at night. So if I wanted to meet Stake, I should go to him.

One day, I almost did. I followed Harvey down the slithery stone steps, leading downward into a hungry stomach of waiting shadows. My back felt hot and cold at the same time, and I was deadly afraid. Nevertheless, I followed. Then I was down, and groping my way, trying to see a thing. Then it whispered A soft, throaty whisper, slimy and unspeakably evil.

'Don,' it whispered my name, in almost unrecognizable words, as if it spoke with a tongue not meant to utter human words.

I cried out, I couldn't hold it back. I panicked, stumbling out of the nauseating cave in a mad flight, and then I ran, away from the forest and the cave with its hellish horror. I never went near it again.

Harvey stopped playing with me altogether from that day on. In fact, he evaded all the other boys and girls of the village, too, and always went out to play alone. Once I overheard a conversation between our parents, and I heard them say that Harvey was always much too late outside. They said he even one night leaped through the window, thinking them asleep, and went out to the forest. Then they started suspecting things about Harvey and girls, which I didn't understand completely, but his father finished the argument, saying that Harvey was still much too young for that. It was just the boy's wild nature, he thought.

But after a while, people began to notice how pale and sick he looked. I had seen it already for a long time, and I knew it to be the bad influence of the thick, stale air in the cellar, and the fact that he was always down there in the dark and never played any more in the sunlight. But I didn't tell on him, and maybe that's my big guilt.

Then he fell sick. The doctor said he had never seen a boy of his age looking so pale. His whole face was thin, almost fallen-in flesh around his skullbones. You could see his cheekbones sticking out. He had lost much weight too. The doc couldn't exactly say what was the matter with him, and that was strange too. Harvey had never been sick before, except the usual children's diseases. The doc ordered plenty of fresh air, wholesome food and some vitamin-pills, and if that didn't help, his parents should go and see a specialist in the city. And Harvey had always been so strong and healthy looking!

The second week of his sickness, I'll never forget. It was the next time I came unwillingly in contact with Harvey's 'friend' Stake.

It was a cloudy, moonless night. The weather was fine, warm and windless, but just not too hot. I had left the window of my room open. I wasn't asleep yet, which was lucky for me. Otherwise I'd never had heard it, before it would have been too late.

It came from the woods, towards the village. Maybe it was bored. Maybe it wanted some company, or just wanted to find Harvey. They were my thoughts then; now I know the much more important and much more horrible reason it had to come out of its cellar.

I heard the slow, dragging steps on the path, and then the crunching of the gravel. Don't ask me how, I just *knew*, with an unsettling clearness, what it was that walked stealthily towards our house through the protecting darkness outside, hid-

den even from the moonlight. In one movement, I was out of
bed and smashed the window shut. The very next second, something whispered very softly outside. There was a rubbing
sound against the window, as if some soft body pressed against
the cold wall, trying to get in, always whispering. There was
nothing to be seen in the darkness outside.

Then the moon came through the clouds for a few fleeting
moments, an eye of ice looking downwards that gave me the
first glimpse ever of the unknown which is always at our side.
The whispering went on and something clawed against the
glass, making sharp lines in it, as for some eternal-seeming
seconds moonlight flooded the scene outside AND THERE
WAS NOTHING THERE.

Real fear runs through your veins like ice, it crawls upwards
under your skin to your neck. It feels like suddenly standing
on the brink of an abominable deep pit with crawling emptiness. Something was there and yet wasn't. I don't know how I
managed to move, but somehow I shrunk backwards, never
letting the window out of my sight. I couldn't breathe, unseen
claws seemed to grope in my stomach and lungs. I'll never
know which reflex or instinct made me reach for the chair. I
was very young then, and I had never had any experience with
the unseen. I had reached in those few seconds a breaking point.
I cried out and threw the chair towards the thing beyond the
window. The glass splintered, as I ran to the door. It wasn't
necessary, it moved outside, very quick, away from the house.

I got a spanking for having broken the window, and then
they had to call the doctor to give me a sedative. Nobody paid
attention to the glass splinters, which all lay inside the room.
I had seen how the glass cracked and broke, just before the
chair reached it!

Then Harvey died. Very suddenly, in the middle of the night.

The doctor said, his heart unexpectedly gave up, for no
special reason at all. He had grown very weak and thin, almost
just skin over his bones. He just simply passed away, from
this world into another. I hope it was into a better one.

Two days later, he was buried. Everyone I knew from the
neighbourhood was there. Serious-looking people everywhere.

Many people wept. I don't know if I cried. When you're nine years old, there's no real understanding of the word 'death'. I only felt Harvey was far, far away from me now, and he would never come back. Yes, maybe I did cry.

The next day, a free afternoon, I went alone to the church-yard to look at Harvey's tombstone and all the pretty flowers on it. Then I heard it again. Now it wasn't sneaking, covered by the dark of night and a moonless sky. It came as an angry thunder-storm, angry, mad, towards Harvey's grave. I jumped away, ran a few steps and let myself roll behind a large tomb-stone, where I stayed hidden, shivering with uncontrollable fear, while the raving terror came nearer and nearer, until it was so close I could hear it, the loathsome, angry whispering.

Much, much later, I came home, to break down in my mother's arms, raving and crying, trying to escape from every shadow in the room. They didn't believe anything I said, until my father, to calm me, went to the graveyard and saw what somebody or something had done to the fresh grave and the stone, to the dug-up, broken coffin and to what was now still left of Harvey's little body. I was delirious for two days before I could speak coherently of the cellar in the wood, and Harvey's friend who lived there. They didn't believe it at first, but they went nevertheless, to find out what was true of my story. They went in a crowd, armed with shovels, pick-axes, guns and electric lamps. They came back, late in the night, looking very tired and somehow scared. None of them said any-thing. The next day, my father told me I must have dreamed everything. They had only found a dead dog in the cave.

Only now, many years later, my father, too, has passed away, and before me I have his diary on that day. In his fine and yet strong handwriting, at last I know what they really found down there.

It was something which could have been human once, but I can't be sure. Neither can any one of us. It was a skeleton, smaller than a normal man, and crouching as if it wasn't meant to walk upright. But on those yellow bones, NEW FLESH, NEW MUSCLES AND FRESH, SOFT SKIN WERE

GROWING. Weak ones, nevertheless, the muscles and flesh of a young boy. They could hardly keep the heavy thing moving. It tried to strike us, and it whispered to us, as Don had told us. When Frank and then Wilfrid hit it with their shovels, it whimpered. We crushed it with our spades, split the bones of the unspeakable thing, and all the time it kept on whispering to us and trying to fight us. It couldn't get past us out of the cellar, and we kept it in the white burning circles of our torches. God forgive me, if it was something which had the right to live, but I don't think it had. The life which moved it was stolen, as was the flesh which grew on it. A foul stench of decay came in gulps out of it, when we broke the bones and split the soft skin. There was blood too, thick and spreading a foul stench of something very old and very dead. Harold cut an arm with a blow of his shovel, and the arm and the hand kept on moving, crawling over the floor. Then Frank heard something outside. He and Peter went to look, and they swear there was nothing to be seen, yet suddenly trees were pushed aside and something struck them away from the entrance with a formidable strength. We all heard something come down the stairs, and at that exact moment I split the skull of the moaning horror with my pick-axe. There was a loud shriek, suddenly cut off and then there was nothing beside us in the cellar. The whispering had stopped, and the loathsome parts of flesh, bones and muscles lay silent.

I can't think of that moment, without shuddering. What could the thing have done to us, if by pure luck, I hadn't hit the skull at the exact moment before the invisible projection (I can't think of a better suited word for it) reached us. We burned everything which was on the floor of the cave, and then we made the cellar collapse over the ashes so that now there is nothing there but a heap of crumbling stones.

They never knew what it had been exactly. Neither did they make much effort to find out. There are some things which don't belong to this world. It is best to leave them alone completely.

But I can't forget what is burned in my memory by such a

petrifying fear as I had never known, and hope will never know again. It is that day, when I lay alone behind the shadow of a tomb, shivering madly in the full sunlight, while something unseen crushed Harvey's tombstone and broke open his grave, always whispering, whispering . . .

SMILE PLEASE

Raymond Williams

THE CHIPPED cane chair creaked its protest as Delorice plonked herself upon it to gaze at her reflection in the large mirror. The bright arc of naked electric bulbs around her reflection gave her a pasty white hue. She bent her head forward a little to study her dry, yellow hair in the glare of the light. It was time for another rinse, really, because here and there the darker roots were quite conspicuous. Still, it would do for tonight for thanks to the red spotlights, which bathed her on stage, the audience would never notice. But come to that the clientele one encountered at the El Toro Club were amazingly tolerant of such things. As long as their very own Delectable Delorice continued to sway and gyrate in front of them they would be happy, providing, of course, she continued to carelessly lose one scanty article of clothing after another to the steady thumping of the tom-toms – in fact they may even be tolerant enough to forgive the lack of music altogether. Noise does tend to distract one's concentration at times, and during Del's act one needed peace to concentrate in earnest.

'God what a life,' she sighed in unison with the lips of her reflection, 'Mirror, mirror on the wall who's the biggest sucker of all?' She closed her eyes and covered her face with her long fingers. In the past each performance had been easier than the one before but now it was getting harder. Before she went on each night she kept getting these frightening moods of depression. She was already thirty-four which was far too old for this game but what alternative was there – an escape into the business to which many of her friends had already turned? Was supplying instant sex to frustrated paying clients a better proposition than this? True the money could be better but her gin bills were already high enough and the change to prostitution would hardly bring them down.

She had tried hard to save as much as she could over the years but like the others in her profession she enjoyed living it up. What she needed was some kind of Sugar Daddy to come along and give her a few thousand so that she could pack the business in here and now and fade away into a plush comfortable home far from the dazzling spot light. But she had given up believing in Father Christmas at a very early age. Two sharp raps on her dressing-room door startled her back to the present. The eunuch-like voice of Ted the call boy squeaked through a, 'Two minutes to the off Miss Delorice'. She squeezed a sick grimace at the mirror as his chuckle floated away down the passage way. Dirty Pig! He was all eyes and grubby little fingers whenever you passed him in the corridor. One of these days she'd – oh what was the use in getting herself in a state, he just wasn't worth the bother, anyway she needed all her strength for the act. Ah well, once more into the breach and all that sort of thing. She pulled open the drawer and took out the ever ready gin bottle. She hastily half filled her blue plastic mug and greedily gulped the cold bitter liquid. The bottle glugged again as she replenished her empty mug. A drop of mother's ruin always seemed to do the trick, the only snag was the quantity needed each time seemed to increase. Still as she wasn't a mother there was no harm was there? She could feel her circulation stirring into life as she returned the bottle to the drawer. A quick check in the mirror on her red and black lace costume and she was on her way.

She hurried down the draughty corridor clutching her dark blue velvet robe tightly around her. As she got to the wings Fat Max, El Toro's resident comedian compère and part time barman was just winding up his act. During the splatter of applause his little round eyes rolled quickly on his red wet face towards her. Seeing her ready and waiting he held up one hand to stem the noise of the lone clapper and continued, 'And now Ladees and Gentlemen, the girl you've all been waiting to see – and believe me there's a lot to see,' he chuckled thickly into the microphone but stopped abruptly when a plaintive voice cried out, 'Stop yapping, Fatso, and get on with it.' Max's grin hardened for a second but with the proficiency that comes with experience he continued as if he had not been interrupted, 'Here she is—' 'Where, I can't see her,' came another voice from the gloom amid a burst of laughter, 'Your very own,' continued Max, 'de-lectable, de-lovely, de-veloped, DE-LORICE.' There was a click as the tape recorder started up then the club was filled with the steady throb of muffled tom-toms. The smiling mask disintegrated from Max's face as he reached Delorice in the wings. 'Good luck, Del, old girl, there's a few bloody-minded bums out there tonight, you're welcome to them. God do I need a drink.'

Delorice steadied herself against the pillar for an instant as if hoping for some strength to ooze from the cold stone to help her into the spotlight. Max wasn't the only person who needed a drink. She cursed herself for not absorbing more gin before leaving the dressing-room – just another half mug full would have made all the difference. 'Go on Del they're all wait-ing,' hissed a voice from behind her.

The next moment she felt herself stalking seductively into the shimmering pool of pink light. Instantly cheers and a few whistles hurtled out of the black abyss towards her but for-tunately all she could see were the two pink suns glaring their rays directly at her. Clicking one of her stilleto heels in time with the beat she drew open the neck cord of her blue robe then suddenly with the deft touch of a true matador she whirled the robe free of her body around her head a few times before leav-ing it to flutter to the ground between herself and the exit from the stage. She knew without looking that it was perfectly in position for her to snatch up to cover her nakedness at the end of the act. A single wolf whistle just managed to pierce the drone of the music. But Delorice was immune to noisy dis-tractions, she proceeded to turn and sway forcing her close-fitting costume taut over whichever curve of her body was visible to the crowd. Then at the desired moment she turned her back on the inquisitive eyes and proceeded to play with the zip on the back of her costume. The zip had been gently lowered to half way when the voice from the wilderness called, 'Unzip a banana,' and a blast of coarse laughter dimmed the tom-toms for a moment. Completely unperturbed Del slid the zip to the small of her back and after turning to face the two pink eyes again wriggled tantalizingly free of her costume. Cheers and calls flooded the club as she kicked herself free and waved her arms high above her head. Her tight silver bra and briefs glinted as they reflected the light. Even the thick curtain of blue smoke seemed to be curling slower in the shafts of pinkness as if it was aware that the best was to appear at any moment. Apart from the drum, there was now an expectant hush lying heavily in the atmosphere. Delorice could sense the sea of blinkless eyes focused on her as she slowly slipped the metal clasp of her bra behind her back. Still swaying her hips rhythmically she crossed her arms across her chest and firmly taking a shoulder strap in each hand she eased the silver covering slowly towards the audience. Then just as they were beginning to glimpse the rounded sides of her breasts she suddenly flicked the bra high into the air giving a well-timed skip forward herself so that her breasts quivered violently up and down. The effect on the audience was shattering. Screams of delight mingling with cries of admiration thundered through the music. Del completed the climax of her act by twitching her tinted body in a wild frantic dance towards the side of the stage. Then with a quick swoop she snatched up her robe and amid desperate cries of despair vanished into the wings.

'Smashin' performance Del,' said Max giving her bottom a friendly pat as he passed her to get the rest of her clothes from the stage. Still panting from the effort she had put into her appearance she put her robe over her shoulders and waited for the rest of her things. Thank God that's another one over she thought.

'Here we are, Del,' said Max returning her crumpled clothes.

She smiled her gratitude and clip-clopped happily back to her dressing-room. For a while she just sat there exhausted taking an occasional sip from her blue mug. Oh, it was a wonderful feeling when it was all over. She could feel all the tenseness and strain leaving her body. She sighed contentedly and stretched back in her creaking chair. In a little while she'd summon up enough energy to get dressed and go home but not just yet. It was just as she was putting down her mug after draining the last few drops that she saw it. There in the middle of her dressing-table was a neat brown paper parcel with 'To Delorice' printed clearly on it. She was surprised that she hadn't seen it as soon as she'd come in – it had been left as conspicuously as possible. Still in her hurry to get the bottle out it was understandable really. She picked it up curiously and turned it over a few times to see if there was anything else written on it. But apart from 'To Delorice' the paper was unmarked. She dug her long silver nails into the Sellotape and ripped away the covering. Her eyes widened and her mouth opened at the sight. Held tightly by a thick red elastic band was a pile of new crisp five pound notes with a neatly-typed yellow card on top. Her brain struggled to contend with the increased thumping of blood through her temples as she focused her eyes on the print. It simply said: 'Please find enclosed one hundred, five pound notes which I trust will be sufficient recompense for awaiting a telephone call from me at 10.30 PM tonight.' The card was unsigned. Five hundred pounds from someone just for waiting for a telephone call? This was ridiculous.

She ran a finger down the edge of the notes. Well they all looked real enough to her, so if it was some kind of joke she didn't mind in the least if it was worth five hundred pounds. She picked up the brown paper and checked her name yet again. Yes, it was clearly addressed to her and she was the only Delorice at the El Toro Club so unless it had been delivered to the wrong place then the money just had to be hers. All five hundred of it for her just if she waited for a telephone call. There must be a catch somewhere she thought but where, that was the question. 10.30 tonight that meant in about – she looked at her dusty travelling clock, 'Hell, it's nearly half past ten now,' she gasped. She pulled the card free of the elastic band, bundled the notes and paper into her handbag and dashed to the door. The cold air in the corridor reminded her to pull her robe together to cover her exposed front as she rushed to the little office at the end.

She burst in half expecting to hear the phone ringing but all was quiet. The only noise in the room came from Ted who was sitting behind the desk scrunching his way through an apple.

'Has the phone been ringing, Ted?' she asked anxiously.

Ted sucked some crushed apple to one side of his mouth and said, 'Not since I've been in.'

Del looked up at the wall clock: it was 10.29. Ted was eyeing her curiously.

'Expecting a call, eh?'

'Mind your own business,' she answered curtly.

'Sorry I spoke I'm sure,' said Ted obviously hurt by the rebuff. 'I thought you was good tonight, Miss Delorice,' said Ted curling his lips back to smile at her.

'You've got bits of green apple peel stuck to your teeth,' she cut back. Ted half turned his face away from her while he stuck a grubby finger into his mouth and swivelled it to and fro like a tooth brush. Del was too busy watching the big hand of the clock creep slowly towards 10.30. Ted wiped his slimy finger on his sleeve then edged his hand slowly towards a gap in Del's robe which his sly eyes had been surveying ever since she came into the room. He thrust his hand into the gap and fumbled his fingers around as much of her breast as he could grip before the smack to the side of his head sent him reeling back into his chair. No sooner had he landed than Del sent his head reeling in the other direction with a blow from her left hand then her right crashed in again. By now he had a hand over each side of his face for protection while Del continued to stand over him swiping one way then the other. At first Ted whimpered and squealed as she lashed him but then for no apparent reason he began to gurgle out little grunts and sighs of ecstasy. By this time Del was beginning to run out of steam and her hands were getting sore but determination enabled her to go on with the treatment until she realized that Ted's eyes looked as big as the glass eyes in Madam Tussaud's. She followed his gaze and saw that with the effort of striking him her robe had been hanging open and Ted had had a grandstand view of her bare breasts all the time, which explained everything.

She quickly covered herself again but the pause was long enough to allow Ted to scuttle out of the chair to the door.

'I thought you was good on stage, Miss Delorice, but I never thought I'd get my own private performance. Why I'd go through—'

Before he could finish it was time for him to beat a hasty retreat before the flying wire basket crashed against the door post just where he had been standing.

The clang of the basket hitting the floor was augmented by the sudden shrill of the telephone bell. Del's pulse was already racing after her encounter with Ted. Her whole body felt hot and clammy and she felt in no mood to answer a mystery telephone call but prominent in her mind was a crisp bundle of blue notes which was sufficient motivation for her to tolerate her damp skin and shaken nerves and lift the black greasy finger-printed receiver. A series of pips were torpedoed into her ear before a metallic crackle ended them as abruptly as they had begun. Well whoever was calling was using a call box, she thought, not that that discovery was much help.

'Hello,' she cooed expectantly.

'Miss Caine?' inquired the voice.

'Yes, that's right. I'm Delorice Caine.'

'Ah, then good evening, Miss Caine,' continued the well-spoken voice sounding far more confident now that the identification had been completed to his satisfaction.

'First of all, may I thank you for awaiting my call. I gather you received my message?'

'Well, yes, I did but I don't know—' Del's hesitancy was interrupted.

'All in good time, Miss Caine. Allow me to introduce myself. I'm Edward.'

'Oh er, hello, Edward,' said Del completely baffled by it all. 'Er, Edward what?' she inquired.

'Just Edward,' chuckled the voice.

'Oh I see,' replied Del realizing that her best plan was to say as little as possible and allow the voice to get on with it.

'I have been a great admirer of your art for some time now Miss Caine.'

Oh, so that was the game Del thought to herself, another dirty old man who wanted a private showing and anything else he could get, so that's what the money was, just a big fat carrot to get her to play around at any kinky game he had lined up for her back at his penthouse flat probably.

'Now, look here,' she burst in suddenly. 'I don't mind you window shopping Mr Edward whatever your name is, but there's no free samples going so you can—'

'My dear Miss Caine,' came the wounded reply. 'Pray allow me to assure you such a proposition had never crossed my mind. I deeply regret that you have so hastily thought of me as a person who would dare to make such suggestions to such a talented artist as yourself. I fear you have completely misconstrued my small gift of money.'

Small gift – £500. Del was numbed at the thought. He just couldn't be for real. He must have taken her silence as a vote of confidence because he continued.

'If you will allow me to clarify – as I was saying your act has intrigued me for some time and my proposition was that you display your talent before a small select group of my friends at a private party I am holding. If you would consider the fee of six thousand pounds adequate for a single performance then I feel we may be able to discuss the matter further.'

The voice stopped, awaiting her reply. Del forced a croaking 'Would you?' she coughed the frog from her throat, 'would you repeat that again, the money that is?'

'Why certainly, Miss Caine. The fee mentioned was six thousand pounds, obviously that is in addition to the five hundred pounds you already have.'

'Oh, obviously,' said Del mechanically. The figure of six thousand five hundred pounds seeped steadily through her fuddled brain. She frightened herself at what she would really be prepared to do for half that amount and here was this amount offered on a plate to her just for taking her clothes off in front of an audience a fraction of the size of the one she stripped before every night. She clasped the phone tightly in both hands in an effort to ensure that she kept this golden voice coming through it.

'Hello, Miss Caine, are you still there?'

'Yes, yes I'm here,' she rushed anxiously.

'Good. All clothing, props, etc., will be supplied and paid for by myself so may I suggest if you are interested we could arrange a meeting and if you are not interested then it will only remain for me to thank you for your time and bid you good night.'

'I'm interested, yes, yes,' she burst in. 'Please I'd love to perform for your friends. I accept and – er thank you for asking me, I'm – er – I'm grateful honestly very grateful – Edward.'

'Splendid Miss Caine. I'm delighted at your acceptance and I look forward to our meeting. Would it be convenient say, if I arrive at the stage door in shall we say ten minutes?'

'Yes, I'll be there,' Del confirmed eagerly. For this money she'd dash out there now as she was if he'd asked her. 'Good. I'll be driving a white sports car and if there happen to be any others there, mine will be the one flashing its lights when you come out – how's that?'

'Yes, that will be fine, Edward,' she answered softly.

'Until then goodbye, Miss Caine, and thank you again.'

There was a click as the receiver went down the other end. There was no time to lose now. She hurried away back to her dressing room and quickly selected the clothes she thought would be appropriate for her meeting with Edward. Yes her ruby corduroy skirt and black sweater always made her look extremely attractive and she did so want to make a good impression on him. If she played her cards right who knows she might have an opportunity for a second booking sometime and at six thousand pounds a time, boy oh boy this was the life. With a few minutes in hand Del trotted through the stage door into the street, her bulky handbag clutched tightly under her arm. A thin drizzle of rain made the street look more drab than usual. There were a few cars parked outside but no white sports car. She looked anxiously up and down the street but nothing moved. 'Oh God please let him come,' she muttered, 'please don't let anything go wrong, not now anyway. I just wouldn't be able to cope if this fell through.' She strutted nervously back and forth outside the door religiously scanning the street like a radar beam. Fine drops of water clung to her false eye lashes. She was beginning to feel cold, damp and very miserable. A low growl made her look down the street again and there gliding towards her was the sleek white nose of an E-type Jaguar. As it whined nearer the headlamps flashed like two lighthouses in unison. She strolled to the edge of the pavement trying to look as relaxed and pleasant as possible.

The passenger door swung open and Edward's voice called out, 'Do get in out of the rain, Miss Caine.'

She needed no prompting but found it rather difficult to get into the car in a dignified manner. Her first sight of Edward was a clean shaven rather long face with a sympathetic smile while his grey eyes absorbed the generous expanse of inner thigh as she struggled into the car.

His strong white teeth flashed momentarily in the gloom. 'That's one thing about an E-Type,' he said, 'the insurance may be shocking but it's worth it when legs like yours get in.'

Del smoothed her skirt down and pulled the door shut feeling rather embarrassed with her performance so far. But why should she? Surely he was the man she was trying to impress and if he enjoyed the sight of her long legs then it was a point in her favour. She had to remember that keeping him happy had to be her first objective; after all wasn't he the golden goose?

As the car purred away she settled farther down in the seat allowing her skirt to rumple up a few inches.

'And what happens now?' she inquired.

'Well, briefly the set up is this, Miss Caine.'

'Oh please call me Delorice, Edward,' she implored.

'Delorice it is then,' he said. 'Well, I was saying this party is for eight of my friends but unfortunately many of them are rather important bods. You know, the odd MP, Harley Street specialist, business tycoon who is too keen to get his name on the Birthday Honours list to risk any discredit to himself like going to a striptease club, etc. So I lay on a private show at my house and charge them accordingly – which explains your generous fee, doesn't it, Delorice?'

She nodded her consent but said nothing. She merely continued to study him. Surely he was only in his early thirties – well definitely younger than her anyway. Wasn't that a bit young to have such important sounding friends. Anyway he seemed too kind and innocent to be organizing this sort of entertainment – still all he had said so far seemed to fit in with what had happened. It explained the secrecy and high fee. His hand dropped to the gear lever and she waited for the fingers to slip after the change on to her leg in the usual accidental manner but the hand returned smoothly to the wood-rimmed steering wheel. Well surprise, surprise! He wasn't even trying to get any fringe benefits for the money.

'The snag is, of course,' continued Edward, 'they must have a perfect view of you but on no account must you see anything of any of them.'

'That's interesting,' Del remarked, 'what do I do, take everything off except a blindfold?'

Edward chuckled richly deep in his throat. 'Don't you worry Delorice, that won't be necessary.' Then he lowered his voice as if someone were listening behind them, 'It's all done by mirrors. Damn clever these Chinese you know.'

Del couldn't help smiling. She was beginning to take quite a liking to Edward, he was so happy and frank about everything you just couldn't help liking him.

'And what time does my act go on?' she asked.

'Oh I should say about 1.30, if that's all right with you,' he said.

'For that money any time would be just right with me,' she countered.

'Good, that's the spirit and by the way they've all requested an Eve in the Garden of Eden routine. I've got the setting all fixed and your three fig leaves. Will that be all right?'

'I think my artistic talent can cope with that all right,' Del answered confidently. 'But just out of curiosity how many of the leaves do I have to – er lose on the way?'

'Well for that money,' he started.

'Yes I know,' she cut in, 'we're going to finish with a real authentic Eve.'

'I'm afraid so,' he replied.

'Afraid?' she asked in surprise. 'Really Edward I thought you'd be delighted.'

He laughed happily.

'Well I am really,' he said, 'but I thought I'd be polite.'

'Will there be a young Adam chasing me around the bushes?' she inquired.

'No, I'm afraid not – and this time I'm not being polite.' He turned and gave her a cheeky but warm smile.

'Oh well I think I'll try and snatch a little sleep before we get there.'

She snuggled farther down in the upholstery. 'Wake me up when we're nearly there Adam – er Edward.' She opened one eye to look up at him tauntingly as he chuckled then she closed it and was soon lulled to sleep by the steady throb of the engine.

It felt as if she had only just closed her eyes when she awoke suddenly as she slid forward in the seat. Apart from the swish and creak of the three wiper blades on the wet screen all was quiet. She turned quickly in the darkness and could just make out the dim silhouette of Edward's face.

'Are we there?' she asked.

'Home sweet home,' answered Edward switching on the map light. The white glare made her crease up her eyes, but her curiosity at the rustling noise from Edward's direction forced them open again.

'Here we are Delorice,' he said placing three large blue piles one after the other in her lap. 'I thought you'd like part of the fee before you go on so if you'd care to check you'll find each pile contains exactly two hundred five pound notes. Will you settle for three thousand now and the remainder after you perform?'

But Del could only nod her reply. She had been moved by the sight of five hundred pounds in her dressing-room but this was just too much to take in in one go. She scooped the bulky bundles together and lifted them slowly as if they were fragile porcelain to her lips. Edward laughed at her display.

'Well I've heard of the face that launched a thousand ships,' he said. 'But now I've seen the lips that kissed six hundred fivers.'

But Del ignored him. Her excitement over the money had already waned as a result of the smell. Still on the pretext of kissing the notes she held the bundles as near her nose as possible one after the other. All the bundles absolutely reeked of perfume and it definitely was not hers. She lowered them a little and then tried again. The was no mistaking it. Each bundle was heavy with the same scent. She purposely avoided looking at Edward in case her face would betray her thought. Surely he didn't use perfume. She realized many men did but somehow Edward didn't seem the type. After shave, etc., she could understand but this was perfume – ladies' for the use of, full stop. Then it dawned on her if Edward had been using perfume then she would have noticed it as soon as she got into the car and she was sure she hadn't. But wait a minute she wasn't thinking clearly – this was obviously not Edward's money, it was what he had collected from his clients in advance for her appearance.

'Edward,' she said suddenly, 'do you mind if I ask rather a personal question?'

'Try me,' he said.

'You know these eight friends of yours that will be watching me tonight?'

'Yes, what about them?' asked Edward pressing in the cigar lighter on the dash.

'Well are they – what I mean is, they're all sort of normal, are they?'

Edward's thick Havana cigar crackled as he rolled it between finger and thumb. 'Come, come, Del, just because they want to watch a private striptease show that doesn't make them kinky does it?'

'No, no, of course not,' she assured quickly taking the notes to her lips again. 'They all pay, er, in advance, do they?'

'If they didn't,' laughed Edward, 'you wouldn't be holding that little lot now believe me.'

'No, of course not, how silly of me to ask such a thing.' She tried to give a carefree laugh.

'Well, if you're happy with the money I suggest we make a run for it,' said Edward.

The cigar lighter bobbed out a little way with a warning click to show it was ready for action. Edward sucked his cigar greedily at the glowing redness. She watched him uneasily. Happy about the money she definitely was not but it was no good telling him that. In her mind she was still conjuring with these eighty mysterious people. Who or what were they, that's what she wanted to know. Eight men from different walks of life, probably coming here from all parts of the country, all wealthy enough to pay about £750 in advance for a single evening's entertainment and funnily enough all eight using exactly the same brand of perfume – now that was odd.

'Yes, I'm all ready,' she replied.

'Good,' said Edward clicking the surface of one of his fingers against his thumb, 'then let's go.'

Del contorted herself out of the car and stopping for an instant to jam tight the clasp of her bulging handbag hurried after him. She crunched gingerly in her high heeled shoes along the gravel path towards the darkened hulk of a large storm beaten house. Long black deformed branches from the wet gnarled trees forked accusing stumps in her direction. She shivered a little as she followed the trail of cigar smoke towards the front door. Edward was not turning out to be the gentleman he had sounded on the phone. In fact he seemed to have lost interest in her. He had not even opened the car door for her or helped her along the way to the house. Instead he was just striding away in front giving an occasional click with his fingers leaving her to follow behind like a faithful dog. Their feet scratched up four wide steps and then she waited while Edward's key grated the lock open.

'In you come my dear,' he said clicking on a few switches. Huh, at last, she thought, he remembers I'm still here.

'Follow me,' he said closing the door. 'Oh and bring everything with you.' Everything. He must be joking: apart from the clothes she stood up in all she had was a handbag, and she wasn't going to leave that with its precious cargo lying around where she couldn't keep an eye on it.

He led the way through a brightly lit hallway into a very long dining-room. The lighting here was very dim in comparison. All the lights were either encased in thick red shades or were actually red light bulbs. Stretching down the centre of the room was a long polished table laid in readiness for a meal of many courses from the array of cutlery.

'I thought we'd have a look at the set and have a quick run through first,' said Edward over his shoulder. 'Then when we're both happy with the performance we can have a quick snack before they arrive – all right with you?'

'Yes I'd like to get everything sorted out first,' she said mechanically while she tried to work out the number of places set at the table in the blood red gloom. Seven, eight, nine, she counted to herself so that meant Lord lead-the-way-in-front would be dining here with his guests while she would be eating elsewhere, still if it was imperative that she should not see their faces then she'd have to be kept away from them for everything – it did make sense really she thought but her curiosity was beginning to stir about her audience. As they left the room through another door at the end Edward flicked off the lights. She stood there in the darkness waiting and watching the glowing tip of his cigar moving away from her. Then it seemed as if a red rocket had burst silently, shedding all its sparks around the room. This room was smaller than the other and the red lighting was cunningly concealed over three of the walls leaving the fourth completely bare and gloomy. Nine plush armchairs squatted on the thick carpet all arranged in a neat arc so that the occupiers would all be looking at the bare gloomy wall. Del was beginning to feel a little like Snow White only in her case there was nine of everything instead of seven.

At the side of the room stood a large cocktail cabinet bedecked with a very comprehensive selection of bottles. The glasses must have been inside the cabinet but she could imagine neat rows of nine whisky glasses, nine brandy glasses and nine of any other shaped glass that happened to be needed. She followed Edward obediently across the room to a door in the opposite glowing wall.

'Careful on the steps,' he warned as he went through the

door and suddenly dazzled her with a burst of flickering white neon light. He stood back at the top of a flight of stone steps leading downwards. 'After you, my dear,' he mumbled not bothering to remove his cigar. Del was taken aback slightly by this sudden unexpected display of gallantry. Her eyes were still adjusting themselves to the bright glare. She looked at him before passing. His teeth were locked together in a cold grin as a result of gripping his cigar end and attempting an accommodating smile. It was then that she noticed the bright sheen on his face as the neon light reflected clearly each minute droplet on his sweating face. The effect was as grotesque as a cross between a witchdoctor's mask and a death mask. A patter of clicks from his fingers broke her trance and she pushed past him to go down the steps mainly to relieve herself of the strain of looking at him. She heard a click behind her and then the door banged. But when she heard a bolt slide home she stopped in her tracks and looked quickly back. But he was still there so she hadn't been locked in the dungeons as for a fleeting second her apprehensive brain had imagined. His muffled step echoed all the way down behind her broken only by an occasional clicking from his fingers. Maybe that's what was beginning to upset her she thought, this habit of his of clicking when she was alone with him in this strange house and that wet white staring face hadn't helped either. The thing was it wasn't really hot enough to make people perspire. If anything she could feel goose pimples on her skin, not perspiration. And if the effort of walking through a few rooms had that effect on him then it was time he saw his doctor. When she got to the bottom of the steps she saw a short passage ahead of her that ended with brickwork. On the left of the passage there was a single dark green door while on the right with the whole length of the passage between them were two brown steel doors.

She stopped at the bottom awaiting instructions and clutching her handbag with both hands.

'Now then, Delorice,' he said, 'I'm sure you must be a little confused with all this, so allow me to set your mind at rest by explaining my little set-up.' A little of the old Edward seemed to have regained control now but his face still looked damp and excited. His eyes switched quickly from one direction to another as he spoke, as if by doing so they could speed matters up. Delorice noticed to her personal discomfort that the excitement in his voice increased the clicking rate of his left hand. The only anchor she found to sustain herself in this bizarre situation was the heavy bundle in her hands. If it hadn't been for that she was sure she would have made a few imprints on his face with her stiletto heel and shot out of there like a stone from a catapult.

'Hey, come on, cheer up, it's not that bad, is it?' he had suddenly taken her by the shoulders and was grinning comfortingly into her face.

'What? Oh no,' she said startled by his sudden move. 'I'm sorry, I was miles away. I think I must be a little on the tired side.'

'Dear me, we can't have that,' he blustered, 'I must keep you fresh and happy for your performance. Would you like to lie down for a while?' he asked.

'No, no, honestly, I'm all right. I'd much rather carry on and get it over with – that is I mean get on with the show of course – really I'm ready fit and able,' she said as convincingly as possible under the circumstances.

'Good that's the spirit,' he said patting the sides of her arms encouragingly. 'Well, then the green door there,' he said pointing, 'is your changing room, you'll find everything you need, apple and—'

'Apple?' she burst in. 'But, of course, dear, why you haven't forgotten you're supposed to be Eve have you?'

'Of course, I just wasn't thinking – yes, you were saying,' she said looking away from him to the green door.

'Yes, well, apple and your three fig leaves all ready for application so they won't fall off until you want to peel them off, eh?' he winked. 'We have to keep the old eye guessing as long as we can, don't we?'

She struggled a sickly half smile in return to his comment – to keep the eighteen old eyes guessing was her problem, not just one. 'Now the door at the bottom of the corridor is where I've laid the set out – I'll take you in when you're ready,' he

T—H

said. Then lowering his voice as if hidden ears were glued to the other side of it he said, 'And this door here is where I will be with your audience, my dear.'

She nodded to show that she understood.

'Good, in you go, then,' he said opening the green door for her. 'And try to be as quick as you can won't you – we've got a lot to get through you know.' She stepped past him without a word into the confined room, and after pressing down a stiff brass light switch she closed the door.

A weak naked bulb shed its poor light on the wooden table and chair. Struth, this was quite a come down from the opulent air of luxury above she thought, anyone able to pay six thousand pounds a time for an act should be able to supply better amenities than these. The three green artificial leaves and the red apple on the table were the only splashes of colour in the room. There wasn't even a mirror or coat hanger available. She moved the props to one side of the table and plonked her handbag in the middle. She then proceeded to undress folding all her clothes neatly and laying them on the table. She used the mirror of her powder compact to ensure she adhered her leaves properly to her body. Then after a quick touch up to her face she popped it back into her handbag. One last smell of the lovely money she thought would be sufficient to see her through the next few hours. To her surprise however the strange perfume had vanished from the notes, all she could smell now was her own brand of perfume. Still the money had been in her bag for some time now so it was bound to be affected by its close proximity to her own make up compounds. She closed the clasp and arranged her clothes in a covering mound of camouflage over her bag. Then picking up the apple which, unlike the leaves, was real she slipped off her shoes and padded along the cold stone floor to the door.

Edward was waiting for her outside. His face lit up as he admired the effect. 'My word, you do look a picture, my dear,' he said, his left hand giving a few clicks of approval. 'This way then,' he said leading off down the passage.

Del paused for a moment and then before she could stop herself suddenly blurted out:

'Let's have a look in the other room first I'm dying to see how it—' Before she could finish Edward had spun in his tracks and was back between her and the door like a eumuch at a harem.

'Delorice, my dear, all in good time,' he soothed. 'Time is pressing you know, now come along, we'll have a good run through your act and when it's over you can ramble through there to your heart's delight.'

Without waiting for an answer he took her bare arm and guided her purposefully down the corridor. That clinched it as far as she was concerned, the audience was already in there and waiting. Who was he trying to kid, run through indeed. This was the real thing first time she could feel it in her bones. Her cold feet plopped along the corridor ahead of him and after the rusty hinges had growled their protest, she went into the room where she was about to perform.

The room was about six strides long and about four strides wide. Along one of the long walls a sincere effort had been made to create a garden of Eden type background. The wall had been vividly painted with leaves of varying bright greens on slender orange branches all intertwined with an occasional splash of red and purple where the odd apple and grape bunch hung. A clear blue sky reflected the glare of the numerous strong arc lights set at strategic positions on the other three walls. In the floor near the centre of the picture was a small pool of real water, large enough probably for two frogs to encircle each other without actually touching. Around the pool and over parts of the floor lay patches of green artificial grass carpet. But the oddest construction was that of a thick twisted hardboard tree trunk arranged about a foot away from the painted wall. Not that the actual effect of the tree was odd, in fact if anything it blended very realistically with the background; but odd because of the support behind it. The tree was attached to round solid steel girders which obviously had their foundations deep down in the concrete floor. The only girder that was not set in this way was the one that branched off and disappeared into the pool of water. Even this piece of metal had been skilfully hidden from the front by one of the painted hardboard roots of the tree.

Delorice now turned her gaze to the opposite wall: the contrast was staggering. Apart from the fitted spot lamps all it could boast of was a single mirror running from floor to ceiling about three feet wide positioned directly opposite the hardboard tree. Regardless of the impression everything in the room had made on her the only thing she said was 'I suppose that's a two-way mirror.'

'It is indeed Delorice,' said Edward walking over to it and giving one patch a gentle wipe with his handkerchief. 'As I told you' he continued, 'my guests will be able to see you but alas you won't be able to see them – neat isn't it?'

'Oh very,' she answered without enthusiasm. Well if nine people were going to watch her through that then they'd have to sit on each other's shoulders if they all wanted to see.

'I'd like to see how they all manage it,' she said sarcastically.

'Believe me my dear,' he answered, 'each one will be sitting in comfort with as good a view as any of the others.'

'They must be very skinny devils as well as rich,' said Delorice straight at the mirror hoping anybody the other side could hear her as well as see her, all this gadgetry had made her take a greater dislike to this audience than any of the others she had worked in front of. It was as she was doing this that she saw the patch of blackened concrete behind her.

'What's that?' she asked turning and pointing to the floor.

'Oh that,' said Edward dragging a piece of artificial grass across a little with his heel to cover it, 'I had a little accident when I was painting the scene. A tin of paint tipped and caught fire.'

'It must have been quite a blaze to char so much of the floor.'

'Yes,' he tried to laugh light-heartedly. 'It gave me quite an experience I can tell you.' Then as if wishing to change the subject he suddenly took the apple from her hand.

'Now, I'll be able to talk to you through my intercom dear, so I think we'll leave the apple here for now,' he said placing the apple on the grassy patch positioned precisely over the marked floor.

'So just do as I tell you and leave the apple where it is until I give you the okay – right now any questions before I leave you to it?' he asked, backing towards the door.

A rising sense of panic in Del's mind thrust numerous suspicions forward for her to ask for clarification but through the sudden turmoil all that came out was:

'Will my money be safe where it is or had I better—'

'Safe? Of course it will be safe, my dear,' he cut in. 'Now relax. In a little while you're going to be a very wealthy girl you know – now just forget everything and give me the performance of your life, eh?' He smiled encouragingly at her and with a last click of the fingers he had gone, clanging the door to.

If it hadn't been for the presence of that ominous mirror she would have rushed across to try the door but deep down she knew that it was well and truly locked from the outside. To hell with it she thought, they can think what they like behind there; I'm making sure. She walked rather self-consciously to the door and tried the steel handle. As she thought, locked! Maybe he had a good reason for it but how she wished she knew what it was.

'Testing, testing can you hear me.'

She jumped slightly as his voice suddenly crackled all through her acting cell. 'Just nod if you hear me please, Delorice.'

She nodded obediently to the mirror. 'Good, now, cheer up dear, you must force a little smile. You know we mustn't frighten our customers away with those old frowns must we.' His voice continued as if it were coaxing a six year old child.

'Now why don't we walk back and forth across the set a few times to get the feel of it, eh?'

Del marched flat footed to one end then back to the tree thinking how pathetic she must have looked to anyone watching. She gave a wide smile in the direction of the mirror to assure him that his prescription had had the desired effect.

'Much better,' he crooned. 'Now let's keep it like that and they won't know what's hit them.'

Boy I'd like to hit them with more than just a smile, she

rambled to herself, the pack of scented creeps that they are. I bet it smells like a women's hairdresser's in there. Then a sudden thought struck her maybe they were women – all eight of them. That would explain the smell on the notes better than any of her other deductions. Why hadn't she thought of it before? But what sort of women would pay for this type of party? Her brain began to feel sick at this sudden development. Oh God what had she allowed herself to get mixed up in now?

'Ah, ah,' shrilled the voice, 'we're beginning to go again, aren't we? Now come along, Delorice, smile dear – that's it – better better – bit more now, good. Now there won't be any music for the trial run because it will interfere with my talking to you but I'm sure a professional artist like yourself will be able to cope, eh?'

She nodded at the mirror. 'Good that's the spirit. Okay let's go – now we'll start from behind the tree. Come on chop-chop off you go – right. Now emerge slowly head first – good that's it. No, no, not too fast, slowly. Lovely, keep it like that smile, smile, don't forget, that's it. Now let's come out gracefully. You're the first woman on earth remember. Good, smile please dear – do try to remember. Shoulders back, come on fill those lungs let me see those leaves straining. Oh yes! yes! yes! and smile beautiful keep coming like that.'

Del exhaled a short gasp of air from her full lungs. He did rabbit on a bit. She'd be glad when the real thing came so that she only had the music to contend with. Still it was his show really, so she was perfectly happy to move around as directed. This was far less energetic so far than her usual number.

'Smile please.' There it was again. At this rate her jaws might set solid in a smiling position.

'Good, good, now move a little nearer to me.' She moved a few slow steps towards the mirror.

'Enough. Stay there. Good, now bring those hands into action slowly now. Move them up your thighs – slowly. Now sway, come on. Sway your body. That's it, perfect. Relax. Leave the smile go for a minute. Keep moving those hands up. Slowly now, keep swaying, now bring your hands under your breasts. That's it – you want to be free now. NOW free yourself, rip away those leaves RIP RIP – Ah yes now just sway.'

The voice had diminished to a mere whisper. 'Your arms are heavy let them sag to your sides – keep swaying. Oh perfect Delorice just keep that movement. Sway for me dear, sway – now gently ever so gently try a few slow half turns from side to side.' Del let the two leaves flutter to the floor from her hanging hands and turned slightly first to the right then to the left giving the mirror every opportunity to see her from every angle. There was a sharp click and the sound of a few gurgling bubbles behind her. She was about to turn to look when the voice rasped sharply.

'Head, Delorice, keep the head still. That's it – smile please – good now start moving back dear – keep looking this way – that's it now pick up your apple – Ah! Ah! not too quickly now.'

She stooped forward for the apple and picked it up with her right hand.

'Hold that angle, Delorice – don't come up yet. Oh, you look wonderful dear – slowly now up slowly. Despite the rattle of the voice she still sensed a steady rippling noise from the pool behind her but the reflection of her body in the mirror obstructed her view of the back so to see she would have to turn around and that would send talking Edward spare for a bet.

'Farther back now that's it, the tree's just behind you.' She could hear the steel creaking as she came to it.

'You're there now lean back – and relax. Now keep the apple in your right hand. Now slowly take a large bite go on now.'

Del studied the apple suspiciously for a second. It looked like any other rosy eating apple. She sank her teeth deep through the skin spraying the roof of her mouth with the rich juice.

'Now slowly and deliberately move your left hand to your last leaf.'

Ah well this was it, this is what they all had been waiting for. She gripped the leaf ready with her hand. The tree creaked heavily behind her. I'll have to slim a bit of this weight off she thought, or those girders aren't as solid as they looked.

'Slowly peel away.' Edward's voice was a hushed whisper. 'That's it slowly – yes. Right let the leaf fall now. That's it smile, you're free. Smile please, Delorice – another bite, go on lean back as much as you like and bite. Good, good. Now stretch that apple high for all to see. That's it stretch that arm up. Lean it back against the tree – good keep it there – this is perfect my dear – stay there – still now don't move – keep it like that – very still now—.'

Del tried to eat the bits of apple without making it too obvious. She hoped that this was about the end now and that he wouldn't want her to take any more bites because her mouth was choked with lumps of half-chewed apple.

Just then a woollen scarf seemed to slip across the wrist holding the apple. She automatically flexed her arm to free her wrist from the sudden sensation. To her amazement she could not move it. She forgot all about the voice and her own nudity and twisted her head up sharply to see what held her wrist. To her horror she saw a thick dark patterned slithering mass knotted around her slender arm. The apple dropped as her hand opened and her fingers stiffened. A shower of apple bits sprayed suddenly from her mouth as her scream ricochetted around the room. She tugged away as hard as she could from the obnoxious body but to no avail. A large head wavered around the edge of the tree and transfixed her with two bright beady eyes. A long slender forked tongue flicked silently in and out a few times before the ugly cavernous mouth stretched wide above her displaying two rows of great white pointed teeth. Her second piercing scream had just rent the air when the head sprang towards her left shoulder. The sharp teeth plunged into her flesh with such force that her knees buckled completely beneath her. The huge jaws compressed the teeth deeper as the Anaconda consolidated its grip. Slowly and deliberately the thick brown coils looped out from behind the tree and slid methodically around her smooth trembling body. First her legs were locked together then her right hand was freed but despite her desperate effort to clutch hard with both

hands at one of the enormous living coils the quivering round-
ness contined to slither unimpeded on its mission. She had
no strength to spare now for screaming. All her might was
being used to withstand the crushing pain in her shoulder and
the general tightening around her. By now her arms had been
forced into submission and were pinned to her body. All
around her the coils continued their encircling until even her
breasts had been encased in the wriggling shroud. Now that
the body had been securely entwined the Anaconda relaxed its
gripping jaws and swayed its head back as if to study its prey.
Del was having great difficulty in breathing now as she gaped
in stunned silence at the flicking tongue. Only her head was free
from the spiral vice. Her brain was still reeling from the sudden
shock of the attack. Yet she was vaguely aware of the voice
hissing out through the intercom, 'And the Lord God said
unto the Serpent, 'I will put enmity between thee and the
woman, and between thy seed and her seed.' But these words
were short-lived in her brain. The Anaconda was already beginning to constrict her body in earnest. The pressure on her
chest was now unbearable. Her gaping mouth gasped snatches
of air to her tortured lungs. A sharp crack stung her head with
a fresh wave of pain as one of her ribs splintered. Her breathing was now both painful and erratic interspersed with sudden
coughs and splutters. A spark of fire seemed to shoot up her
back and then she realized she could no longer feel any pain in
her legs. That could only mean one thing, that her spine had
snapped beneath the pressure. For one brief instant the thought
of her money flashed into her head, now how pointless that
impressive amount seemed and as if her imminent death helped
her to see things more clearly she thought of how the smell of
the money had confused her just as probably the smell of her
perfume on it would confuse the next girl to be lured along to
this strange stage of terror and death. Another series of sharp
cracks sent spurts of bright red blood spluttering with her
choking coughs. Her protruding dying eyes didn't even blink
as the snake bathed a flow of slippery saliva over them and
other parts of her head in readiness to assist the swallowing
process. Its expanded jaws were already working smoothly

down engulfing her head as her last gurgle of air bubbled fitfully through a mouthful of warm blood. The Anaconda had now reduced her body to the shape of an elongated sausage. It toppled its prey to the ground and using its own tail as a lever proceeded to push her farther into its yawning mouth.

Edward watched fascinated through the viewing lens of his humming movie camera. He had a green eye-shade on his forehead and he puffed away excitedly at his cigar. He didn't know how long it would take the Anaconda to swallow the pink pulp but he would keep filming until he came to the end of his film anyway. Then he would soon have another great epic in the can. At least this time he wouldn't have to dispose of pieces of charred body as he had last week, thanks to the strong digestive juices in the Anaconda which were capable of digesting bones and even shells. Still last week's film which he was going to call the Nudest Joan of Arc was a real gem as well, even if the fire had made a bit of a mess of his studio floor. His close circle of wealthy friends were really going to enjoy these films when he showed them in his theatre upstairs. The beauty of it was of course that unlike a single live performance he could show the films as often as he liked and make money each time without having to pay any artist for doing the job. He let the camera run on its own while he sat back exhausted in his special chair. Like all the famous directors of Hollywood he had his own canvas deck chair with his name EDWARD HITCHCOCK in bold black print on the back. He mused happily how amazed his friends always were at his special expensive film shows and how they kept beseeching him to tell them how he arranged the trick photography. These days the ordinary public always flocked to the cinema if there was an Alfred Hitchcock film showing but in time he was sure the name of Edward Hitchcock would displace that well known master of suspense and every one would be praising his fantastic works of suspense and realistic horror. The amusing thing was it was all so terribly simple to achieve really. Anyone could do it – well anyone as cunningly clever as he was anyway.

The Anaconda was still swallowing its crushed meal. Already its skin was expanding to surmount its newly acquired bulk. He picked up his pad of notes from the empty chair alongside his. He ran his eyes down the long list of detailed notes each with their neatly underlined subheading – Set, lighting, props – ah, here was what he wanted. 'Anaconda details'. Now according to his information the snake would take approximately two and a half hours to swallow her, then about 22 hours to consume the meal. He clicked his fingers meditatively as he worked the arithmetic out in his head. That meant about this time tomorrow the Anaconda would slither back contented into the hidden tank beneath the pool and he would be able to release the lever to close the hatch on it. Yes that seemed all right. Then he would be able to get into the studio and start working on his next set. He already had the drums of concentrated acid ready to pump into the tank after draining the water away, then that would remove all traces of the Anaconda which in turn would have removed all traces of Delorice. He blew a blue cloud of smoke into the air. This had definitely been his best planned and best executed project so far, but enough of this gloating. If he was to surpass the great Alfred Hitchcock then it was time to start thinking about his next great production. He closed his eyes to shut out the squirming tangle through the mirror. He couldn't do justice to his planning and watch that spectacle at the same time. Now what about the story of Lady Godiva – that was always popular and he was sure that his creative genius could devise a fitting end for her. After all it hadn't failed him yet!

COMPULSION

A. G. J. Rough

I REALLY must apologize for this intrusion but I have many faults and my lack of consideration for other people's privacy is just one of them. You're probably reading this curled up in front of a crackling coal fire or tucked up cosily in bed, smoking a cigarette or drinking a hot cup of coffee. Whichever it is you undoubtedly feel warm and secure, settling down to a nice quiet night you might say. Well, don't let me disturb you. Just lie back and grant me a few minutes of your time so that I can say what I have to say. Afterwards, in all probability, your train of thought will have been left completely unruffled and you can forget all about this brief interlude. But right now I must tell you, or at least tell someone, about this terrible compulsion of mine.

I suppose it all started when I was a child. I know that remark sounds rather 'old hat', but they tell me, psychologically speaking, anyway, that during the early years we are all very sensitive, very prone to influence from outside sources. As a child, I was constantly an object of ridicule for my young companions and for some strange reason they found it agreeable to mock me because of my deformity. I didn't find myself quite that amusing.

Undoubtedly, facially speaking, I was very ugly and I was unfortunate enough to have been born with legs of unequal length which resulted in a pronounced limp. But even now, however hard I try, I can think of nothing which can possibly have justified those endless hours of shrieking, merciless laughter, ringing in my ears, haunting my dreams, which sent me scuttling away behind closed doors, afraid to face the world or anyone in it. I thought I'd forgiven them all years ago, putting my persecution down to the callous exuberance of youth once

I had been accepted, on almost equal terms, into the world of adults, the world of tact and discretion. However, when this compulsion of mine first started, I began to wonder if I had ever, in fact, really forgiven anybody.

Had I, for instance, ever forgiven Anne? Working with the same company I often had the opportunity to admire her poise and graceful femininity. While working I had often raised my eyes to find myself staring at her as she slid smoothly through the door from the typing pool, glided across to the desk, put down my coffee, smiled, turned and strolled slowly back from whence she had come. Wondering at the freshness of her complexion, watching the sway of her long, blonde hair, briefly scenting her perfume on the air, I was completely captivated. I had never then, and still never have, known a woman in any sense and this undoubtedly served to sharpen both my admiration and my desire.

After several months of this self-seduction I determined to make my feelings known to the girl. During one of her many visits to my office I clumsily attempted to explain exactly how I felt. I shall never forget the puzzled look that first crossed her face, and then the uncontrollable laughter as she suddenly realized what I was trying to say. The more she laughed the more desperate I became. I grabbed her wrist, pleaded for her to try and understand but she became afraid. Amusement was replaced with a look of both distaste and contempt. She broke free from my grasp and ran from the room. Within a few days she had found work elsewhere, while I was left as alone as I had ever been.

I thought that I had long since grown accustomed to the stares which I often received, yet now I seemed to notice a growing antagonism towards me, written in the faces of those people that I passed in the street or met elsewhere. Each of those countless faces seemed to bear the contempt and distaste that I had seen on that other disastrous occasion. I acknowledged that this feeling was brought about mainly by my own frame of mind and that I was unwittingly exaggerating the attitude of other people towards me. That is, until I first experienced the compulsion . . . and then gave way to it.

It first happened about eighteen months ago. I was taking my usual late night stroll – a habit which offers me some light exercise and also enables me to take in some fresh air without being too concerned with other people. The hour was late and the streets were deserted, silent save for the sharp tap of my walking stick against the pavement. Somewhere, far off, a dog was baying at the moon and a train whistle moaned in the night.

Taking no note of the direction in which I was travelling I eventually found myself striking out across a large area of common land with which I was passingly familiar. I made my way along a time-worn path, winding between stunted bushes that crouched menacingly in the blackness, until finally, some half a mile ahead, I could see the dim lights of the road by which I had decided to return home.

Looking out across the common I could vaguely make out the figure of someone approaching, bobbing towards me along the path. As we converged I was able to see that it was a man, hands thrust deep into the pockets of his overcoat, head lowered and walking rapidly. Soon he was only a few yards away. I could tell from his stride that he was both young and energetic, striking out purposefully, obviously intent on reaching home as quickly as possible. It occurred to me that he was probably some young Romeo who, having bade his lady love a fond goodnight, was now returning home with his head in the clouds. Of course this was pure supposition on my part, but even so I couldn't help but experience a sharp stab of envy.

As we crossed on the path the young man bumped heavily against me. I, in turn, murmured an apology but received no reply to my passing courtesy. The man strode on, not even noticing me nor, perhaps, considering me worthy of attention. For some reason fury and resentment welled up inside me. I, who had been denied so many things in life, had been brushed aside, ignored, by some young hooligan who probably had so many of the things that I had wanted for so long.

For a moment I stood shaking with rage, then I turned and leapt after him. The young man must have heard me approaching, for he had half-turned towards me as I brought my heavy brass topped stick crashing down across his skull. The resistance that it met was slight. The noise of the impact was like the soft crunch of fresh eggs shattering on a hard kitchen floor.

I released the stick and stood back, watching with wonderment as the figure, having made no cry, folded and sank slowly down on to the grass. The walking stick was still embedded in the skull. I lit a match and saw from the guttering light that the face was frozen in a mask of shock and fear, eyes and mouth agape. I think that I smiled. I certainly experienced no regret due to the drastic steps that I had taken a few seconds earlier. On the contrary, as soon as I had calmed myself and began to fully appreciate the situation, instead of sensing fear or panic, I felt positively euphoric. A feeling of satisfaction swept over me almost as if a debt had been partly repaid.

I had to place my foot across the corpse's windpipe in order to brace myself. In this manner, after exerting no mean effort, I managed to tear my ornate but effective club free of its gory resting place. Undoing my victim's overcoat and jacket I then used his shirt to wipe the blood from the brass top of the stick. I then rose, looked once more into those dead, rapidly glazing eyes, and then continued, at a very conservative pace, my stroll home. Before retiring for the night I carefully washed away all traces of blood from the head of the stick, and burned my shirt which was badly stained about the cuffs. The sleeves of my overcoat also required a little attention, but having completed these few tasks I went to bed and slept soundly.

The newspapers, the following morning, were full of it and for once I felt quite important. All over the country people would be reading about my handiwork. Admittedly, nobody would be attributing the crime to me personally, but that was the beauty of the whole thing. I had often heard it said that a crime without motive was the most difficult type to solve. I would be known simply as an 'unknown assailant' but it would still be me that those thousands of people were reading and wondering about. For the first time in my life I was being noticed and I couldn't have been happier about it.

For a few weeks I was in very good humour. As the days passed the papers had given the story very good coverage and had not tried to conceal the fact that the police did not have a single clue to work with. As time went by the paragraphs diminished in size and evenually all mention of the case disappeared entirely. It was about that time that I started to feel restless again. Once more my life was empty and I felt compelled to do something about it. Once again I was beginning to feel unimportant, downtrodden and inconspicuous.

One evening a few weeks later I took a bus to the opposite side of town. I spent a few hours at a film show, went to a pub for a few quiet drinks and rounded off the night with a sumptuous meal at an out of the way Chinese restaurant. One o'clock found me roaming the streets in search of some late-night straggler. I didn't have long to wait.

I was standing in the shadow of a shop doorway when the little blonde girl walked past. I suppose she must have been about eighteen, very petite, very modern and very nervous. I could tell that she was nervous because she was walking very rapidly as do most women who find themselves alone in the street late at night. Her heels rattled lightly over the pavement, at times almost breaking into a run. I remember fiddling with the pyjama cord that I carried in my pocket.

I left the doorway and limped after her, following at a respectable distance, but I quickened my pace as she turned into a side alley which I knew led past a breaker's yard, over a railway bridge and into the street beyond. I was indeed fortunate.

As she approached the railway bridge I was almost upon her. She must have sensed something for as I covered the last few paces that separated us she began to turn and must have seen me bearing down upon her for she would surely have screamed if I hadn't reached her first. The pyjama cord was wrapped sweetly around her throat in a trice and her pretty, gaping mouth could only word the scream. A single flickering gas light, affixed to the bridge, cast its ghastly yellow light upon the two of us. As the cord cut deeply into the smooth skin of her neck I remember thinking how attractive she was, but I watched her beauty fade before my eyes. Her pale blue eyes stood out from their sockets, bulging, beseeching in an unnaturally baleful stare. Her tongue lolled out across her cheek and thousands of tiny blood vessels erupted in a purple web across her sweet, pink complexion. As her eyes slowly glazed her body shook, a final gurgle died in her throat and her heels scratched a feeble and final tattoo against the ground. Finally she hung limply in my arms.

I pocketed the cord, lifted her body and cast it over a low fence and down the railway embankment. It took me almost two hours to walk home.

As I said earlier, all this has been going on for something like eighteen months now. Four or five times I have killed in my own town, but now and then I have ventured farther afield. On one occasion I simply clubbed a pedestrian while passing on my bicycle. Another time I poisoned somebody in a restaurant. It was broad daylight, the place was crowded and I chose a random cup. In one decidedly rash moment I pushed an elerly man in front of an underground train at the height of the rush hour and then disappeared into the crowd. You'd be surprised if you knew how easy it really is.

I would like you to know that I have sent this story to the publisher anonymously. It is completely true in every detail and, as I gave no address, I will never have any way of knowing if it ever reached print unless I happen to find myself reading it somewhere. If the man has had the courage to publish he will receive both my admiration and my gratitude.

You see, I just had to tell somebody how things really are. I just want you to understand that if I ever meet you somewhere late at night there will be nothing personal in what I do. It's just that I like being noticed.

CROCODILE WAY

Mary R. Sullivan

I WENT home in '51 but was posted back in '55, and went up to Ellis's place in Kluang to visit. On a night so sticky that the clouds were too tired to relax and let the rains come, he told me about it. He told me of the night Jock Buchanan and Haji Noor died. Maybe the oppressive atmosphere or the intensity of his talk had its effect. He sat in a great basketwork chair, the darkness concealing his body and the disembodied voice pierced the gloom between us seeking somewhere or someone to pick it up and exorcize it from the brain. It seemed like some compulsive confession rather than a statement of fact.

'I was sitting in the jeep, nursing my shotgun and watching the headlights playing hide and seek with the jungle as we passed by. We were on the Kuala Lumpur–Klang road on the way to Swettenham. I was half expecting to see a big cat as one always does, but apart from the odd Sambhar skittering away into the thick I saw nothing. Jock was driving, if our method of progression could be covered by such a term. He drove as if potholes and traffic did not exist. Indeed for him such dangers never seemed to intrude to impede his foot flat-down progression.

'We were after croc in the Klang river. You know it. It drains from K. L., all points North and East, rolls through or rather squirms through Ulu Langat and into the sea at Port Swettenham. About Thames size or a bit bigger at Klang which was our jump off point. It is muddy, deep and tidal nearly up to its source.

'We got into the village about ten-thirty. The place was still a bit tired looking then from the war. The wet pontoons were still being used, replacing the bridge we blew in '42. Jock stopped the jeep alongside the old bridge which was resting its belly in the river and we looked around for Haji Noor.

'He was sitting, unsmiling as usual on the bank. He was still surprised by people being stupid enough to pay him for that which he liked doing. Admittedly, using shotguns, harpoons and lights in the middle of the night was a silly way to kill crocodiles, but the queer English seemed to object to using a rope baited with a live dog as did Allah's beloved people on the river. His wonder did not affect him adversely as a night on the river brought money, the feet of the croc for sale as aphrodisiacs to the Chinese and invariably some compo which helped to feed his ever increasing family. Bars of chocolate were not unknown if the shooting was good.

'Jock took the sealed headlight and battery from the jeep. I carried the guns, harpoon and food. Haji Noor carried the great flask of coffee. He would have had hysterics if he had known that half the coffee he enjoyed so much was Scotch. Perhaps not. He was a very sophisticated Malay for a villager and the only aspect of his religion he seemed to abide by, even enjoy, was his four wives.

'We trooped down to the pontoon, got into the kolek and Haji Noor pushed off. He stood in a half crouch at the stern of the boat pushing out towards the main stream. Jock sat in the middle with the lamps and ready to act as harpoon man. I lay in the prow with the two guns. I had my usual jitters that the freeboard was insufficient, the craft inherently unstable which it was and the current too fierce for us to survive. However we had all done this many times, and as before, Haji Noor guided his small boat through the maze of floating trees, river débris and innumerable swirls to the relative calm of the main stream. It was a glorious night. Not the fairy-book equatorial night of myriads of stars and a giant Hollywood moon, but a dark, dark hunter's night. It was like moving through velvet and one could almost feel the absence of light on the skin.

'The ebb tide was slackening when we got down to the big bend about a mile and a half below the pontoons. Although dark the fifty-yard wide stretch of mud on each side of the water glittered with phosphorescence from its heterogeneous collection of small occupants. We swung on the tide and Jock switched on the headlamp.

'Immediately four blood red diamonds, unwinking, returned the light to us. One thrust on the paddle and we glided through the water, now oily and sweating in the glare of the lamp, towards the crocodiles. I slipped the safety catch on the twelve bore, and as usual my guts shuddered up into a knot while mosquitoes chased each other madly around the resultant emptiness below my chest. At about twenty yards the beasts' eyes went out and their bodies came into view. They were lying half in the mud, half in the river. They lay unmoving, their snouts open, the water flowing through the hideous gap between upper and lower jaw. Their nauseating bellies, like time-expired ice bags, were spread out clutching the mud while their corrugated tails lay quiescent on the outer edge of the light. Both were about eight feet; too big for good skins but small enough for us to tackle. We glided, slowly now as the thrust of the paddle died, towards them. Nothing moved. Even the slap slap of the water against the hull of the boat merged into the surrounding stillness. At five yards the crocs twitched preparatory to moving. I squeezed the trigger at the nearest beast. Through the flame and smoke I saw my heavy shot slam into its face just above the eyes. The whole scene exploded in sound and fury of movement.

'The reptile contorted itself into a galvanic mass of hate, and in a convulsive effort to reach the water, and us, came right off the ground, its giant tail thrashing and twitching to gain power. Haji Noor swung the kolek broadside on as Jock hurled the spear. Left to its own devices the headlight beam swung away into the sky like a maddened Cyclops and the river scene went dark. With no light the beast seemed to be thrashing among us in the boat. After an eternity of noise and fury – silence. Then as Jock pulled on the rope another outburst just as violent but of shorter duration. We pulled in the croc, knifed it in the water and lashed it to the boat. My stomach slowly unknotted and the cold sweat, a product of fear and excitement combined, poured down my back. Jock recaptured the headlamp and in its light I could see his shirt stuck to his body like a black skin, and there was moisture pouring down his face.

'We stopped then, awaiting the tide with the boat just resting on the mud and ate some food washed down with the coffee. When the tide turned, small waves hammered insistently on the boat as if seeking admittance. We pushed off up the river then with Jock in the prow and myself amidships with the light and harpoons. We went up river with the tide and soon reached the inside of the big bend. Perhaps you know it? Lim Cheng was killed there by the Fijians.

'About fifteen yards from the bank I switched on the beam. The bank burst into life. I should have switched off the light. Stopped Jock from shooting. I did not. I was paralysed with shock. I think we all saw the enormous estuarian crocodile at the same time. I do not know if Jock was conscious of its size or even cared. My scream, 'Don't shoot', and Haji Noor's prayer were both unavailing. Our cries mingled with the reverberating percussion of the shot. One of the giant diamonds on the bank abruptly disappeared as the shot went home.

'The monster reptile on the bank jerked convulsively with pain, hurled itself into the water and slammed into the boat.

'The impact hurled me into the bottom of the craft in a mess of legs and harpoon ropes. I heard Haji Noor cry out and the stern lifted as he fell into the water. The boat lifted even more as Jock went overboard. The headlight caught in the rope toils and locked on to the water, its beam illuminating the bank. I scrambled up and looked over the side. Jock was running fast over the mud flat for the safety of the bank. For a moment my relief was intense, and then the full horror of what was about to happen struck me as indeed it must have penetrated Jock's mind at the same time. For the first time in his life he had let fear overcome his reason. He had panicked and lost his nerve. He had swum for the bank, and then, deceived by the nearness of the bank and the innocent appearance of the mud gleaming like golden sand, had tried to cross that deadly flat.

'Like a man with magnets on his feet, his steps got slower and shorter as if the mass of his body was too much to carry. His feet first, then his ankles sank into the slime with each step. The crust broke, he went in up to his knees and then could go no farther. He half turned towards the water. I saw the look of relief on his face transformed to one of terror as he realized he could not return to the boat. He looked back again towards the bank now impossible to attain. Shock then flattened his face into a rubber mask devoid of all expression. He did not speak or cry out, his head dropped on his chest. He may have been praying. I do not know.

'Without conscious thought I found the second shotgun. I do not remember either raising or aiming it. I did not hear the sound or feel the kick as I squeezed the trigger. Jock pitched forward on to the mud from his waist. The slime gripped him, sucked the body down and closed its smooth innocent-looking surface over the indentation. Even his footprints had been washed out.

'My mind started to function again. I swung the beam in a wide circle over the water. Haji Noor was swimming strongly for some overhanging branches which reached down to the water. I seized the paddle and furiously drove the boat towards him.

'Even as I saw it happening I did not believe it. I had heard all the planter's tales of crocodiles drowning their food. I had never believed them. Haji Noor was making all the necessary swimming movements but was not getting anywhere. He was slowly sinking into the water. One had the impression he was swimming forwards but going backwards. Before I could reload his head went below the surface. It reappeared for a moment. His scream was cut short as water flooded into his mouth and he sank again. For a second or so I saw his hand waving furiously above the surface. Then nothing. No sound, no mark of their passing. The orchestra of the jungle started up as the foreign sounds died. I was alone. I am still alone, except at night, then, in a nightmare of sleep or wakefulness, I know not which, they are with me again.'

THE GREEN UMBILICAL CORD

Jamie McArdwell

ANDREW lived in his studio, atop the garage, in back of a huge desolate house that faced the ocean.

The main house had remained empty – boarded up – since Margarite's disappearance some four years before.

The studio was Andrew's only home now. To reach it, he had to walk through what once had been his wife's garden ... past rose bushes that had long since gone to seed and strangled themselves on their own roots, past a couple of undernourished and decadent pyracantha bushes whose berries were of such poor quality that neither bird nor bee professed an interest in them.

And then, there was a patch of sunlight ... and a brilliant green fire. The ivy! It ran up the south side of the garage, streamed across the roof of the studio, and flowed like a sluggish jade river down the north side. The leaves were monstrous; they crowded, pushed, shoved, and vied with each other to be the largest, the shiniest, the ones closest to the sunlight.

Some of the main creepers were the size of a strangler's wrist!

On the east side, streamers had grown through an old porch swing and lifted it up until it now hung askew – suspended in space – some three feet from the ground.

When an offshore breeze was blowing from the southwest, the entire garage and studio looked as though it were alive – festooned with millions of green vampire bats all quivering their little wings as they fed at an unsuspecting host.

Ivy had slithered through the eaves into the studio room itself. Streamers had crept through the window sill and grown until it was quite impossible to open – completely close, or even see through — the glass. It had fearlessly invaded the chimney during one summer, and fanned out so rapidly that it choked the draught and made the fireplace much too smoky to use.

The creepers inside the studio hung down — swaying, always in movement — like the trailing tentacles of a hungry Portuguese man-of-war. In some sections of the room, ivy was entwined on chair rungs, through bed springs, and looped around lamps. It had insinuated itself on the bookshelf, shoving off paperback novels and scholarly works alike.

When Andrew lay in bed and gazed up, he saw a solid carpet of green across the ceiling and beams.

He liked what he saw.

The ivy was his. It had always been his — ever since the day the first cutting had been brought home by him and placed in a water tumbler. Even Margarite admitted the ivy was his . . . the house was hers, the car was hers, the bank account hers . . . the ivy could belong to Andrew.

All of the other flowering plants and trees, however, were his wife's possessions.

She had won a fabulous number of prizes at the County Fair for her green thumb; if ribbons had been passed out for black hearts, she would have won one of them too.

Because she considered herself unequalled as a botanist, Margarite sneered at Andrew's pathetic little ivy plant. When he appeared undaunted by her taunts, she sneered at his pathetic little body and spirit.

She predicted the ivy would wither and die. Once, Andrew caught her sprinkling salt around the plant. Silently, he nursed his baby back to a spindly undernourished existence again.

Then one night — in a fit of pique over something else — Margarite had struck at him while he was peeling potatoes. For the first time in their marriage, he hit back . . . unfortunately forgetting to put down the knife before he struck.

And while she lay on the floor, gasping like some huge bulging-eyed gutted fish, he proceeded to finish the job by filleting her. The deed took five hours and thirty-two minutes;

it would have taken only five hours, but Andrew paused to watch *The Beverly Hillbillies* on television. Once the deed was completed, the bones were placed in an old plant fertilizer sack and carried to the ocean.

The *fillets de Margarite* were buried alongside the garage, right next to the ivy plant.

A most remarkable thing occurred within a few days. The ivy, which had been puny and white until then, suddenly began to take on a healthy green colour. It strengthened. It grew. In one day alone, it put out ten new creepers and stretched upward with eager little fingers for a distance of eight inches. At the end of three months, the ivy had covered the entire south side of the garage.

Inexplicably, however, on about the first anniversary of Andrew's bereavement, the ivy's upward growth stopped. It began to lose some of its lustre. Frantically, Andrew started extra waterings; he purchased the very best commercial fertilizers and plant foods available. He mothered the plant as best he could. It was all to no avail.

Andrew was not a scientist, but even a layman can understand simple cause and effect. Thus it was that he soon came to the conclusion that the plant was suffering from lack of organic nutrients similar to that which had been added a year before. He tested this hypothesis by grinding up a particularly loathsome yapping little Pekingese that had kept him awake for some nights running by its shrill and totally uncalled-for barking.

The ivy reacted. Not as strongly, or as rapidly, as Andrew wished, but enough to prove that he was correct in his basic assumption.

A Siamese cat was the next to go. The ivy did not care for Siamese cats; it developed ugly black blotches on some of its leaves. The marks went away shortly after a huge St Bernard disappeared.

At the end of three months, enough domestic pets had been reported as missing that even the newspapers felt compelled to comment on it.

Although the ivy remained fairly healthy during these

ministrations of organic nutrients, its spectacular growth had ceased. Naturally, Andrew was concerned . . . as would be any conscientious mother who sees her offspring suffering from malnutrition.

After considerable deliberation and several days of scanning the vital statistics pages of his newspaper, Andrew paid a visit to the churchyard . . . by moonlight. The digging was surprisingly easy. Just as the moon was gingerly lowering itself into the cold waters of the sea, Andrew lugged his newly-acquired plant food out to his bicycle and placed it – bent in the middle like a rolled up rug – across the back rack. He then pedalled somewhat apprehensively home.

Finally, Andrew's theory was proven. His baby grew again – rapidly – pulsating with a new life. It swept in a green tide across the roof of the studio and had made it halfway down the north wall when it ran out of steam.

A short time later, a gas company employee became entangled in the ivy while reading the meter outside the garage. His shouts for help brought Andrew blinking down into the sunlight. He decided the meter reader was a gift from the gods . . . one of those things obviously ordained . . . one of those wonderful coincidences that one simply does not question. By now, Andrew had become quite proficient; the deboning process took less than two hours.

How the plant grew. It completely encircled the building and began its intrusions through windows and cracks. The creepers became thick and one could almost feel the power surging through those green arteries.

Of course, the increased size did present certain problems. Food for example!

A shapely, red-headed bank teller named Mellissa was the next to become fodder. Then, in quick succession, a myopic pigeon-toed writer with a red beard, a radio disc jockey, an English lady watercolourist, an argumentative lady Christian Scientist, a newspaper editor, and a nosy police inspector.

Even Andrew was forced to admit that the last item on the menu was a mistake. Never before had there been such a hub-bub. The neighbourhood swarmed with newspapermen, television cameramen, FBI agents, insurance investigators, and curiosity seekers. One newspaper sensationally stated in a copyrighted story by its science editor that a sea monster had been sighted by usually reliable sources, and that the beast – 150 fet long and three sets of sharp teeth – could have been responsible for the missing persons.

This report frightened Andrew so much that he ceased his nightly walks along the seashore.

As a result of all the publicity, *table d'hôte* entrées for the ivy plant became very scarce . . . although, by Herculean efforts and taking some tremendous risks, Andrew was able to scrounge up a small boy as an *hors d'oeuvre*.

And finally – on a Sunday – after a week of no new food sources being found, Andrew was forced to put the ivy on a cold water diet. Feeling empathy for his beloved offspring, he himself went to bed that night after a dinner of only cold water.

The offshore breeze sprang up about ten o'clock; it caused the ivy leaves to rustle like vicious little rats scurrying hither and yon in agitation. The wind brought a cloud cover with it; the moon was veiled in film at first, before being blotted out altogether.

Policemen – walking in nervous pairs on the beach – heard the high thin horrible screams but were unable to place the direction from whence they came.

It was two days before the police hacked their way into Andrew's studio.

The ivy creepers were everywhere; they hung down from the ceiling in great undulating curtains of greenery. Their leaves – like the tiny hands of babies – seemed to be waving 'bye-bye'.

On the couch, the police could see Andrew.

Ivy grew out of his mouth, his ears, out of his pyjama tops and bottom.

And right in the middle of poor old maternal Andrew, the largest sucker root of all was firmly attached to his navel – like a green umbilical cord.

EUSTACE

Tanith Lee

I LOVE Eustace although he is forty years my senior, is totally deaf, and has no teeth. I don't mind that he is completely bald, except between his toes, that he walks with a stoop, and sometimes falls over in the street. When he feels it necessary to emit a short sharp hissing sound, gnaw the sofa, or sleep in the garden, I accept everything as quite normal. Because I love him.

I love Eustace because he is the only man who has not minded about my having three legs.

THE BOSTON STRANGLER   7/6

GEROLD FRANK

'Impossible to read without being horror-struck . . . DeSalvo's own dreadful background, plus his insatiable sex urge, fills out a picture of mass murder as pathetic as it is shocking' *The Birmingham Post*

'This is no book for the squeamish. Gerold Frank has chronicled the hunt for the killer in all its tragic and occasionally grotesque detail' *The Yorkshire Evening Post*

'An unnerving book, which I do not advise any woman to read alone in the house' *New Statesman*

In 20th Century-Fox's new film version of the book, Tony Curtis plays the Strangler and Henry Fonda the Assistant District Attorney who conducted the greatest manhunt in the history of crime.

Science Fiction in PAN

Rosemary's Baby 5/-

IRA LEVIN

The book that topped US and British bestseller lists for months and is now a terrifying Paramount picture, starring Mia Farrow, John Cassavetes and Ralph Bellamy.

'At last I have got my wish. I am ridden by a book that plagues my mind and continues to squeeze my heart with fingers of bone. I swear that Rosemary's Baby is the most unnerving story I've read.'
KENNETH ALLSOP, EVENING NEWS

'The pay-off is so fiendish, it made me sweat. Diabolically good.'
PETER PHILLIPS, SUN

'... if you read this book in the dead of night, do not be surprised if you feel the urge to keep glancing behind you.'
QUEEN

'a darkly brilliant tale of modern deviltry that, like James' *Turn of the Screw*, induces the reader to believe the unbelievable. I believed it and was altogether enthralled.'
TRUMAN CAPOTE

A SELECTION OF
POPULAR READING IN PAN